TAKING THE FALL

Also by A.P. McCoy

A.P. McCoy: My Autobiography
McCoy: The Autobiography
The Real McCoy: My Life So Far

TAKING THE FALL

A.P. McCOY

First published in Great Britain in 2013 by Orion Books,
an imprint of The Orion Publishing Group Ltd
Orion House, 5 Upper Saint Martin's Lane
London WC2H 9EA

An Hachette UK company

1 3 5 7 9 10 8 6 4 2

A CIP catalogue record for this book is
available from the British Library.

ISBN (Hardback) 978 1 4091 2957 8
ISBN (Export trade paperback) 978 1 4091 2972 1
ISBN (Ebook) 978 1 4091 2971 4

Typeset by Deltatype Ltd, Birkenhead, Merseyside

Printed and bound by CPI Group (UK) Ltd, Croydon, CR0 4YY

The Orion Publishing Group's policy is to use papers
that are natural, renewable and recyclable products and
made from wood grown in sustainable forests. The logging
and manufacturing processes are expected to conform to
the environmental regulations of the country of origin.

www.orionbooks.co.uk

TAKING THE FALL

1

December 1979

Duncan was hauled out of sleep by the sound of his bedside phone. It came into his dreams. As he sat up in bed, someone tapped him lightly on the head with a thirty-two-pound mallet. With eyes still pasted shut, he grabbed the phone and licked his dry lips.

A voice said, 'Duncan, you dog!'

Duncan made to check his surroundings, but as he moved, he took another light knock from the mallet. He winced. He was recovering from a Young Jockeys' Christmas party at the tail-end of 1979 that had started with them all getting thrown out of the Lamb and Flag and finished in the Wherever nightclub.

'What was the last thing I said to you last night, Duncan?'

Duncan smacked his dry lips. 'Goodbye?'

'Funny. Think again.'

Duncan actually tried to think sensibly, but his headache discouraged the effort of remembering. His tongue had sprouted a thick-pile carpet and that put him off speaking too.

The voice on the phone said, 'Platform two for the eight forty-five. Be there, I said. Didn't I? Well, didn't I? Now you just listen to this.'

There was a dull roar on the phone. Like the sound of a train approaching.

'Did you hear that, Duncan? Did you? That's the eight forty-five coming in, steaming.'

1

'Kerry, you don't fool me. That's an electric train. Electric trains don't steam.'

'It's the feckin' eight forty-five whatever you say and I'm on it and you're not; and you can forget about your ride today. For God's sake don't tell me you ended up with that red-headed bird you were flirting with all night.'

Duncan looked over his shoulder. Under the white cotton duvet a sleeping figure lay curled, but all he could see of her was a pale and elegant foot poked out from the bottom of the bed. Her toenails were painted flamingo-pink. He sniffed and delicately pulled back the corner of the duvet to reveal the shiny chestnut curls and slightly freckled brow of a very pretty red-headed girl.

'No,' he said. 'It's a blonde.'

'You're a lying toerag. I saw her climb into a cab with you when we left the Exchange Bar.'

'Is that where we ended up?'

'Oh yes. And she had to put you into the cab with a spoon.'

'Kerry,' Duncan said, 'I'll make it down for the next train. Sit tight. Wait for me. Be a good pal.'

'Hell with that. You're on your own, son. What was the last thing I said to you last night?'

'Platform two. Eight forty-five.'

'No, before that. The last thing before the last thing. I said don't get mixed up with the redhead. Didn't I? Do you know whose feckin' daughter she is? Do you? Do you know? Now I'm on this train. You better get your arse there for the first race or you're on the skids, pal, on the skids. I'll cover for you as far as I can. Just like I always do. Jesus, man, do you know whose daughter that is?'

'Kerry, I'll get there.'

'You're a damned nuisance is what you are.'

Duncan heard a whistle blow and then the line went dead.

Both he and Kerry were jocked up for the first race at

Doncaster. The last time he'd raced there he'd been pulled up by the stewards for excessive use of the whip, which was just ridiculous because the ride he was on was already dead before they'd dragged it out of the stables. The steward, Pointer, was one of those failed trainers in green wellies: a by-the-book military type with a hatred of every promising young jockey who showed a high seat and a bit of style. Duncan had got lippy with him, and that bit of lip had cost him dear.

He didn't want to go back to Doncaster. He had the mother of all hangovers and there was a fine-looking girl in his bed whom he'd quite like to meet. No, he didn't want to go to Doncaster, but on days like this you had to take what you were given.

Unless you were at the top of the game, that is, front of the pack with plenty in hand, and then you could pick and choose. And the top of the game was where Duncan planned to be. Time was – for a while – when that looked to be exactly where he was heading. He'd been one of the most promising – no, scratch that – *the* most promising young jockey in the country. He was hacking up everywhere. Runner-up for the 1978 Conditional Jockey Championship; though he rode fewer winners, his strike rate was ten per cent higher than the champion's. Everyone knew damned well he was the better jockey. Then when he'd moved on to becoming a fully fledged jockey, he'd found out the hard way that the best jockeys didn't always come by the best rides, and that had cost him dearly.

There was just stuff in his way. Connections, for example: owner loves you, trainer hates you; or trainer likes you but owner for some reason won't even let you ride his prize pig. Other things counted too: old friendships, former stablemates, debts being paid, secrets protected. Jockey Club favours. Form; and not the form of the horses, either.

Then there was the darker stuff: arrangements, handshakes, bookies' specials, say nothin'. The whole lot of it nothing to do with who could gallop down that last straight with their nose in front. It should be so simple, best jockey gets best horse, but it never was. You got what you were given, and if you had a bit of lip and a bit of spunk about you and spoke out of turn just occasionally, you might find yourself saddling a can of Pedigree Chum for all the chances you had.

But Duncan was one for winning rather than whining, and he knew it would come good in the end. He was just going to have to work through it and prove himself. He had the touch. He could feel a ride quicken under him, and not every jockey knew when to tuck in and wait and when to let the horse open up. Sometimes he could even take a horse on the downgrade and flash past a favourite. He had it. He had what it took, and he knew it.

First he had to dig in and ride the gaff tracks, and ten dozen other gaff tracks, and learn to button his lip. His friend Kerry had that lips-sealed thing off much better than he did. Knew when to shut up. He and Kerry went way back, had been Conditional jockeys together, still a rivalry there, but good mates. They had looked out for each other, and after they had finished their time as Conditionals it had been Kerry who'd warned him he'd be disqualified for excessive use of the lip if he wasn't careful.

But so often he just couldn't help himself. His gob always ran away with him. 'Not exactly a pigeon-chaser, is it?' he might say to a trainer when given an outsider. 'Why am I so bloody lucky?'

'Just take the trip,' Kerry had told him. 'Ride what you're given and you'll get your chance one day.' But still Duncan would complain and mouth off to the trainer if he was told to do nothing more than get round.

And of course Kerry was right. He and Duncan were both twenty-one years old but still kids as far as the owners and the trainers were concerned. But knowing that you should shut your gob and doing it were two different things. Sometimes it seemed that his mouth worked independently of his brain. It was like there was a little monkey-demon that got inside him and said the things he said, half in fun, half in jest, but usually at some cost to himself. Maybe he should have his jaw wired shut.

And maybe he should have his zipper wired shut, too. He turned to the girl sleeping beside him. Gently he tugged the covers from her, revealing her breasts. He leaned over and kissed a pink nipple and she woke up, blinking at him. She smiled happily and sat up, propping herself on one elbow.

'Duncan, do it again, will you?'

'Listen,' Duncan said. 'Do you have a car?'

'A car?'

'I'm late for a meeting at Doncaster. I was wondering if you could drive me.'

'Drive you? How could I drive you? I don't have a licence.'

'What?' Duncan's head pounded again. 'How old are you?'

'Eighteen. In January.'

Only just the right side of legal. Duncan blinked. At least there wouldn't be a stewards' inquiry. 'You might have told me.'

'The subject never came up. Anyway, you're not so much older.'

'I feel like I'm a hundred this morning. And I've got to get to Doncaster.' He swung his legs out of bed and found his way to the toilet. There was a bathroom scales on the floor and he weighed himself. It was close. He didn't have a couple of hours for the sauna, so he was going to have to pop a pee pill to get rid of that extra two pounds. He got off the scales and inspected his face in the mirror. His eyes were bloodshot and he didn't look like a winner today. But he would, soon. In a few hours' time he would put on the silk and he would glow and he would fly.

He threw some cold water on his face. When he came out of the bathroom, patting his face dry with a towel, the girl pulled the sheets around herself but in a manner he knew was inviting

5

him to whisk them away from her. She shook her head coquettishly. 'Anyway, how come *you* don't have a car?' she said. 'You can't go everywhere on a horse.'

'It was repossessed last week. I'm sunk.'

'I can get you a car easily enough.'

'How's that, then?'

'My dad. He's got loads of cars.'

'Loads? What is he, the local Ford dealer?'

'Don't be silly, Duncan. He's in the same business you're in. Racing, I mean.'

'Oh I remember now.' *I could hardly forget, could I?* he thought. *Major scumbag number one.*

'And,' she laughed prettily, 'he's got about twelve cars in the garage. What do you like? There's a Lamba … Lambra …'

'Lamborghini?'

'That's it. And a Porsche. A shiny black one. And some others. He never uses most of them, so he won't miss one for a day.'

He flicked the towel at her buttock and she squealed. 'Get dressed. We're on our way!'

They took a taxi from Duncan's place to hers, and all the way Duncan tried to figure out a way of asking her name without sounding impolite. After all, if you've just had sex vigorous enough to make you lose half a pound, you really ought to know what she's called. 'Your dad,' he tried. 'Does he have a pet name for you?'

She made a face. 'No. Why do you ask?'

'Well, it's just that most dads have a special name for their daughter, don't they? I wondered if he called you Bunny or Pumpkin or some such thing.'

'Bunny?'

Duncan shrugged.

'You're weird,' she said. She looked out of the window at

the grey sky. After a while she said, 'He just calls me Lorna like everyone else. To be honest, he doesn't care about me enough to give me a pet name.'

Lorna. Of course. He'd thought it was Laura or Lara and it was important not to get it wrong. Now he remembered moving in on her in the nightclub and making her laugh, and Kerry beckoning to him and saying, 'Now you keep away from that if you ever want to ride for the Duke.'

She'd been wrong about her father. 'Duke' Cadogan wasn't exactly in the same business as Duncan. No more than a soldier fighting in Northern Ireland was in the same business as an international arms manufacturer. Where Duncan was a jockey, Cadogan was a racehorse owner, one further step removed than a trainer. He bought the horseflesh and sponsored a stable the way that a businessman might buy himself into being the chairman of a football team. His nickname had nothing to do with the English aristocracy.

When the taxi drew up at Lorna's house, Duncan got out, paid the cabbie and stepped back to take in the size of the property. 'Anyone home?' he said nervously.

'Only the staff,' Lorna said. 'I'll get the keys to the garage.'

She hurried off, leaving Duncan to take in the sweep of the lawns, the outbuildings and the great Georgian columns trumpeting the front of the house and its gravel driveway. Just one of those outhouses was bigger than the old cottage he'd shared with his dad as he'd grown up.

Dad it had been who had raised him and put him in the saddle. Dad who had taught him everything he knew, who'd showed him the way. Yes, he was a lot older than all the other lads' fathers, in his late forties when Duncan was born. And when his mother – who by all accounts was a screaming basket case – had upped and left when Duncan was only five years old, it had been Dad who had taken over and done the whole damned thing.

7

His dad, Charlie, was a small-time trainer. Not any more, but back then. Struggling to make it, always struggling. He didn't have big-time players investing in his tiny stables: no football managers, no business tycoons, no fake dukes. He did everything the hard way. Went over to Ireland, or even to France – something no one else was doing at the time – to find a prospect, bring it back, get it fit, race it and sell it on. Some of these trips Charlie pulled Duncan out of school and took the boy with him.

'I love you, Dad,' Duncan heard himself whisper as his eyes surveyed the four-million-pound property. 'And I will fucking get them. All of them.'

He was brought out of his reverie by the sound of Lorna trudging across the gravel. She beamed at him, dangling a big set of keys in front of her. 'Shall we see what's there?'

He followed her over to a modern garage with steel doors. She unlocked a side door, hit a switch and the doors rolled upwards, purring as they went. A row of lights flickered on, one after the other, to reveal Cadogan's collection of motors.

They walked slowly between the silent vehicles, Lorna lightly trailing a finger on the slightly dusty paintwork. She seemed to be waiting for him to choose. The motors looked sort of sad and sleepy and forgotten, like beautiful courtesans in a harem no one ever visited, losing their best years. There was a Mercedes-Benz 450 SL soft-top; the Porsche and the Lamborghini she'd mentioned; a 1960s American Dodge Dart and an early seventies Chevy Camaro. There were a couple of vintage classics like the 1939 Simca 5. Heck, there was even a new Volkswagen Beetle in the mix, and for a moment he felt like taking that just for perversity. But the Lamborghini had more curves than a *Playboy* centrefold.

'I think you'll look pretty in the sunflower,' he said.

'Oh good,' Lorna said. 'I've always fancied the yellow one.'

She went over to a cabinet, unlocked it and puzzled over

the rows of keys until she found the right set. She tossed them through the air and Duncan caught them. He weighed them in his hand for a moment before unlocking the Lamborghini doors. He stepped round to the passenger door and held it open for her.

She blushed. 'You're a gentleman!' She sank into the low-slung plush leather of the passenger seat and it made her skirt ride up her legs.

'Oh yes, every inch a gentleman.' He unclipped the seat belt and reached across her to fasten it in place. Then he pulled the strap across her chest.

'Not too tight!' she protested.

But he tightened it anyway, then leaned down and kissed her, putting his tongue in her mouth at the same time as he slipped his hand between her legs. She wore thin tights but no knickers.

Moments later he was outside the garage, listening to the motor purr. He depressed the accelerator and the purr turned to a big-cat snarl. He looked at his watch. This was going to be good.

'This has grunt!' he said. But then he was distracted by a whirring noise from overhead. He looked up through the tinted glass of the windscreen and saw a helicopter high in the sky. It looked like it was descending.

'That will be Daddy popping in for a few things,' Lorna said. 'Probably best if we shoot off.'

The Lamborghini did have grunt. It ate the motorway. They were so low in the seats that it was like riding in a snake's belly. Duncan felt his own body weight pressing on his kidneys, and the diuretic pills meant he was going to have to stop pretty soon. He wished he'd stopped at the last services, but time was short if he was going to make the race. He looked at his watch and gave the accelerator a little more toe. The motor spat in response.

He wished he could pile up enough money to give his old dad one of these things. Not that his father was at all interested in cars. There was only one kind of horsepower for Charlie, and that was the kind where you pumped oats in one end and shovelled shit from the other. But when he made it, he would give his dad one of these anyway.

He looked at his watch. He was going to have to floor it to make the race in time.

School had come and gone and had barely touched Duncan. It wasn't that he didn't get along with his teachers – though the old lippy problem had got him into a couple of scrapes with teachers and older boys alike – it was just that all that geography and maths and other stuff didn't seem to stick.

'Don't you worry,' his dad had told him. 'You're too sharp for 'em, that's the problem. You've got brains enough. It's just a different kind of brains.'

And his dad was right: Duncan did have a brain. What kind of brain that was became clear one day when he was just nine years old and Charlie took him along to a race meeting in Leicester in the East Midlands, not far from the stables. It was a day of sunshine and the jockeys' bright silks were shimmering and flying like flags at a gala. Duncan was mesmerised by the tic-tac men and the antics of the bookies' runners. His dad gave him a brief explanation of what the signs meant, explaining that some of the gestures were secret. Duncan went over and stood by the white-painted rail dividing Tattersalls from the Silver Ring. He watched the signs and observed the runners, and then he studied the bookies' chalkboards as the odds tumbled or went way out. Pretty soon he had it all worked out.

His dad was sceptical at first. 'You can't know that,' he said. 'Not for sure you can't.'

'Yes I can. It's a pattern.'

'I know it's a pattern, but—'

'I can tell when this one in Tattersalls is talking to his mate

10

in the Silver Ring. He's telling him too many people are backing one of the horses.'

His dad, who always wore a sporting trilby and a moth-eaten sheepskin coat, tipped his hat back on his head and thought for a moment. He studied the form in his folded newspaper. A minute later he said, 'You little beauty! You sodding little beauty!' and gave him a tenner.

Duncan, small for his years, had approached a bookie with the terrific name of Billy B. Bonsor. Billy B. Bonsor had a beautifully painted fairground-style board with the slogan 'Payment as a Matter of Honour'. Mr Bonsor (so Duncan took the man to be) stood on an upturned wooden crate and announced as if to the entire racetrack, 'Very young fellow says ten on Midnight at sevens and who knows it?' Another man standing behind the crate recorded the bet in a ledger and Duncan was handed a betting slip. Before he released the slip, Billy B. Bonsor gave Duncan a weird look. Then he ran a finger under his nose and wiped the board, dropping Midnight Rambler from 7–1 to 5–1. Then he wiped the board again and changed it to 9–2.

Duncan ran back to his dad and gave him the betting slip. 'Why did he drop the odds?' he asked.

'He thinks someone sent you with the bet.'

'But you did!'

'Yes.'

His dad told him that there was good money and mug's money in gambling and that theirs was mug's money, even though they were in the business. Mug's money it might have been, but Midnight Rambler strolled home, and after deducting the stake, his dad let Duncan split the take. Thirty-five pounds was an inconceivable amount of money for a nine-year-old boy.

But what mesmerised Duncan even more than the tic-tac men and the painted boards was the racing itself. There was something unearthly and magical about the jockeys. He got up as close as he could to them and studied them. Some were tight-lipped before a race, and some would be wisecracking and all smiles. But Duncan knew it was the same thing. It was the tension. The excitement. They glowed with it.

And when he stood with his dad roaring them in near the whitewashed rail at the home stretch, there was something beyond beautiful in the growing rumble of the approaching riders. There was a moment when the silks flashed past, when the hooves thundered on the turf and the jockeys and their mounts seemed to be locked into position. If he could have frozen the world in time it would have been at that moment. It was perfection. It was life itself.

This was the obsession. Not so much with gambling, though that was part of it, but with the racing. He wanted in. He wanted to be bathed in that glowing thing.

He told his dad he wanted to start saving and would put his thirty-five pounds towards his own pony.

His dad laughed and tipped his trilby back on his head. 'Well, you're about the right size and weight,' he said, 'so long as you don't grow too much over the years. So long as you keep your weight down.'

'What is it?' Lorna said.

'It's no good. I need to pee. I'm going to have to pull over.'

'Can't you wait till the next services?'

'It's a desperate situation. I've got to go.' The pills didn't take any argument. He was already slowing down and indicating for the hard shoulder. He stopped the car, got out, went round and faced away from the motorway, and unzipped. The release of pressure was indescribable. His body sagged with relief. He stood there pissing heartily, in full view of passing traffic. He didn't care. It seemed to go on. And on. He looked at his watch. He was still pissing when he sensed another car cruising along the hard shoulder to draw up behind the Lamborghini.

12

The police officer was already getting out of his car. It made no difference.

The officer walked towards him with slow, measured strides. 'Not exactly discreet, is it?' he said. 'Not exactly discreet in a big yellow sports car, relieving yourself in full view on the Queen's highway, is it?'

Duncan finished the task in hand, vented a huge sigh and zippered himself up. He turned and offered the policeman a smile that went the full distance.

'I mean,' said the officer, 'it's all a bit of a circus, isn't it?'

'You're right, officer. And I'm not going to try to argue my way out of this one. Let me say this: you fellows do a fine job. I've always said so. So I can't complain when I'm found out myself, now can I? But in my own defence, I wouldn't be standing here like this if there was any other way on this earth. Believe me, I wouldn't. Now without taking anything away from you, or without trying to stop you from doing a proper job, will you give me permission to tell you how I came to be here, like this, on the Queen's highway and all that?'

The officer blinked very slowly. 'Try me,' he said.

A few minutes later Duncan got back in the car, still smiling.

'Did he book you?' Lorna said.

'Nope.'

'What did you say to him?'

'What did I say to him? He's a racing fan. I gave him a winner.'

'You did? Isn't that a bribe?'

Duncan toed the accelerator and got another big-cat squeal out of the engine before pulling on to the motorway. 'Oh no. I just told him I was a jockey and that I was late for the two thirty at Doncaster and I was riding a mare called Trojan's Trumpet and that it was guaranteed to at least get a place but that I needed to get there and that I was really sorry. That's all I said.'

'He went off pretty quick.'

'Oh yes. He's off now to find the nearest bookie.'

She looked at Duncan with a mixture of admiration and disapproval. 'How do you do it?'

'How do I do what?'

'That. People like you, doesn't matter where you fall, you come up smelling of roses, don't you? How do you do it?'

'Ah,' he smiled. 'If only that were true.' He pulled out into the fast lane and put his foot down to the board.

Doesn't matter where you fall, she'd said. He'd fallen off horses enough times, that much was certain. He'd forgotten falling off more times than he remembered. Duncan started riding when he was five and owned his first pony shortly after that first day at the races. He'd ridden gymkhanas and juvenile events until he was impatient for the real thing. He was always falling off. But it wasn't all roses.

Keeping a small training concern going was hard for his old man. It broke your heart and it broke your back. They had occasional help but mostly they had to do everything themselves. Even so, his old man always put Duncan before himself.

Then one year things started to look up. His dad's hard work began to pay off and in one great season he had a slew of point-to-point winners. Then in the next season he started competing with the National Hunt big boys. He had winners at Cheltenham, took fourth place over the giant fences of the celebrated Grand National and finished a great run with victories at Punchestown in Ireland and at Sandown. People started looking their way. Owners were always dissatisfied if their expensive animals weren't pulling in the prizes, and it was easy and lazy to blame the trainer; and so one or two owners were always moving their horses along. Some started to come to Duncan's father.

And one or two big-time trainers didn't like it. Duncan wasn't aware – at the time – how easy it was to make serious enemies in horse racing. Ugly enemies.

At the track, the stewards pointed him to the car park reserved for owners and trainers. With the Lamborghini purring, he crawled into the parking area. He could see Kerry, already in his jockey's silk, standing outside the entrance, puffing on a cigarette and anxiously looking the other way. He slipped on some dark glasses and inched the motor as close as he could to Kerry and wound down the window. Kerry glanced over. He obviously didn't recognise Duncan in his shades, nor the car, because he looked away again. Duncan hit the horn.

Kerry looked over again.

'How are we for time?' Duncan asked him.

Kerry's handsome Irish jaw opened but he didn't say anything. He tossed away his cigarette and stalked over to the car. He peered inside and the skin crinkled around his steely-blue eyes as he took in the red-headed Lorna in the passenger seat, and the plush interior of the car. Then he stepped back and folded his arms, shaking his head in disbelief. 'And you can wipe that bloody silly smirk off your face.'

'Was I smiling?' Duncan said. 'We'll have to stop that, then.'

'How in hell do you do it?' Kerry said. 'Go on. Tell me. I'd really like to know.'

'I've no idea what you're talking about.'

'Really? No? Well tell me something else. Is that a nippy car?'

'Lamborghini? You bet it is.'

'Good. Because when you've finished your race, with the amount of shit you're in today you're going to need to get away from this place very fast.'

2

He'd told that copper on the side of the motorway that Trojan's Trumpet would finish in the frame, and he thought he might. The race was a seller, and Kerry was riding the fancied horse, but there wasn't much in it across a field of six over two-miles-and-four. He got off to a poor, leaping start and was slowly away with four in front, the field already lit up by Kerry. After the second fence a horse called Mountain Block moved up close by and Duncan felt a sudden impulsion from his mount. He gave her a squeeze and she followed Mountain Block. Duncan sensed that she'd got a good turn of foot. He decided to wait and bide his time.

Trojan's trainer Billy Miles had told him to stay on the outside, but Mountain Block tracked to the inner. He was going with it; fuck Billy, it was him riding the horse, not the trainer. Trojan had enough to go past Mountain Block, but Duncan held her, kept her back. He knew she'd got plenty.

It was something his dad had once told him. *Never disappoint a horse.* What he'd meant was that although a horse would often want to leap to the front and you had to hold it back, there were other moments when its mood and form flashed like white heat and you needed to let it go.

It was still about his dad. Well, that and the fact that Duncan was a competitive, bloody-minded and obsessive son-of-a-bitch who didn't like getting beaten at anything, whether it was a donkey derby on Skegness sands or the Gold Cup at

16

Cheltenham. Not that he'd ridden in the Gold Cup. Not yet. But that was coming.

Duncan wanted to give it all back to his dad. He wanted to repay him for all the sacrifices, the loyalty, the things he'd gone without. But time was not on his side. Dad was showing early signs of losing his memory. His own father had been a victim of early dementia, and both Duncan and Charlie knew that he was going the same way. There had already been a clinical diagnosis, and it was not good. Duncan didn't know exactly how many years he would have before the idea of repayment became meaningless. He wanted to do things for his dad before it was too late. He only knew that if he was to achieve any of this and soon, he'd better make smart use of the whip.

He was very certain of what had quickened his father's professional demise. Three terrific seasons had started to pull in the good horses. His dad changed his business model. Instead of scouting, buying, training and selling on quickly, he started to hang on to his winners and look upwards on the National Hunt calendar. The top races brought big cash prizes, and that in turn would attract still more owners.

It was all going so well. Then in a single season it all crashed spectacularly. Failure followed failure. Bad luck stalked bad luck. Then came the doping charge that destroyed him. It was crazy: there wasn't a more honest trainer in the country, but Charlie was hauled up and found guilty. He became ill with the stress and the worry of it all. His burgeoning training business collapsed.

They hit the halfway, the pounding hooves picking up in tempo now, and took a fence together sweetly, Trojan still tucked in behind Mountain Block. From there he moved past two of the other runners, who were never going to be on terms. Kerry was still way out in the lead with the second horse just a length in front, kicking up a lot of shit into Duncan's goggles, half blinding him. The jockey on Mountain Block must have thought the same thing, because he squeezed up, and Duncan followed, still with plenty in hand, and they were through the shit-storm with only Kerry out in front but starting to look tired.

Duncan felt a familiar blood-surge in his brain. This was the moment. He lived for this precise moment. The sound of the hooves blotted out all other sound; the smell of the sweat on the horse's flanks obliterated all other smells; the grip of the reins in his hands and the balance of his toes in the stirrups were the only things he could feel.

We go, thought Duncan, and the horse, picking up his message, just breezed in front of Mountain Block and was soon pressing on Kerry.

Kerry looked back at him. 'Where the fuck did you come from?' he shouted.

'You've fucked it!' Duncan shouted, and he laid his stick over Trojan's haunches. 'You dropped your pants!'

'You're not having this one!' Kerry yelled back.

Duncan was fifteen when he left school. His dad gave him the choice and he leapt right out of the ring. But Charlie figured he'd already taught Duncan everything he could. With things going well, he had taken on other hands, and could afford to send Duncan to a stables where he might learn some new tricks. He'd chosen Penderton, run by an old friend, Dick Sommers. But mainly he had wanted Duncan to work with Dick's head lad.

To call a man closing in on retirement a 'lad' was just one of the many odd things about the racing industry. Head lad Tommy was the wrong side of sixty. A former jockey himself, he'd seen pretty much everything from the days long before TV cameras had featured at the tracks and changed the game. He knew horses, and he knew where all the bodies were buried. He was a fierce taskmaster and had little to say to anyone, preferring to communicate by means of a growl and a curse and a stinging slapped ear.

But it was Tommy who found Duncan crying behind one of the stables at Penderton the day after the doping charge was made to stick. Tommy knew exactly what it was about. The grizzled old boy came up to him and fixed him with his unblinking green and yellow eyes.

'Stop your snivelling. Now listen. Charlie's a good 'un. He didn't let anyone down.' He held his hand up and Duncan backed off a little, thinking he was going to get a slap from the old man. 'See that hand? Your dad can have that hand any day. I owe him. But I'll tell you this for nothing, son. For nothing. He was done over.'

Ashamed to be caught crying Duncan tried to dry his eyes on the back of his hand. 'What?'

'You heard me, son. They got at him.'

'Who?'

Tommy shook his head. He had eyes like ice in a yard bucket on a frosty morning. He poked Duncan on the shoulder with a hard, leathery finger. 'Your old man's a good 'un, and don't you ever forget it.'

But the next time Duncan went up to Penderton, Tommy sent him to bring out a horse called Stormbringer. There in the stable, on the wall, was a dead betting slip. On the reverse were three names. They were the names of three top players in the field: a trainer, an owner and a major jockey. The handwriting was clumsy, almost childlike. Duncan knew that Tommy could barely read or write, but could do so well enough to write down the names of horses. This note was his work.

The dead betting slip was one issued by none other than Billy B. Bonsor, the bookie who had taken Duncan's first ever bet. There was his slogan. *Payment as a Matter of Honour.* Duncan memorised the three names and then tore the slip into tiny pieces. Then he walked out Stormbringer and looked across the yard.

There was Tommy, watching, giving him a look that was as old as time.

Old mates that they were, after the race Kerry and Duncan always exchanged banter and occasionally offered a little flick of the whip when one bested the other. The competition between them as conditionals had been keen. By the time they were full jockeys it was mustard. Now they'd skin a horse with a thin whip to get in front of the other, even if it took them through the gates of hell.

'Close thing.'

'Closer than you think.'

'No, I had you.'

'No you didn't.'

'You let me win, then?'

The stable lads led the horses away, and as Duncan carried his saddle back to the Weighing Room, Billy Miles came over. Billy was a decent trainer and Duncan didn't mind him, though he liked the owner of the horse, George Millichip, a lot less. Billy wore a brown fedora and a Berber coat and he had a way of squinting at you when he talked. 'Not bad,' he said.

'That's what I thought,' Duncan said.

'If you'd kept her on the outside you'd have won that race.'

'Not a chance, Billy.'

'You'll not be told, Duncan, will you?'

'Listen, I've just put a couple of thousand pounds' selling value on that horse for the owner and here you are looking like you've lost a fiver.'

'You can tell him yourself. He's on his way over and he's not best pleased with you.'

20

George Millichip, also wearing a brown fedora but with a camel-hair coat, came striding across the grass. He was already purple in the face. 'What sort of a game do you think you're playing?' There was spittle on his lip.

Duncan saw Billy look away. 'Well done, Duncan. You rode that nag to a good second place, Duncan. You made me a good few quid there, Duncan. Thank you, Duncan, here's a drink for you, Duncan.'

'I'm not talking about the race,' Millichip spat. 'I'm talking about your appalling behaviour. You were so late I was lining up another jockey. You left us no time for instructions. You made us look a pair of fools.'

'How about that! With no effort on my part!'

'What was that?' Millichip replied, angry.

Duncan stopped walking. From behind his saddle he said, 'You should never disappoint a horse. Did you know that?'

Millichip turned to his trainer. 'What the hell is he on about?'

'I'll tell you something else,' Duncan said. 'Did you realise you were breaking one of the rules of horse racing?'

'What?'

'You and Billy here. You're both wearing fedoras at the same time. You can't do that. Only one of you can wear a fedora. The other has to wear a flat cap or something.'

'What?'

'I mean, did you ever see Frank Sinatra and Dean Martin both wearing a fedora together? No. It looks wrong.'

Millichip stared back at him. Billy, chewing on his lip, squinted even harder and looked away again. Duncan hitched his saddle up. 'I've got to get weighed in, so's you can claim your prize money.'

They didn't follow him, but after a moment Duncan heard Millichip shout, 'That's your lot. That's the last ride you'll have for me.'

*

Duncan weighed in and started to strip off his sweat-soaked silks. As he was about to go into the shower, he got a message from his valet that another trainer, a man called Petie Quinn, wanted an urgent word.

Hair still wet and gleaming from the shower, he found Quinn waiting outside the Weighing Room. He was a stocky Irishman with a bullet head of close-cropped silver hair. He was a bruiser, but well-respected, if only middle-ranking. He pretty much kept himself to himself.

Quinn stepped up to Duncan, but from the side, as if he preferred to stand shoulder to shoulder. 'I saw how you rode that seller. Will you ride in the last race for me?' he asked.

'What's going on?'

Quinn looked round like there might be an enemy listening. 'I'm running Brighton Taxi in the last and she's good for a place at least, but my idiot jockey has broken his wrist.' He linked his arm through Duncan's and muscled him away from some eavesdroppers in the corridor. 'We're telling everyone he slipped in the shower, but the fuckin' idjit was making an early weigh and he dumped himself off the scales.'

'He did what?'

'Will you ride for me or not?'

'You're joking! He's riding steeplechasers and he fell off a weighing machine?'

'Yes or no?'

'You've got it.'

Quinn's big face broke into a huge grin. The skin crinkled around his eyes and he offered Duncan a shovel of a hand to shake. 'You do this favour for me and there'll be more rides for you. Plenty more rides.'

'One thing,' Duncan said. 'You'll have to tell George Millichip.'

'What? He doesn't have you exclusively.'

'No, you don't need his permission. Let's say it's a courtesy. Don't discuss it with him. Just let him know.'

Quinn shrugged. 'I'll find him in the owners' and trainers' bar and tell him right away. See you in the paddock.'

So it was one contact lost and another made. No change there then. But it did feel good to be driving out of the reserved car park in the sunflower Lamborghini with Lorna tipped back in the passenger seat as he toed the accelerator. The Lamborghini gargled fuel as he crept out of the gate, getting him attention he could take or leave. He'd made his mark on the card today.

'A first and a second,' Lorna said. 'Are you pleased?'

'It'll do nicely. I came here only expecting to get round on the first one.'

'What's it like to ride a winner?'

He looked at her as he edged out of the racetrack grounds and on to the high road. Her eyes were wide and she darted her tongue to moisten her lips. She wanted an answer to the question no one could ever really answer; the question posed by every lazy journalist who shoved a microphone or a note-book in your face. *How does it feel?* She was a beautiful and naive young thing; it didn't seem right or fair that he was going to have to hurt her just to get revenge on her father. He glanced at her again. Her hair was long and wavy and nut-brown, with natural red highlights; her skin was pale, but her lips were the same rosebud pink that appeared in her cheeks. Her hazel-brown eyes had a delicious sparkle, impossible not to see as an invitation.

He'd pushed Brighton Taxi with hands and heels to an easy victory. All Quinn had said to him in the paddock was to keep him near the front, then give her a squeeze when he felt the time was right. He liked that: a trainer who trusted a jockey to do the job. And it was the horse itself who'd told him when she wanted to go. Duncan had whispered *go on, then* and had given her the squeeze, and it was enough to run out an easy

23

winner. Quinn had been overjoyed and had hugged him like a bear in the winners' enclosure – this man he'd only met an hour earlier – and stood for the champagne afterwards. Duncan had one glass and Lorna had three. But the best part of it was to be raising his glass to the purple-faced George Millichip across the carpet of the owners' bar.

'What's it like to win? I can't tell you,' he said.

'Try.'

'If I told you it was like Christmas Day and your birthday and the first day of the summer holiday all rolled into one, it still wouldn't get close. How does this thing work?' he asked, indicating the eight-track tape-cartridge player in the dashboard.

She flipped the glove compartment open and found a cartridge the size of a paperback book. It had never been played. 'Old stuff. Jimi Hendrix. Do you want to stick it in?'

He smiled at her and asked her to turn up the volume. He drove out of Doncaster towards the motorway, and as he took the country lane approaching the slip road he noticed a muddy old sunken track between the trees. He bounced off the road and bumped the Lamborghini along the track, which was just about wide enough.

'What are you doing?' Lorna shouted.

'You want to know how it feels to win? Wait there.'

He got out of the car and walked around to the passenger door. When he opened it, Lorna's eyes were blazing at him. There was a soft smile on her lips, like she knew exactly what was about to happen. Duncan reached down the side of her seat, pressed a catch and the seat fell back, taking Lorna with it. She screamed in surprise and then giggled. But she stopped giggling when he reached both hands under her skirt and hooked his thumbs around the waistband of her semi-opaque black tights, tearing them from her in one deft movement. Her exposed legs were milky white and the neat triangle of pubic hair confirmed she was a genuine redhead. He parted her legs and stuck his tongue deep inside her.

She was shocked. 'Don't do that!' she shouted.

He ignored her. She grabbed his hair, trying to pull his head away from her pussy. He resisted. At last he came up for air and said, 'It's what grown-ups do.'

'Really?' she said. Then she surrendered. 'Jesus!'

He forced down his trousers and got into a tangle until she helped him. He lifted her ankles over his shoulders and plunged deep inside her. They both howled as the psychedelic sounds of Jimi Hendrix blasted from the open doors.

Pretty soon he turned her over so that her pale rump was sticking up in the air. The smell of new leather seats and the smell of sex somehow got mixed up in his mind. He was trying to work her dress free over her head so that he could grab her tits at the same time. He managed to get it over her freckled shoulders, but the unbuttoned neck stuck to her skull like some kind of exotic headdress and wouldn't go any further. He gave up trying to rip the thing free. At last he swelled to double his normal size and came inside her.

He lay across her, his head on her shoulder as they waited to recover.

Finally Lorna said, 'Is that what it's like to ride a winner?'

'Pfff mhhh,' he said.

'What?'

'Pretty much.'

He dropped Lorna back at her mansion, but only after checking that Daddy Cadogan's helicopter wasn't on the pad. He wasn't quite prepared to meet the Duke just yet. Lorna told him to come in while one of the staff summoned him a taxi, but he didn't much fancy hanging around for the small talk, so she said she'd get a cab to pick him up on the road.

'When will I see you again?' she asked with spaniel eyes.

'I almost can't wait,' he said, kissing her. 'I'll call you.'

He walked up the long driveway and waited at the gates for the cab to appear. It started to rain, so he took shelter in the trees, looking back at the lights of the grand house. He was already feeling a little sorry for Lorna. He didn't have to be a psychologist to see that a kid like that was throwing herself at him because she had no decent family life. She was sweet. *But don't go soft on her*, a voice in his head warned. *You're here for a reason.*

The headlights of an approaching car washed over him, but he was hidden under the trees as it slowed and turned into the driveway. It was driven by a chauffeur in livery. And not in a helicopter this time but there in the back seat was Duke Cadogan himself, living it large.

That was close, thought Duncan as he watched the red tail lights recede up the long drive. After a minute the cab arrived. He flagged it down and got in, giving the cabbie his address.

'Had a good day, sir?' asked the cheerful cabbie.

'It's a struggle,' Duncan said. 'But you mustn't weaken.'

'Quite right,' said the cabbie, who then went on to tell him what was wrong with the country, the government, the tax he had to pay, the immigration policy and the lousy through-flow of traffic.

There were worse things you could be, Duncan thought, than a winning jockey.

3

When he got back to his flat, the first thing he did was call Kerry. His friend had been unseated in the fifth race. When Duncan saw him he was fine, but there was a fear he might have torn ligaments in his ankle.

Falling from a horse was an art form. The art was not getting an injury if you could get away with it, and pretending that it didn't hurt if you had. His old man used to tell him that if nothing was broken he was to get back on the horse. Duncan learned to hide pain even from himself. After a while he drew admiring remarks from his father. 'You're the iron boy,' Charlie would say. Duncan almost started to welcome the next fall so he could prove to himself exactly how hard he was.

But though the falls almost always hurt, that wasn't a problem for a jockey. It was the damage that kept you out of racing that really mattered, and the course doctor had told Kerry he was going to be out for a few weeks.

'You're joking,' Duncan said over the telephone. 'That's fucked.'

'The bastard of a quack,' Kerry said. 'I got up and walked away but he saw me limping. He took off my boot and I hit the roof. It's torn.'

The implications for Kerry were serious. He sent every penny he earned back to his family in County Kildare, where he had a seriously ill mother and three younger siblings to worry about. If he wasn't racing, he wasn't earning.

'You know that Petie Quinn fellow?' Duncan said. 'He was so pleased with me winning that last race he gave me a good bonus, cash in hand. You can have that and pay me back when you're riding again.'

'I can't ask for your winnings, Duncan.'

'No, you can't. And you can't refuse me either.'

'Fuck off with you.'

'No, you fuck off. That's settled then.'

Kerry went quiet on the other end.

'Are you okay?' Duncan asked him.

'Sure. Pissed off. You're one o' the best, Duncan.'

'Fuck off now. Talk to you later.'

The next day he took a bus to see his dad. Charlie was living in a care home called Grey Gables. It was one of God's waiting rooms, and Charlie knew it. The smell of urine was just about masked by the smell of bleach. There were about sixty residents, ranging from fun, sprightly pensioners to the barely breathing. It wasn't what either of them wanted but it was governed by their income, and the staff seemed caring enough.

Duncan tapped on the door. Charlie's eyes opened wide with delight to see his son. He put a finger to his lips and beckoned him into his room before gently closing the door after him. 'You'll never guess what's happened here, Duncan. Sit down, sit down.' He made Duncan slump into the soft upholstered chair while he drew up a hard-backed chair for himself.

'What's gone off?'

He folded his arms. 'They've give me an *injun*!'

'What?'

'My new carer. She comes and does the bed and checks up on me. *Injun*.' He waved his palms in the air – jazz hands – as if that denoted extraction from the Indian subcontinent.

'Is she all right?'

'Bloody beautiful. Lovely. Some prat up the corridor wouldn't have her 'cos she's an *injun*. They asked me. I said I don't mind. Glad to see the back o' that other lazy sow. Did I tell you about that pound note left on the table?'

Charlie claimed that his previous cleaner had been lifting small change left around in the room.

'You did, Dad, you did.'

'They think you're ga-ga if you're in this place. Nothing wrong with my memory.'

Most days, thought Duncan.

In fact Charlie's long-term memory was superb. He could remember every detail of each horse he'd ever trained and raced. He knew its place, the prize money, the condition of the track and the wear and tear in the saddle leather. He was a one-man horse-racing almanac.

Charlie uncapped a bottle and poured himself a whisky. He didn't offer his son a glass because Duncan didn't like the stuff. Charlie wanted to hear all about Doncaster, and Duncan told him everything except how he got there in the Lamborghini and his Jimi Hendrix experience in the woods afterwards.

'To hell with Millichip. He's going backwards. So who is this Petie Quinn fellow, who you rode for in the last race?'

'I don't know much about him, Dad. Gave me a good drink on top of my fee. Owns and trains.'

'How the hell does he afford that?'

'No idea. Doesn't spend it on fancy suits, that's for fuckin' sure. Looks like a dosser.'

Charlie tapped his bottom lip. 'Irishman. Petie Quinn. Wait! I've got him! Rough-looking fellow, comes up to you sideways.'

'That would be him.'

'Can't say I know much about him either. But I know he once got into a row with Osborne. No love lost there.'

Osborne. That was one of the dangerous names, along with Cadogan. Osborne was a trainer. Any mention of those names could bring on a black mood and a bout of bitter recrimination, sometimes even leading to heavy whisky-drinking and an episode of dementia. Duncan had become expert at steering the subject away from the three names he'd found on the back of the betting slip. He was about to change the subject, sharp, by talking about Kerry tearing the ligaments in his ankle, but he was saved by a delicate knock on the door.

It was Charlie's Indian carer.

'Ah, Mrs Solanki,' Charlie shouted. 'We were just talking about you. I want you to meet my son.'

'Don't get up!' Mrs Solanki was in the house uniform. She wore lots of gold rings and had a brilliant crimson spot in the middle of her forehead.

But Charlie and Duncan were already on their feet. 'Pleased to meet you, Mrs Solanki. You're looking after my dad? That's a tough job.'

'He keep ask me to marry him,' she giggled. She had a strong Punjabi accent. 'But I say no, I have husband!'

'She comes into my room like a beam of light,' Charlie said.

'I come to make bed. I come back later.'

'She seems fun,' Duncan said after the woman had excused herself and left.

'She's a doll. What were we talking about?'

'I was just telling you about Kerry ripping his ankle, Dad.'

Duncan spent all afternoon with Charlie, sifting through the details of the day's racing at Doncaster and at all the other track meetings around the country. They talked about the big Boxing Day meeting at Kempton with the wonderful Prince Dagobert Chase, a glamorous Grade 1 National Hunt fixture open to horses aged four years or older. It was the second most prestigious chase in all of England. A ride in that sort of exalted company was what Duncan wanted; but he was dreaming. The best he might hope for was another race on the same card, but no one had picked up on him. Kerry was booked for a ride that day. Duncan brushed away a selfish hope that he might not be ready in time. There was always the possibility that Kerry would persuade the trainer to give Duncan the ride.

Charlie had the same thought. 'Who is putting Kerry up? At Kempton, I mean.'

Duncan mentioned the name of the trainer.

'I know him. I'll call him.'

'No, Dad, best not.'

'What? Is that another one you've been mouthing off to?'

'Kerry might have a word. Best leave it.'

The fact was that having his dad put in a word was sometimes counterproductive. Charlie was innocent of everything that had been said about him. Charlie knew that; Duncan knew that. But the trio who had stitched him up had done such a good job, there was still plenty of doubt everywhere. Even amongst folk Charlie might count as old friends and allies. Reputations in horse racing were hard won but easily ruined. Duncan heard how people talked. In the Weighing Room and the owners' bar. In the bar and at the gallops. Jokes. Whispers. Rumours.

Hell. Sometimes you mentioned a name and all you got was a raised eyebrow or a flared nostril and that was it.

If he were a killing man, he would have done the job by now, for what they'd done to his dad. But he wasn't. He didn't want blood. He only wanted what was fair, but which no court of law could ever give him. He wanted revenge. He wanted justice.

Duncan had learned about summary justice as a lad, when he was at Penderton with old Tommy. When he was taken on, he cycled the seven miles there and back every day. He never saw the owner, Dick Sommers, and at first the job was mainly about shovelling shit. But when gruff Tommy saw that he was interested and knowledgeable, he started to let him do more than groom the horses and pick their hooves. If Duncan did

31

well, Tommy would bare his teeth and nod; if he was careless, he'd get a cuff round the side of the head. It was a shock to be slapped like that: his dad had never once hit him. But it only made him more attentive, more determined to get things right.

One Saturday in March when Sommers and his team were away at Cheltenham, Duncan arrived early for work and leaned his bike against the fence. There was a gallops adjacent to the stables where the horses were trained up an incline, and one of the stable hands, a fox-faced girl named Dawn, was putting a horse called Patroculus through his paces. Duncan knew there was something special about Patroculus and that he had been rested for several weeks after going lame ahead of a big race. Tommy and another man in a sporting trilby were leaning against the rail watching the animal race up the hill.

Being early, Duncan approached the men from behind, whereupon they both spun round and stared hard at him as if he were a spy.

'I wondered if I could watch,' Duncan said.

'Fuck off,' Tommy said.

Duncan tried to gabble a word of apology.

'Fuck off,' Tommy said again, through gritted teeth.

Duncan felt his scalp flush. He didn't need to be told three times. He turned on his heel and walked back to the stables. He could hear the men talking. After a few moments one of them called him back. The two men were still regarding him steadily: Tommy scowling from under his cloth cap and the man in the trilby looking amused. This other man beckoned him.

'How long you been with us, son?'

'Eight weeks.'

'Eight weeks. What Tommy means, son, is that when you work at these stables, you keep your mouth shut about every-thing you see and everything you hear. Yes?'

'Yes.'

'Good lad. You can stay and watch, though we're about done.'

Tommy shook his head, but both men turned their attention back to the horse. Dawn was cantering Patroculus towards them, and when she drew abreast, she pulled him up and walked over. She looked meaningfully at Duncan.

'It's all right,' said the man in the trilby.

'He was pulling my arms out. He hasn't even broken sweat.'

'What about his pipes?' said the man.

'Nothing wrong with his pipes,' Tommy growled.

Dawn shrugged.

'Six weeks,' said the man in the trilby.

'Eight,' said Tommy.

'Six.'

The two men turned and walked back towards the stables. Duncan was left standing alone. He turned to admire the horse, but Dawn was already trotting away.

A couple of weeks later he was cycling to Penderton. A light mist hung over the fields and he had to climb a hill before he could freewheel down to the stables. As he took a bend, he spotted a car parked between some trees. Its driver had a pair of binoculars trained on the gallops in the hollow.

When he got to the stables he immediately told Tommy.

'Where?'

'There's an old farm track at the top of the hill. It's overgrown. But he's taken his car up the track. There's a gap in the trees and you can see the gallops from there.'

'What car?'

Duncan told him it was a Wolseley saloon.

'Yep.' Tommy said no more but whistled up two rugged young men who also worked at the stables. They piled into a Land Rover and with Tommy at the wheel they lurched out of the yard. It was the first time Duncan had seen Tommy smiling since he'd started working there. Just outside the gate the Land Rover suddenly braked. Tommy got out and waved for Duncan to go with them.

Duncan climbed in beside Phil, one of the young men, who looked at him and sniffed. They drove up the hill and Tommy stopped to let Phil out, so that he could come up behind the spy. Then they cruised to a stop by the gap in the hedge and the rest of them got out quietly.

When the spy with the binoculars saw them coming, he turned away and walked straight into Phil, coming up from the rear. Phil grabbed the man's collar.

'Now then, Derek,' Tommy said.

Duncan had seen lads roughed up at school but he'd never actually seen adults give someone a beating. He stood back, hardly sure whether he was supposed to join in. But Tommy stood watching with his hands on his hips. The man called Derek seemed to accept his fate.

One of the young stable hands held the spy's arms behind his back. The other squatted down and offered three quick, hard jabs to the stomach. Duncan heard all the air wheeze out of the man and then saw him collapse to his knees. He was released by the stable hand pinning him from behind, who stepped round and dealt another hard blow to the side of the man's head, landing near the ear, and a further blow to the neck.

The man collapsed on the woodland floor. It was all brutally efficient.

'He's fakin' it,' said one of the young men.

'Either that or he's soft as shit,' said the other.

Duncan didn't think the man was faking it at all. There was a small flow of blood leaking from his ear. He was making noises like he was straining to breathe.

'Now that's just a taster,' said Tommy. 'You've got the message, haven't you, Derek?'

Derek, his face in the dark woodland mulch, wheezed a kind of reply.

'That'll do,' Tommy said.

When the Land Rover returned to the yard, the three men

got out in high spirits, laughing, boisterous and with shining eyes. Duncan got out too. Tommy nodded at him and made a playful feint of a punch in the ribs. Reading Tommy's feelings was harder than reading those of a horse; even so, it was evident that the head lad was pleased.

'I wanted you to see that,' Tommy said. 'There's a thing called loyalty. That chap Derek used to work for us. It might have looked a bit rough, but it's finished now. Finished. He's been paid back and he won't come again.'

'What if he goes to the police?'

'He won't. Loyalty, Duncan.'

Tommy was pleased enough, a couple of weeks later, to give Duncan an exercising ride out on a retiring champion chaser called Jabberwocky. The difference between Jabberwocky – long past his best – and anything he'd previously ridden was the difference between a Porsche and a pedal bike. Duncan's loyalty – and his future in the racing game – was sealed. Another thing that was sealed for him was the idea that if you wanted to right a wrong, you took it into your own hands.

Duncan left Grey Gables but only after giving his father a little hug – something that would never have been acceptable to either of them in the old days. Soft, Charlie would have called it. These days they had more time for a bit of soft. He also left two new tenners on the table, even though Charlie said he didn't need it.

He said goodbye to Mrs Solanki and took the bus home. When he got to his apartment he felt a sudden pang of hunger, like someone grabbing his intestines with sharp fingernails and twisting. He had a glass of juice and smoked a cigarette instead. He told himself that he might have a spoonful of soup later on that evening.

He made a couple of calls. Not much doing. The way for a

freelancer to get rides was to get yourself down to a stables and ride out first thing in the morning, until they got your trust and gave you a chance. Of course, getting in there in the first place was the trick. The higher up the pecking order for the good horses you went, the less they needed you to ride out with them.

Much more recent to the sport was the idea of getting an agent. He wasn't so sure about that. Agents were often known as 'characters' in the business. Characters were people who suddenly and impulsively made a dash to Rio de Janeiro. Anyway, there were only a few agents in the country, with most people getting their rides the old-fashioned way. Getting an agent – a sound one – wasn't as easy as you might think: an agent might take you on if you were already getting the rides coming to you, in which case why the hell would you need one? Still, Duncan was desperate enough to try anything. Petie Quinn had promised him there would be more rides, and on the strength of that and his win in the last race he left a couple of messages saying he was looking for a change of agent. Change from not having one, that is.

He felt a stab of hunger again so he decided to go and spend a couple of hours at the sauna. He had read somewhere about Continental jockeys using saunas to lose weight. It wasn't exactly a popular idea with his contemporaries, most of whom preferred to pop a pee pill, but Duncan found it worked well for him if he spent enough time there. It was also somewhere he could go to try to calm his racing mind, and to work things out in his head.

He had a membership at a local gym and they had a decent pool and sauna set-up. If you chose the right time to go, it wasn't crowded with blokes picking their toenails with a penknife or sitting with their legs apart to advertise their fat willies. He slung on a jacket ready to make the twenty-minute walk to the gym.

Before he left, he noticed that Lorna had left a bracelet on the bedside table in the bedroom. He thought he should call her, but then checked himself. He didn't want to appear keen; and if she'd left her bracelet, she'd probably done so deliberately. She would call him. He was still looking at the bracelet when the phone rang.

He had an intuition that it would be her. He let the phone ring. Then he decided to pick up in case it was one of the agents returning his call. It was a male voice he didn't recognise.

'Is that Duncan?'

''Tis.'

'Hi, Duncan mate, how are you doing?'

'Who is this?'

'I'm told you're looking for an agent.'

'Who is this? Peter Fraser?'

'No.'

'Ernie Calmun?'

'No. Ernie told me you'd called him. He's not taking anyone on just now so he passed your name on.'

'And you are?'

'Mike Ruddy.'

'Never heard of you, sorry.'

'Yes you have. I used to be a jockey. Before I was an agent.'

Duncan thought about it. 'Oh hell, yes, I do know you. I've ridden against you once or twice. I didn't know you were an agent now.'

'That's right. What you doing right at this moment?'

'I'm just on my way to the hot box.'

'The what?'

'The sauna.'

'What the hell is that all about?'

'Helps you lose weight.'

'Which one? Which sauna, I mean.'

Duncan told him the name of the gym. Ruddy knew it. 'I'll

see you there in half an hour. I'll join you in the hot box. Ha ha! I like that: hot box. Not that I need to any more. I'm an agent: I can be a fat fuck, right?'

'Wait a minute, wait a minute! How long have you been an agent?'

'About five minutes. See you in the box. I mean hot box.'

Click.

He didn't notice the girl at the desk beaming at him when he signed in and took a towel for the sauna. He was still wondering how he'd been manipulated into meeting Mike Ruddy. It was already out of the question. There were only four really big agents in the country and he needed to be with one of them. Beyond that there was a handful of second-tier agents that he might have to go with. They didn't include Ruddy, who as far as he knew wasn't an agent at all.

He had the sauna to himself and turned the dial up high. Apart from anything else, it was a good way of discouraging company. He relaxed back with his eyes closed. But within a few minutes the door opened and a small, dark, wiry figure with a towel knotted at the waist came inside. He didn't look at Duncan. He took his seat on the bench, put his hands on his knees, leaned forward and vented a theatrical sigh. He breathed out heavily three or four times, then turned to Duncan.

'Yep. I'm Mike Ruddy.'

Duncan's eyes were still half closed. 'You're not an agent at all.'

'Yes I am.'

'No you're not. I looked at today's cards. You were riding earlier today at Leicester.'

'That's right. I was. It was my last race ever.'

'What?'

'I quit. I'm no longer a jockey. I'm a jockey's agent. Phew! Hot!'

38

Duncan took a harder look at the man. He was gazing back at him, headlights full-beam, offering a huge smile. He looked like a more handsome version of an orc.

Ruddy reached out and touched Duncan on the wrist. Duncan looked at the spot and Ruddy withdrew his hand. 'Listen. I've been a jockey for twelve years. I've had some winners but I'm never going to get near to being a champion. I know that; everyone knows that. My own agent is – was – Ernie Calmun, who you phoned earlier. Well he's been saddling me with losers. Today's horse blew up on me and the last one had a wind problem and it's all over. Going nowhere. So I'm in Ernie Calmun's office late this afternoon giving him a bollocking and having a right old fallout about the rides he's giving me. Then his secretary pipes up. He thinks he's a big shot so he has one of those intercom things on his desk and she goes, "What will I tell Duncan Claymore?" And he goes, "Tell him I don't have a place on my list right now." An' it's like lightning! I think: no, I can't ever be a champion jockey, but I can be an *agent* to a champion jockey! And I quit there and then. On the spot.'

'You're mad.'

'And you know who that future champion jockey is?' Ruddy held out a hand that wanted shaking. 'Congratulations, Mr Duncan Claymore!'

Duncan looked at the hand, but the only thing he shook was his head. 'You don't have any clients. No office. No track record. You don't have anything.'

'You're not listening! I have loads of contacts. I've ridden for every owner and trainer you can name. I've got three jockeys who will come with me. No, four. Four. Christ, you like it hot in here. It's the future, honestly, Duncan, I can see it coming. Every jockey will have an agent pretty soon. Don't get left behind.'

'Which four?'

'What?'

'Which four jockeys have you got?'

'Palmer will come if I ask him. He's a pal. And Jangers. You must know Jangers.'

'Both good jockeys; both past it.'

'Not for two more years. Which is all I need. Plus I've got the two top conditionals will come with me.'

'Conditionals!'

'You're only just out of conditional yourself! What's more, if you say yes, they will all come. They know you're good. But ask yourself why you need an agent.'

'Oh yes. To take ten per cent of my loot. I need that.'

'Don't be a drip! I'm not talking about that.'

'Enlighten me.'

'Excessive use of the lip, old son!'

'That's an old joke.'

'But it's true. You can't shut your gob. But here's the thing, young jockey. They like me! The owners and the trainers, they all love me. How the fuck do you think I've been getting so many rides all these years when I'm second-rate? So I'll do all the talking for you. I'll be good at it. I'll get the rides for you, wait and see. You'll be turning this one and that one away, you will! It's 'cos I'm so fuckin' likeable.'

Duncan sighed. There was a logic. He looked at Ruddy and the sweat was pouring from his temples down the sides of his face. 'This is a fuckin' crazy idea.'

'Do you always have it this hot? Listen. It all adds up. You say yes, the others say yes, it snowballs. I've got contacts in the press. We announce a new agency. They don't know I'm riding bare-arse, do they? It's all how you tell the story, Duncan. I make out it's exclusive, picky. Play hard-to-get. I know who is unhappy with their agents. We'll tap 'em up, like they do in football. This is going to be great! A new agency! A dynasty! What do you say?'

'I say I'd have to be fucked in the head to agree to that.'

Ruddy leaned in closer. His eyes were like the backs of shiny black beetles. His smile got wider. 'Six months. Give me six months to make it work.'

'That's a long time.'

'No it ain't. Christ! I might have to get out of here in a minute! I know someone who went to sleep for six months.'

'What?'

'He went to Ibiza and drank himself into a coma. Came round six months later. Says he feels much better for it. You won't notice six months.'

'It's a long time from where I'm sitting.'

'You're not listening! You know you'll get nowhere before Christmas. January is a washout for business. February before you even start a conversation. No one will talk in March while the Cheltenham Festival is on. That's April before they even think about it. There you are. May. June. Six months.' He blinked, wiped sweat from his brow and leaned in closer. His eyes were wide with a mad gleam. 'Well?'

Duncan blinked.

'I saw you blink! Is that a yes? Is it?'

Duncan looked at this madman smiling in his face. The sweat streamed from him now. He was like a child with his enthusiasm. 'I must be fuckin' mad,' Duncan said.

Ruddy let go a roar of triumph. He jumped off the bench, whipped off his towel and danced around the sauna. He punched the air. He clapped his hands. He performed a Mick Jagger dance, hands on hips, back and forth in front of Duncan.

'Put your tackle away,' Duncan protested, 'before I change my mind.'

Then Ruddy fainted from the heat, hitting the tiled floor with a slap.

4

The rides came in for him over the Christmas period. Kerry, good as his word, managed to get some of his lost rides assigned to Duncan. Then Petie Quinn called him with a surprise. It would be impossible to speak sideways into a telephone, but somehow Quinn managed it.

'That idjit who fell off the weigh machine. He's out for a couple of weeks and I want you to take all his rides.'

'All of them? How many is that?'

'Hold on. I'll be putting my spectacles on to read it to you. I don't want to get it wrong.' The exercise of putting on glasses seemed to take a lot of time and a fair bit of laboured breathing. Duncan waited patiently. 'We go to Ludlow on the eighteenth; then I've two running at Exeter the next day; then a seller at Worcester; then on the twenty-first nothin', but the day after, two again at Lingfield . . .'

'That's a lot of horses,' Duncan said.

'Is it too many for you?'

'Hell, no.'

'Then on Boxing Day at Kempton—'

'You're joking!'

'Don't get excited. It's only the first race. Then I've got two more the day after at Wetherby and then at Punchestown across the water if you're up for it on the twenty-ninth, and that's it, and we'll see how you do before we get into the new year.'

Duncan almost dropped the phone. 'I didn't know you had so many horses.'

'I'm coming into my time, Duncan. Is it yes or do I have to look for someone else?'

'Look no further, Petie. I'm your boy.'

'We haven't talked terms. I've never met a jockey who doesn't talk terms first.'

'I have a feeling you'll do right by me.'

'Well ...'

'Listen. I've got myself an agent.'

Petie growled. 'I'm not much of a one for agents.'

'Never mind. But I'll let him pretend that he got me all these rides. Okay by you?'

'That's your funeral. So it's yes to everything? I've got some new colours, by the way. We'll have them for you for Ludlow. The daughter designed them. They're not rubbish or anything.'

'Right.'

'You'll want to come and see the set-up?'

'Sure.'

'How about tomorrow?'

Duncan's head was buzzing. He'd gone from three rides over the Christmas period to fifteen. He had to sit down and map it all out to see where the conflicts lay. Any more rides and he would need a secretary to co-ordinate his schedule. Luckily for him there were only two conflicts. One of them could be dealt with if he could leave quickly and get to the second track for a late race. It occurred to him that a fast car – not unlike a Lamborghini – wasn't essential but would be helpful. The other conflict was with one of his own rides. He would have to call the trainer – a man he liked a lot – and explain.

It occurred to him that he could hide behind his new agent, Mike Ruddy. After all, that was what agents were for. But it went

43

against Duncan's nature. He preferred to do his own dirty work, so he called up the trainer and explained his predicament. The trainer, a small-time operator, was disappointed but understanding; halfway through the conversation, though, Duncan remembered that Ruddy claimed to have two senior jockeys on his books. He asked if one of them would be an acceptable substitute and the trainer said he would be thrilled to have either.

Next Duncan called Ruddy. He broke the news that Quinn had offered him eleven rides.

'Eleven!'

'Yes, and you get no commission on them either, so don't ask.' The normal arrangement was for an agent to net ten per cent of a jockey's fee plus ten per cent of any win bonus. But since Ruddy hadn't found the rides, he wasn't about to argue. 'But if it helps, you can go and brag that you got the rides for me.'

Ruddy was happy with that.

Duncan said, 'Where are you with Palmer?'

'Oh, he's with me. Or he says he will be officially as soon as I can offer him a ride.'

'I've got one for him.'

Ruddy checked Palmer's schedule and there was no conflict. 'It's working! I'm in business!' he shouted down the phone.

'Whoa, Bess! It's only one commission,' Duncan said.

'It's my first of many. Wait till you see. I'm going to talk to Palmer.'

'Another thing. I'll be riding at Kempton on Boxing Day.'

'You're joking! Can I tell 'em I got that one for you too?'

'You can tell them what the hell you like.'

'I'm sorry I'm late,' Duncan said, kissing Lorna before he sat down. They were having lunch at the Ritz. Not because either of them liked it, but because Lorna's father had an account. The name of Cadogan carried weight with the staff and got them a good table. But it didn't allow Duncan to eat without being 'correctly attired'. With seconds of his arrival, the maître d' asked him if he could have a word. Duncan had arrived wearing a neat grey suit but with an open-necked shirt. The maître d' offered him the loan of a tie and escorted him out to the reception area, where he was given a choice from several.

'I should wear it as a headband,' Duncan said when he sat down again.

'Is it awful?' Lorna said, glancing round the restaurant as if she hadn't seen it before. 'This was the only place I could think of, and anyway, the old bastard will pick up the bill, won't he?'

'Is that how you think of him? The old bastard?'

Lorna had called him. She wanted to meet him again. It was she who had suggested central London.

'I suppose I shouldn't talk about him like that. But you don't know what he's like.'

'No, I don't.' Duncan scowled at the card in front of him. 'Can you translate this menu?'

'The food here is ghastly. Anyway, you said you never eat much.'

'I don't. They can't muck up the soup, can they?'

She wrinkled her nose. 'I saw the Prime Minister eating here one day with some of her cabinet. She hardly touched the food.'

'She should be a jockey.'

Lorna reached across the table and stroked his arm. 'Why have you been hiding from me, Duncan? Didn't we have a great day out at Doncaster?'

Duncan ordered something called *potage aux carottes* and Lorna had *foie gras*. She also ordered a bottle of Chablis. She'd obviously been there many times with her parents. Duncan wasn't made uncomfortable by the stiff formality of the place, but neither was he particularly impressed by crisp linen and heavy crystal glassware. He could take it or leave it. It was just

45

that he felt he had more in common with the waiters than the diners.

Lorna read his thoughts. She looked a little sad. 'It's dull here, isn't it? Next time I'll think of somewhere more exciting.'

Duncan smiled to himself. She was already projecting the pair of them into the future. 'It's fine. Let's have a glass of wine.'

During the meal Lorna dropped her napkin. Duncan, watching like a hawk, saw how the waiter's nostrils flared as he dipped down beside her to retrieve it. The waiter put the napkin back on the table but saw Duncan looking at him. He'd been caught and he knew it.

'That man was sniffing you,' Duncan said after the waiter had gone.

Lorna preened the hair at the back of her neck. 'That's disgusting.'

Duncan looked at her. She was wearing a short, skimpy black dress with black tights and shiny black heels. She also wore poppy-red lipstick. 'Go to the ladies' room and take off your knickers,' he commanded.

'I can't. I'm not wearing any.'

He leaned across and stroked the side of her dress, feeling the coarse line of suspenders under her dress.

'Stockings, not tights,' she said.

'You gorgeous slut.'

She licked her poppy-red lips. 'Do you want to get a room?'

'What? At these prices?'

'I can put it on account.'

'How do you do that?'

'I have Daddy's code word. All I have to do is tell the staff. It covers room, dinner, everything.'

'Tell me the code word.'

'No.'

'Tell me.'

'No. You'd only abuse it.'

'How would I abuse it?'

Lorna narrowed her eyes at him. 'Bringing women here and things like that.'

'Do you think I'm seeing other women?'

'I'm sure you do.'

'You're wrong. The only woman I'm seeing right now is you.'

'Right now?'

'Tell me the code.'

The room in the Ritz was enormous. It had a marble mantel-piece, elegant sofa, furniture of polished mahogany and heavy red velvet curtains. The gold tie-ropes for the curtains were missing. These had been used, at Lorna's suggestion, to tie her wrists to the enormous king-sized bed. She lay face down on the bed, nude but for her black stockings and suspenders. Her ankles were similarly tethered, with her legs stretched wide apart, but with the white cotton belts from the bathrobes supplied by the hotel.

Duncan, having carefully tied the knots as requested, was slowly undressing. He'd had more Chablis than soup, and the wine had made him heady. The sight of her peachy pink bottom already had him on fire. He was hard as a rock. He was just determined not to rush things.

'I'm not telling you the code,' Lorna said, petulantly.

'Did I ask again?'

'I'm not telling you, so don't ask.'

'Okay.'

'So don't ask.'

You're being slow, thought Duncan. *She actually wants me to make her spit it out.*

Naked, he got on to the bed with her and ran his index finger slowly down the length of her spine. 'Well tell me this, Lorna.

How is it that an eighteen-year-old girl has such … sophisticated sexual tastes?'

She sighed. 'Kiss my neck. Daddy has a Betamax with a nice collection of what he calls foreign art films.'

'Foreign art films?'

'Hmmm. Do that again. He keeps them locked in his office. But his estate manager cut me an extra key in return for a favour.'

'I can imagine what that favour was. You're a naughty girl, aren't you?'

'Yes. I am. And we know what happens to naughty girls, don't we?' She swayed her bottom a little, as if to tell him what she wanted. Instead he kissed her neck and ran his tongue down her spine. When she purred, he spanked her buttock hard.

She cried out. But then said, 'You can spank me harder.'

He slapped her again, this time raising a neat red handprint on her white buttock. She tensed but pushed her bottom in the air for more. She purred again and he rewarded her with another slap. With each slap he pushed his way a little further inside her.

'You're divine,' she said.

He nibbled the side of her neck and gently bit her shoulders. He reached round to pull at her nipples, which had become like hard berries. She shuddered under him. He'd never known a woman who could come so easily.

He had her spread out like a starfish and she occasionally pulled at the restraints as if she wanted to break free, but would give in and bury her face back in the pillow. At last he came inside her and lay face down on her back, feeling their sweat mix and cool under his body.

They lay like that for a long time. Eventually she said, 'You okay?'

'Now give me the code.'

'Ha! Not a chance. You should have wrung it out of me.

Don't you know a woman will give you anything just before she comes?'

'Really?' He climbed off her and moved across to the shower. He switched it on and above the sound of the rushing water he heard her call to him.

'Untie me, Duncan. I want to get in there with you.'

He ignored her and stepped into the shower. When he switched it off, she was still calling him.

He got dressed quickly.

'Where are you going?'

'I have a meeting. I'll be back in an hour or two.'

'Untie me!'

'Relax.'

'Untie me, you bastard!'

He walked across to her and made to untie her wrist. Then he kissed her instead. 'Don't go away.'

He could still hear her muffled shouts as he walked down the corridor to call the lift.

He met up with Mike Ruddy at the Pillars of Hercules on Greek Street in Soho. It was a smoky joint padded out with tired professionals and creative types. Ruddy said he'd rented a tiny office around the corner and was in the process of equipping it. So far he had a telephone, a desk with no chair and a paintbrush. Duncan suspected he was living there.

When Duncan arrived at the pub, Ruddy was already three quarters of the way down a mug of bitter. At the table with him but drinking white wine was Aaron Palmer, the senior jockey who'd also thrown in his lot with Ruddy. Ruddy crowed at Duncan's arrival and scuttled off to get him a glass of wine and another beer for himself. The two jockeys nodded at each other.

'He managed to talk you into it too?' Duncan said, glancing round. All jockeys had a habit of checking out the faces seated about them in a bar. Just in case they might say something that could be misconstrued – or correctly construed – as inside information.

'Ah, fuck it,' said Palmer.

Palmer was thirty-eight. He was already cruising to retirement. With most jump jockeys retiring around the age of thirty-five, he maybe had a couple more seasons left. Unlike flat jockeys, who were more likely to ride until they were fifty, jump jockeys started to feel the pain of hitting the ground at thirty miles per hour on a regular basis. About one in every ten rides you ended up with your face in the wet grass, hugging your ribs. You could see that Palmer had lost his appetite for mud pie. In the Weighing Room some of the jockeys called him the Monk, not just because he had a severe haircut like a tonsure, but also because he was a loner with an intense stare.

Duncan wondered if sticking at a job for long enough changed your face. He'd seen fishmongers who looked at you like a haddock on a marble slab. Palmer had a ridiculously long, thin horse-face, which made you wonder if he'd started out like that. He also had a habit of chewing on nothing at all. He had everything but the bridle and the blaze.

'So how did he talk you round?' Palmer wanted to know.

'I'm still not sure. Plus I didn't already have an agent.'

'That's ridiculous. Lad with your talents.'

'I can't bite my tongue.'

'Then get a tongue-tie.'

'Ha.'

'I rode a couple of times for your dad, you know.'

'I know.'

Palmer glanced right and left. Then he slowly leaned across the table and spoke very quietly. 'I don't know what went down that time. But I know what I know and Charlie was always a straight shooter.'

'It's good to hear you say that. Not everyone thinks so.'

'I know what I know. And so do others.'

Ruddy came back with the round of drinks. Wine for Duncan. 'You've no idea what a relief it is,' he said, 'to drink as much beer as you like. What are you two talking about?'

Palmer looked at him with glittering eyes. 'Up Your Bum to win the three thirty at Buggertown. Cheers.'

Yes, one or two big-time trainers hadn't liked it when Charlie had begun to do well. Not least because Charlie wasn't one to mince words. That was where Duncan had got it from. Charlie served it straight up. If he thought someone was a liar or a cheat, he told them. He said: *I don't care if the mare is in foal or the stallion breaks its neck, a liar is a liar and a cheat is a cheat.* He'd taught Duncan to speak straight, too.

But what he'd failed to teach Duncan was that you couldn't do that in horse racing any more than you could do it at the town hall hustings. Eventually the liars and the cheats and the knaves would move against you.

While Duncan was at Penderton, Charlie was having his best year. But maybe he was doing too well. He had winners over in Ireland at Punchestown, at Kempton, at Cheltenham in front of all the cameras, and then finally a spectacular and thrilling second-place photo finish with a horse called Dieseltown Blues at the Grand National, on the day when every granny in the country placed a bet, the ultimate test for horse, jockey and trainer. And then they started coming.

High-profile owners who were maybe dissatisfied with their trainers – in the way that high-profile owners often were dis- satisfied if they weren't winning everything – brought some serious stock along for Charlie to look at. And if the animals weren't fit, he told them so. Fitness and diet and a different but uncompromising training regimen for each horse was what Charlie was all about. But the original trainers were disgruntled to hear that Charlie had told so-and-so that their horses were unfit. Some of them took it personally.

And when one owner decided he wanted to pull all six of his horses from their current stable and move across to Charlie, that was when he got the hex.

'You've got a visitor,' his head lad said.

Charlie let go of the fetlock of the bay he was attending to and saw a man in a sheepskin coat and a cloth cap getting out of a Jaguar XJ6 luxury saloon. He recognised the man from televised horse racing, though they'd never met. It was William Osborne. There were two top trainers in the country at that time, battling for supremacy. Osborne was one of them.

Osborne, a fox-faced man, tucked his chin into the collar of his sheepskin coat as he walked across the yard, so that his warm smile was half hidden. From across the yard he offered a handshake and greeted Charlie like they were old pals. 'Charlie,' he said. *Charlie!* 'How come we've not met in person before now? How's that then, hey?'

'It's Mr Osborne?' Charlie asked, shaking the hand, still wondering what the hell this was all about.

'Will, please, Will to you, Charlie. We trainers are one of a kind.'

No we're not, thought Charlie. 'What can I do for you?'

'Cup o' tea would be grand,' Osborne said. He stuck out a long tongue to advertise how parched he might be.

Charlie kept an electric kettle and a box of tea bags in the tack room, so he led the way through. Without being invited, Osborne took a chair. Charlie leaned his back against the wall, arms folded, while the kettle boiled.

'I've got a filly. Very sweet. Should be doing much better. Big hopes for her. But she keeps fizzling out. I've done everything and I want you to have her, see what you can do.'

'What?' Charlie said. 'Why am I so honoured?'

Osborne wrinkled his eyes. 'You've got a hell of a reputation for ironing out these things.'

'Have I?'

'Oh yes. Oh yes. Have a word with Charlie about her. That's what they've all said.'

'Who? Who said?'

Osborne tapped his nose. 'Those who know.'

Charlie sighed. 'If she's fading, you can't always straighten 'em. Depends how she's been treated. If she's injured, that's another thing.'

The kettle boiled. Charlie made tea in two chipped mugs.

'Milky and sweet, if you don't mind,' Osborne said. 'Will you take her, Charlie? I'll pay top dollar. That goes without saying.'

Charlie handed over the mug of tea. 'Of course I'll bloody take her. I'll be glad to.'

'Good man! That's what I was hoping to hear.' He slurped the tea nosily. 'Lovely.'

They talked for a while about the season, and some of the successes both men had had. Osborne was very complimentary about the race run by Dieseltown Blues at the Grand National. He said it could win it next year. He wondered where Charlie was sourcing his stock.

'I've been over to France a few times. Looking for something different, you know?'

Osborne said he did know. He even suggested Charlie might keep an eye out for him on his next run across the Channel. He got near the bottom of his mug of tea before he said, 'George McEwan's on about pulling his six horses out of my place and bringing them down here.'

Suddenly all the flattery fell away and Charlie saw right to the heart of this surprise visit. 'Happen,' he said.

'It's a lot of horses for me to lose right now, Charlie.'

'It is that.'

'Six horses. We're near the end of the season. And me and

you-know-who are neck and neck for the Champion Trainer.'

'That you are.'

Osborne laughed, a curious bark of a laugh. 'He got a treble at Nottingham on Saturday while I had a bad day. You see it's not just the six, Charlie; it's that tongues wag and people lose confidence very easily. Then another follows him. They're like bloody sheep, you know? Anyway, it's a very bad time for me to lose any horses. Very bad. Worst possible timing, to be honest.'

'Yes, I can see that.'

'The rate you're coming through, Charlie, and all the great things you're doing right now, you're going to need some good mates around you. Believe me, it cuts up rough. Well, I'm just here to say that I'm very interested in being a friend to you. I can see how we both need each other.'

'Well, to be honest,' Charlie said, 'I don't really see how I need you.'

'Ha! You say that now. You say that now. But – and no dis-respect to you, because you've done a great job with this small set-up you've got here – you've never been in the thick of it at the top level. And that, Charlie, *that* is when you need friends. I'll be honest with you – George is a fucking idiot. He's the worst kind of owner. He wants to tell you what size hoof pick to use. He's a fucking pain in the arse.'

'But you want to keep him.'

'At the moment. As I've explained to you, it's very bad timing right now.'

'Mr Osborne—'

'Will, please, Charlie!'

'Will. If you want to bring your filly down here, that's up to you and I'll be very pleased to try and straighten her out for you. And if George wants to bring one, two or six of his horses, I'll be pleased to take them, too. I don't mind telling you, I need the money. The building has already started on my new stables. It's a done deal.'

'That's not what I want to hear, Charlie.'

'We don't always get what we want, Will.'

Osborne sighed. 'You don't understand how things work in this business. You think you do, but you don't.'

'I've a fair idea.'

'No. You don't get it.' He swilled the dregs of his tea around the bottom of his mug. Then he flung them across the concrete floor of the tack room, where they splashed dangerously near to Charlie's boots. He stood up and walked to the door, where he turned before leaving. 'I've come here trying to help you, and there it is. You think you've thrown a six, but you haven't. You've thrown a big zero. You mind how you go, Charlie.' Then he was gone.

Later that evening, Charlie told Duncan about the whole thing. He tended not to keep things from his son.

'What are you going to do then, Dad?'

'What am I going to do? I'm going to do this.' Charlie picked up the phone and carefully dialled a number. 'Hello, is that George? It's Charlie Claymore here. Yes, I'm good. I've just rung to tell you the new stable block will be completed over the weekend. You bring your six horses just as soon as you're ready. You will? That's grand. I'll see you next week, then.'

He put the phone down with a light click. Then he grinned at Duncan, showing his teeth, like a horse.

Duncan had been gone from the hotel maybe two hours. When he let himself into the room, he thought Lorna had gone to sleep. She was still tied to the bed exactly as he had left her, spread-eagled with her pale bottom presented to him like the centrepiece at a banquet. There were slight chafe marks on her ankles and wrists where she'd struggled to break her restraints. She lifted her head and looked back at him and her hair fell

55

across her eye. It was difficult to say whether she looked angry or submissive.

He sat on the bed next to her and gently ran his ring finger along the length of her spine. She shuddered. The palm of his hand cupped her buttock and he trailed it across the swell of her bottom. Then he leaned across and nuzzled her neck, and traced the length of her spine with his lips. He kissed the backs of her legs, starting with the delicate folds at the backs of her knees.

'There should be a word for the back of the knee,' he said.

'You're a swine.'

He moved up to kiss the back of her thighs.

'While you were gone, a hotel waiter came and found me like this. He fucked me. It's all your fault.'

'Did you give him a good tip?'

He put his fingers inside her. She was still wet.

'I need a pee! I'm desperate. Duncan?'

Duncan relented. He started to loosen the cord at her wrist.

She stopped him. 'No. I want you to fuck me again before you untie me.'

Some time later, when they were both getting dressed, Lorna pouted and said, 'Duncan, do you have any feelings for me at all?'

'Of course I do. I wouldn't be here with you now if I had no feelings for you.'

'But you never show your feelings. I don't even know if you like me!'

'Come here.' He kissed her. 'I won't lie to you: I'm not in love with you. I'm not going to mislead you. But I love being with you. Isn't that enough?'

'No. Yes. I don't know.'

'Get dressed. I'd better go and settle the bill.'

'Just tell them "Oscar".'

'Oscar?'

'Oscar.'

Duncan went down to the hotel reception area and asked to pay the bill. He was relieved that Lorna had parted with the code word. He suspected he didn't have enough in either his pocket or his bank account to cover lunch and a room at the Ritz. 'It's the Cadogan account.'

'Certainly, sir.' The receptionist took out a file, spread it before him and asked for a reference.

'Oscar.'

'Thank you, sir. That's all taken care of.'

5

At Ludlow, Duncan rode a second-placed novice called Billy Blake for Petie Quinn. There was an exciting level of fitness to Petie's horses, whether they were being brought on or were the more finished article. It reminded him of Charlie's training techniques. Petie went for a good broad chest and plenty of muscle in the back end. He was less concerned with how pretty or stylish the animal was in the gallop. He knew power when he saw it.

They had the new silks designed by Petie's daughter Roisin, a nervy, doe-eyed colleen in her mid-twenties, slim as a reed. The silks were sky blue with dark blue chevrons on the sleeve and a dark blue star on the body. These would be his colours every time he rode for Petie.

At Exeter the next day he rode a winner and a third. He won the seller at Worcester, and that made Petie very happy. Three days before Christmas they were at Lingfield. Petie had him on a mount called Wellbeing in the second race, a Class 5 handicap hurdle for four-year-olds and upwards, but his big race of the day was the Abercombie Stakes, the fifth race on the card, a Class 1 chase for five-year-olds and above.

Littlewoods the bookmakers owned the racetrack. They were working to pull in the punters and had organised a Christmas gala day. With a bit of wining and dining and a few free bets for the producers, they'd managed to bring in the TV cameras, too.

The Weighing Room had an extra air of excitement, beyond the usual nerves and tension and banter.

'Have you seen that tart they brought with them?' one naked jockey was shouting, scratching at his balls. He seemed to be talking to the whole room. 'Women sports commentators, can you believe it? What the hell next?'

'Get her in here,' shouted another naked jockey. 'I'll interview her.'

Someone flicked a wet towel at his arse.

It had been two years since the first female jockey had competed on equal terms in the Grand National, and the television company had responded by commissioning a former model – but one with a family background in racing – to co-anchor their racing programme. Her name was Mandy Gleeson. Duncan had seen her interviewing jockeys on the TV. She was no slouch. She knew her stuff all right.

Duncan stayed out of the banter. His nerves only expressed themselves inwardly. He liked instead to get focused and descended in on himself. He didn't like to talk much with anyone before a race.

The weigh-in was sound – but only just, thanks to more pee pills. What with the big one at Kempton coming up on Boxing Day, there wasn't going to be much of the turkey and pudding for him. Outside in the paddock, Petie was waiting. At 10–1 Wellbeing was not much fancied. He was on the small side, with legs that didn't seem all that well constructed. He was also physically nondescript. He didn't stand out, not in any sense, and the average punter trying to size him up would probably consider him physically average or below average.

But Petie Quinn wasn't your average punter, and Duncan too knew that this horse had reserves. In the parade ring Petie told him just to go for it and gave him a leg-up on to the horse. Duncan made his way to the start, where there was a white camera van ready to track the race from the rail. Something about it spooked Wellbeing, but Duncan walked him round a few times and the horse settled.

Wellbeing got off to a strong start. Duncan knew that whatever he decided, the horse was going to take some holding. He was straining to get out there in front. Duncan felt that sudden and familiar knock of blood to the brain where the instincts took over. Petie had said to let him fly. Wellbeing didn't need asking. Duncan let him go and the horse streamed out there in front. It was glorious. From that moment early in the race Duncan knew he'd got it won. The horse was like a flag in the wind and Duncan felt like he was doing nothing more than holding the pole. His own heartbeat and the pounding of hooves underfoot were inseparable.

Wellbeing led the whole way round. Nothing else in the race had an answer. In fact Duncan eased up well before the post because he was afraid the margin of victory combined with the outside odds might have looked suspicious to the stewards. As it was, he had nothing to worry about.

'Would you believe that?' Petie said to him back in the paddock. 'Would you believe that? We'll be looking for a better class of race for this fella!'

Duncan jumped down. He was still patting the horse when he saw a camera crew heading towards him across the winners' enclosure. They were being led by Mandy Gleeson. She held a microphone with a furry windsock, like it was a torch lighting the way in front of her.

'Here's the press,' Duncan said.

Petie turned and looked startled. 'Oh, fuck that,' he said, and scuttled away, leaving Duncan to handle things.

'Where you going?' Duncan called after him. But Petie had already melted into the crowd.

It was the first time Duncan had had a microphone stuffed under his nose like that. He was still holding Wellbeing by the rein. Mandy Gleeson was a tall, dark-haired beauty and she fixed him with intelligent eyes. A breeze blew her hair across her face and she smiled as she scraped it back with an elegant fingernail. 'Just having a word now with the jockey, Duncan Claymore: Duncan you had it from the off.'

'Sure enough, we knew what the horse was capable of, but even we were a bit surprised. I just steered him home.'

'Modest, I'm sure. You're having a good few days and let's hope it continues for you. Perhaps we can have a word with the trainer when he gets here? Tell us a bit about him.'

Duncan cast about to see where Petie had gone. The cameraman and the sound man circled. 'Petie Quinn is a terrific trainer and you'll be hearing a lot more about him. He's not one for the cameras, if you know what I mean, but when it comes to the game, he's right up there. He's firm and he knows what he wants and he knows how to get the best out of both jockey and horse.'

'And you're riding again for him later today. We hope that goes well for you. If we can track down Petie Quinn we'll have a word, but meanwhile we'll hand you back to the studio.' She was counted out by her director, and the cameraman and the sound man relaxed. Mandy smiled at Duncan. 'You did good,' she said.

Duncan, not a great one for smiling, said, 'You did good too.'

'Sorry, I didn't mean the race. Obviously you did well in the race. I meant the interview. It's not every jockey who can do a good job for the cameras.'

'I meant the interview too. It's not every TV presenter who can do a good job for the cameras either.'

She paused, wrinkling her brow. The wind blew her hair across her face again and she scraped it back a second time. 'Are you taking the piss, by any chance?'

'Why would I need to do that? I just won a race.'

Mandy turned to her crew. 'Let's leave Mr Claymore to enjoy his victory.' They turned and left as a group. The stable lad who'd been hanging back came to lead Wellbeing away. Duncan watched Mandy go. He saw her look back, briefly, over her shoulder at him.

Duncan weighed in after the race result was announced so that the betting punters could collect. He got a few slaps on the back from his fellow jockeys, and it felt good. But amid the hearty congratulations he felt a stir in the Weighing Room. Another jockey had come in, a seasoned campaigner. His gaunt face and pinched features, along with his slightly crouched manner of walking, made him instantly recognisable.

He'd been the country's Champion Jockey for the last nine seasons. It was Sandy Sanderson.

There was a chorus of 'All right, Sandy!' and 'Good to see you, Sandy!' and 'Surprised to have you here today, Sandy!' Sanderson lapped it up without so much as a bit of eye contact with the jockeys greeting him. If it wasn't for the fact that the junior jockeys stepped aside for him, it looked like he was pre-pared to muscle his way through. He was a little man who took up a great deal of space. He said something brief and dismissive to his valet. He looked like he was doing everyone a favour by showing up.

Duncan turned to one of the jockeys he'd just beaten in the last race. 'What the fuck is he doing here?'

'Last-minute change,' the jockey said under his breath. 'If you ask me, the racetrack wanted him here for the cameras. Hey – you'll be up against him in the fifth.'

Sanderson was very popular with the public. He knew how to work the media and he always made out he was on the punters' side against the bookies. Maybe he was and maybe he wasn't. But while Joe Public adored him, Sanderson was less popular with some of the jockeys, despite the apparent adulation from the Weighing Room. He'd cut you up in a race, or box you in. There were stories, from untelevised meetings, of him using his whip across the face of a neck-and-neck competitor.

Duncan had no problem believing the stories. Along with Osborne and Cadogan, Sanderson had been there conspiring to destroy his father. He was the third man on his list.

Perhaps Sanderson caught Duncan staring at him; or maybe Duncan made the mistake of thinking Sanderson didn't know who he was. Why would he? He was way out of Duncan's league. But he'd underestimated the man. The Champion Jockey seemed to sweep past him, but at the last moment he turned. Sanderson had a habit of speaking through almost gritted teeth. 'Claymore, isn't it? Soaking up the sellers and the bumpers, is it?'

Duncan recovered quickly. 'Just like you did early in your career. You're a role model.'

Sanderson sucked his teeth and moved on through the Weighing Room.

Sellers, yes, he took selling rides, and bumpers too. Sanderson knew that was where he got some of his winners. But the comment had been enough to let Duncan know that he posed – at least somewhere in the Champion Jockey's mind – a threat to Sanderson. Duncan couldn't wait to challenge him in the fifth race.

The Abercombie Stakes was the main race of the day and the cameras made a lot of the parade ring and the betting patterns. The excitement level swelled, but Duncan felt very little of it. He was gone into the zone. He didn't want to talk to anyone or be spoken to by anyone. The noise, the banter, the weighing routine, it was all debris on his way to the green grass. He was riding a beautiful six-year-old liver chestnut gelding with a star called The Buckler, and he couldn't wait.

Unlike the heroic but funny-looking Wellbeing, The Buckler looked the part. He had terrific balance and symmetry of build and a lovely, fluid stride.

Petie was there in the ring. The Buckler was on his toes, ears pricked forward, already hungry for it. He circled and Petie led him round. 'You've to ride him covered up. Keep back. You'll know when to go,' said Petie. Duncan heard him but said nothing.

He took a steady canter down to the starting gate. Sanderson was already there on his chestnut, along with the favourite, a grey called Owner's Consent, and one or two other horses circling. The Buckler was a bit flighty and excited by the crowd, so Duncan took him round in a wide circle. The horse wanted to go; so did the jockey. Sanderson stopped his horse, stretching, standing in the stirrups for a moment, and looked across at Duncan. It was a mean look. Duncan wondered if Sanderson knew that he was Charlie's son.

I can take the evil eye, he thought, *and I can spin it right back at you.*

The starter's assistants came over to make a girth check and let the jockeys know they had half a minute to go. A lot of mud had been kicked up in the previous races. Duncan pulled on his goggles. He heard the loudspeaker echoing without having to hear the words spoken by the starter. It was just detail, all smoothed out. There was only the race ahead of him as he stepped his horse up to the tape. Sanderson came in right next to him. The horses inched forward in a tight, controlled bunch.

The white tape flew up like a startled bird and they were away. Duncan got a nice start and he let the front runners go ahead, tucking in behind comfortably. Over his shoulder Sanderson was doing the same, with the favourite Owner's Consent in a similar position. The race was three miles and two furlongs. There were a lot of jumps and a lot of heavy mud to get through.

But The Buckler was full of running and he took some holding. It was like riding an electric current, and Duncan knew he had a good horse. If he could get his timing right, he fancied himself. They jumped cleanly and made good ground and the mud was flying. Duncan took a clod of wet earth in the face kicked up by one of the front-runners. At about the halfway marker he felt a shift of gear around him and he knew the leaders were tiring early and the covered runners still had plenty left. He could spot Sanderson's colours keeping good pace on his left hand and Owner's Consent on his right. Visibility was poor, but there was the rumble of hooves over heavy ground to keep him in the zone.

Three hurdles from home, one of the front-runners fell but he took nothing down with him. Owner's Consent shifted up in front, but still with plenty in hand. Duncan kept pace and Sanderson hung in there with him, and already Duncan knew it was going to be between one of those three. They headed up to the second-last hurdle and still the mud was flying. Owner's Consent was making ground, and although it was sooner than Duncan would have liked, he knew he had to stay with him or lose it altogether.

As they approached the jump, Sanderson deliberately brought his mount tight in to Duncan: so tight you couldn't have slipped a cigarette paper between them. Duncan snarled but stayed focused: he figured that Sanderson was just trying to put him off his jump. A few lengths on from the jump Sanderson got himself forward a little and hooked the heel of his boot in front of Duncan's stirrup. The Buckler lost a little momentum as they hit the jump. Sanderson got over clean, but The Buckler landed badly and lost two lengths in the run to the final fence.

Owner's Consent was pulling away and Sanderson was on to him. *Now we go*, Duncan told The Buckler, giving him a little squeeze. He took the final hurdle just behind Sanderson. Owner's Consent had opened up a lead on both of them, but Duncan thought he might just catch him. The Buckler wanted it as much as he did, and he was a horse with a big heart. Duncan heard the roar of the crowd as he caught Sanderson and passed him in the last half-furlong. It just wasn't enough to catch Owner's Consent, though, who galloped in with a length to spare; Duncan second; Sanderson beaten into third place.

The crowd was buzzing. The favourite had come home, the bookies would pay and they'd been treated to a fine race. Duncan knew the winning jockey a little and he wanted to congratulate him. The camera crew, led by a windswept Mandy Gleeson, were already moving in to interview him, so he decided to hang back and not steal the fellow's limelight. But as he did so, he spotted Sanderson moving in with no such modesty, so he thought, *fuck it*. He got between them and leaned over to shake the winning jockey's hand. The winner was so elated he would have kissed anyone's grandmother, and he received Duncan warmly.

They exchanged a few flattering words, all of which the TV crew were delighted to pick up. Duncan spun it out, knowing that Sanderson was held back in the line. It pleased him to nark the old bastard. Not until he was good and done did he peel away. With the winner now dismounting, Sanderson had lost his photo opportunity and turned away.

'Don't disappear,' Mandy said to Duncan. 'We'd like some words with you after.'

'I'll be talking to my trainer,' Duncan said, and walked The Buckler over to the ring.

Petie Quinn was waiting for him. He couldn't have been more delighted. His face was wreathed in smiles. Though one of his stable lads was buzzing around, he took The Buckler's reins himself as Duncan dismounted. 'I'll fuckin' well take that!' he shouted. 'Can you believe that?' He was practically dancing a jig. 'I'll take the second prize and there's a lot more to come from this horse, I'll tell you. He's just starting out!' He saw Duncan scowling. 'What's the matter with you?'

'Did you see what happened at the second last?'

'I saw you stumble on landing. So what?'

Duncan told him about the stunt that Sanderson had pulled before the jump. 'We could have had it. If it wasn't for that.'

'No way, son. No way. I saw the winner come in there and he

still had plenty in hand. I'm happy with what we have here.'

'We could have had it.'

'And I'm telling you you're wrong. We were well beat. And listen to me: I didn't want to win this race with this horse. He's only going on seventy per cent of what I can get out of him. You wait and see. He'll be up for bigger things and we don't want everyone knowing it. His best is yet to come.' And with his big rubbery lips the Irishman kissed the horse's neck. 'This is a great day and we're on the pig's back!' He looked up, his eyes shining with delight. Then his face clouded over as he saw Mandy Gleeson and the camera crew heading towards them. 'Oh Jeez! Here they damn well come! Chuff chuff chuff!' He stuffed The Buckler's reins into the stable lad's hands and was gone.

Gleeson was already talking into the camera as she approached and Duncan was aware that they were live on TV. The camera loomed behind her along with the sound man and her director. 'If we can have a few words with Duncan Claymore, who rode a brilliant second place ... Duncan, you had enough there to beat Sandy Sanderson into third but you were pegged back at the last.'

Duncan was generous in praise of the winner. 'Marvin's a great jockey, and I didn't have quite enough to pinch it. But this was a great race and as I was saying to you earlier, Petie Quinn is a fine trainer and there's more to come from him.'

Mandy tried to steer him back on to the race. 'There was a lot of mud flying out there and you had Sandy nipping at your heels.'

'That's right. I had the Champion Jockey breathing over my shoulder. It was a great race.'

'Coming up to the second last it was all getting a bit compressed there.'

Duncan paused. She jiggled her eyebrows at him. She – or her crew – had seen the incident. She was encouraging him to

67

have a go, live on air. 'Yeah, well, that's the game, you know. Sometimes it does get a bit tight, but you have to find your way through it.'

'You faltered there at that hurdle.'

'We did. And we recovered. The Buckler is all heart, you know? You can go anywhere with a horse like that.'

'Okay, we'll let you go and shower the mud from your face. Well done to you.' She turned away and spoke her next words directly to the camera, before they cut and she handed the microphone back to the sound man.

Duncan was already lugging his saddle back to the Weighing Room when Mandy caught up with him. 'Thought you might be signalling an inquiry with that one,' she said airily.

'Not my style.'

'What is your style?'

'Winning the next one and the one after that.'

'I'd say you're the kind of man who likes to get his own back.'

Duncan stopped. 'Did your cameras track the whole race?'

'Of course.'

'Would you be able to get me a copy of that?'

'Maybe.'

'I'll buy you lunch in return.'

'No thanks, I've seen a jockey's lunch. I can get my own stick of celery.' She peeled away and returned to her camera crew.

Duncan returned to the Weighing Room. Marvin, the winning jockey, was already there, and so was Sanderson, looking sour. The Clerk of the Scales was a self-important fusspot who made them weigh in in strict place order, which left Duncan standing alongside Sanderson for longer than he would have liked. There was a one-pound discrepancy allowance and Duncan wondered if he was carrying that much in mud. But the clerk was satisfied.

'I see you've got a taste for the camera,' Sanderson said.

'It's only what I see you doing,' Duncan replied.

'That's true enough. Though there are things you wouldn't see me doing.'

'Such as?'

'Such as riding money laundered for the IRA.' Sanderson turned away and was already stripping off his silk, heading for the shower.

Duncan stopped dead in his tracks as he heard the clerk's public announcement echoing through the tannoys around the track: *Weighed in, weighed in.*

6

Maybe Sanderson knew something that Duncan didn't know. Duncan wasn't a great one for politics, but you'd have to have been brain dead not to know that the 1970s had been a battleground between the Irish Republican Army and their fight to get the British authorities to withdraw from Northern Ireland. Every now and then they would trigger a spectacular and deadly car bomb, not just in Northern Ireland but on the British mainland too. Manchester, Birmingham, London. Just a couple of months or so before Duncan rode The Buckler at Lingfield, the IRA had blown up Louis Mountbatten – a member of the British aristocracy related to the royal family – on his yacht. Sandy Sanderson's assertions were more than a little sensitive.

Duncan had read in a newspaper that the IRA were laundering the money they were getting from the US and Libya. He'd talked about it with Kerry. But he'd never for a single second made a connection with Petie Quinn.

He said nothing to Quinn about Sanderson's comments. He had a glass of wine with Petie in the owners' bar after the races were over and then made his way home. He had three days before his next ride, which was the big meeting at Kempton on Boxing Day. He took saunas and long hot baths, starving himself so that he could have a bite or two on Christmas Day with his dad. He might have consulted his pal Kerry, but Kerry

70

had taken his busted ankle back to Ireland to be with his family over Christmas.

He'd managed to get his car – a Ford Capri – out of repossession and arrived at Grey Gables on Christmas Day to pick up Charlie. They'd arranged to have Christmas dinner at a local hotel. The door was opened by Mrs Solanki, who bid Duncan a cheery Happy Christmas and led him through a reception area where a string of cards on the wall and a plastic tree in the corner seemed to be the only concessions to the festive season.

'How's he been?' Duncan said.

'Yesterday he cry for something,' she said. 'But he wouldn't tell me why. Today much better.'

Duncan wanted to be kept informed about all of these things but it shredded his heart to hear them. Charlie could be fine for weeks at a time and then might have one bad day. There was no predicting any of it.

Charlie was scrubbed, smartly dressed and ready for his excursion. He was bright-eyed, rubbing his hands together when Duncan came into his room. The radio in the corner was softly playing carols. 'Here's the TV star,' he shouted. 'Come on. Have a glass of sherry.'

Duncan didn't like sherry any more than he liked a glass of engine oil, but Charlie had a bottle and two glasses waiting on a low table. Slightly shaky, he poured them a glass apiece and handed one over. 'Happy Christmas, son.'

'Happy Christmas, Dad.'

They clinked glasses.

Charlie popped his lips in appreciation. 'Did you see Mrs S out there?' He put a finger to his lips and then spoke in a hush. 'They don't do Christmas, you see. 'Indu. That's why she's working today. 'Indu. They do another thing. What is it? Dibli.'

'Divali, Dad.'

'Something like that. Anyway, look at this.' He picked up a plastic Tupperware box and flipped open the lid. Inside were a number of dark pastry triangles. 'These will blow your bloody socks off. Samosas. Something like that. She's been smuggling 'em in for me. Have a go.'

'I can't eat that, Dad. I won't make the weight.'

'I'll cut the corner off of one.'

'Don't bother.'

But Charlie insisted, just as he did with the sherry. Duncan tried a bit of the samosa. His face quickly turned red.

'Christ, that's hot!'

'Bloody marvellous, eh? You could marry a woman who makes things like that. Want a bit more?'

'Let's go to the hotel. We have a table booked.'

'I've got you a Christmas box. Let me get it.'

'Get your coat on, Dad.'

'I don't need a coat. It's like a spring day out there.'

'Yes you bloody do. Get your coat.'

Finally Duncan got Charlie outside. 'Christ, those things are hot,' he said again.

'You wait until it comes out the other end,' Charlie said, getting into the car. 'It'll blow your bloody arse off.'

The hotel restaurant was full. They had a roaring fire going and the waitresses wore paper crowns. Dinner went well, at least for the most part. 'All the trimmings,' Charlie kept saying. They shared a bottle of wine. Duncan ate a bit of his turkey and some of the vegetables. For a jockey's dinner he would call that hearty. They discussed his last few races. Charlie was thrilled to have watched the televised races at Lingfield. When Duncan told him about Sanderson's antics, he almost leapt out of his chair. 'I knew something had gone on! I knew it!'

'Listen, Dad,' Duncan said when all the plates had been cleared away. 'Petie Quinn says he'll get you a VIP spot at Kempton tomorrow.'

'No,' Charlie said flatly. 'I'll not go.' He wiped his mouth with the cotton napkin and dropped it to the table.

Duncan knew he wouldn't be persuaded. They'd been here too many times before. Charlie hadn't set foot inside a racetrack since he'd been discredited. It just hurt too much.

'I'll watch it on TV, though,' he said. 'I shall enjoy that.'

'There's something I want to ask you, Dad. It's about Petie.' He told Charlie what Sanderson had said about IRA money.

Charlie blew out his cheeks. 'What do you think?'

'Well. He's an odd bloke. There's not many who can keep a big stable without investment, yet I don't hear of any owners. He seems to own them all and train them too. Plus he's got a decent set-up in Warwickshire. The money's got to be coming from somewhere.'

'Ask him outright,' Charlie said.

'What? If he's laundering money for the IRA he's not likely to admit it, is he?'

'You've got to give the bloke a chance. Either way he'll deny it. But you've got to listen to *how* he denies it, and make up your mind. You either decide it's fine to ride for him or it's not. There's no middle position.'

They talked about it a bit more. Duncan had already spent a little bit of time at Petie's set-up. He was due to go there again two days after Kempton, just before they were supposed to go to Punchestown together. He and Charlie decided that he would get the next day's races under his belt before confronting Petie head on about what Sanderson had said.

Charlie had plenty of sound Irish friends in the racing game. He said he would ask one or two what they knew about Quinn. 'What's more,' he added, 'Sanderson is a turd who'd say anything.'

The subject of Sanderson was dangerous. Charlie was looking too hard into the bottom of his wine glass, so Duncan distracted him. 'Look, Dad, I brought you a present. Here you go.'

He handed over something he'd had gift-wrapped. Charlie tore open the paper and fumbled with the box. He seemed puzzled.

'It's a Polaroid. A camera. Here, give it me. Watch this.' He took a picture of Charlie across the table and the instant photo rolled out of the bottom of the camera like a tongue. 'Just wait a minute as it develops.' Duncan watched the snap as the colours came up. It was a good picture, except that Charlie looked baffled, even a little frightened. Duncan handed it over.

'How do they . . . ?'

'Progress, Dad.'

'Here, I've something for you.'

Duncan unwrapped his gift. It was a pair of racing goggles. He already had several superior pairs but said nothing. 'That's great, Dad. Could have done with those at Lingfield.'

Charlie was still gazing at his Polaroid. 'I look old.'

'No you don't. Hey, you'll be able to take a snap of Mrs Solanki.'

'Huh?'

'If she lets you. Okay, maybe it's not the best present. I've got you a dressing gown too. It's in the car. It was too big to bring in.'

'A dressing gown?'

'Yep. Nice warm fancy one. With a big C embroidered over the breast pocket.'

'You got me a dressing gown last year.'

'No I didn't. That was . . .' He was going to say, *That was ten years ago, Dad*. Instead he said, 'No, your old one is frayed. Chuck it out. This is a really smart one.'

Charlie looked over his shoulder. 'She's taking her time, isn't she?'

'Who?'

'Your mother. Where's your mother? Wait.' Charlie suddenly seemed to notice the other diners in the busy restaurant as though for the first time. He started to stand up. 'Who are all these people?'

Duncan got up and went round the table. 'Dad, sit down. Relax. Let me get you another drink, okay?'

Charlie sat down again. Duncan called the waiter. He asked for a brandy. 'Dad, Mum left us a long time ago. We're having Christmas dinner here at the Tavistock Hotel.'

Charlie looked around him again.

'You live at Grey Gables now. With Mrs Solanki and all those other people.'

'Who is Mrs Solanki?'

'She's the Indian lady who cleans and looks after you at Grey Gables.'

'Oh yes. I like her.'

'Yes.'

'What is this thing?'

'It's a camera. Instant camera. I just gave it to you as a Christmas present.'

'Really? I'm sorry I didn't get you anything this year, son.'

'Yes you did! You gave me these great racing goggles. Look!'

'Really? I gave them to you?'

Duncan had had a long talk with Charlie's doctor who had warned him that these episodes would become more frequent. Charlie was deteriorating. He could be fine for a long period, then he would unaccountably get unstuck in time or become confused about where he was and who he was with.

Duncan felt he was running out of time. Bad enough that he had to face the idea of losing Charlie bit by bit. But there were other things that had to happen before time ran out. He wanted to achieve so much for his dad. He had to become Champion Jockey while Charlie could still appreciate the achievement. Hand in hand with that he had to get his revenge on certain men in the racing business so that Charlie could savour it. He wanted to sit across the dinner table with his dad discussing old times as they tore up those men's bones.

The waitress arrived with Charlie's brandy. 'Everything all right with you good-looking gentlemen?' she said.

'Everything's fine,' said Duncan. 'Thank you.'

After she'd gone, Charlie said, 'I'm sorry, Duncan. These days I just get so confused.'

'It's okay, Dad. Enjoy your brandy and then we'll go back and see Mrs Solanki. Everything is fine.'

'Come over here, Duncan.'

Duncan, then aged seventeen, had cycled back to his dad's stables from Penderton. Dusk was settling, but he found Charlie out in the yard next to the drive leading to the cottage, tending to a chestnut gelding called Hiawatha that had suspected laminitis – far more common in small ponies than racehorses. Charlie dismounted and laid his bike on the gravel track.

It was about four weeks after Charlie had received his visit from William Osborne. Of course he had ignored Osborne's veiled threats. The new horses had arrived and Charlie was expanding his business on all fronts. The lame Hiawatha had to be scratched from a big race.

Any stables could be blighted with unusual cases of lameness, and the causes are various: an immature horse raced too often, for example, or the trauma of racing on hard ground. Another cause was overtraining, generally on firm ground. When Hiawatha's case was followed by a second horse and then a third with the same symptoms, bad luck began to be seen instead as careless or incompetent horse management. Word quickly got around the racing community.

Hiawatha had been in tip-top form before being scratched. When the third horse was found to be lame, Charlie knew it was nothing to do with his horse management. But he'd drawn a blank.

When Duncan laid down his bicycle, his father was gently

running his hand up and down Hiawatha's leg and over the fetlock joint. 'Come here,' he said again. 'See if you can feel anything.'

Duncan took over. He too gently ran his hand up and down the animal's lower leg and around the hoof to feel for any heat or abnormal pulse. There wasn't either. He said so.

'Feel your way again,' Charlie said.

Duncan went slower this time. He shook his head.

'What if I tell you there is something.'

Duncan tried again. Then his finger snagged on something very fine. 'Oh!'

'Yes.'

'It's a wire!'

'It's not wire. It's fine fishing line.'

One of Charlie's part-time workers was an old fellow they called Gypsy George. He was indeed a gypsy, with black eyes and monstrous bushy eyebrows, but one who had settled. Somewhere in the mists of time he'd either abandoned or been banished from the Irish gypsy community for reasons never discussed. Now he was neither true gorger nor true gypsy. He'd been with Charlie a long time and what he didn't know about horses wasn't worth knowing. Charlie called him over.

George got down on his knees and examined the horse himself. Eventually he found what Charlie had found. It was superfine nylon fishing line. It had been pulled tight and knotted, and then the hair around it had been smoothed over.

'Anyone could miss that. But I've seen it before. They'd sneak in and put it on a horse before a sale to make it look like the horse was suffering from the founder,' George said, using the old word for laminitis. 'Then you could buy it for a song, you know?'

'So there's nothing wrong?' said Charlie.

George got up. 'As soon as we take that off there'll be nothing wrong. So long as it hasn't been too tight for too long. But there. That tells us another thing right enough.'

'What's that?' Duncan said.

George's bushy black eyebrows waggled. 'It means we have ourselves an enemy. Someone is out to fuck us up.'

7

Boxing Day at Kempton and the weather was grand. The air was cold like chilled wine but a bright yellow winter sun flared across the track, lighting up the green grass. The going was soft and that suited Duncan's ride – Delacroix, a big strong gelding bay Petie had bought from his French bloodstock agent. With Christmas still in full swing there was a festive, tipsy air about the track. The cameras and Mandy Gleeson were there again, and the owners' bar was packed with many beautiful women dressed up for the occasion.

Mike Ruddy showed up in a new suit and with a shirt collar a size too large. He was buoyant, showing off, out to get new clients. Aaron 'the Monk' Palmer was there, riding in the big race against Sanderson. Somehow his association with Ruddy seemed to have given him a renewed enthusiasm for the game. He'd won the race he'd substituted for Duncan and the two others Ruddy had found him beside. A hundred per cent record so far for his partnership with Ruddy.

In the Weighing Room, as Duncan approached the scales, Sanderson appeared from nowhere, squeezed past him and said, '*Boom!*' in his ear. A harsh whisper, nothing else. He was gone before Duncan could answer.

Petie's daughter was there in the paddock with her father. She smoothed the silk at Duncan's shoulders. 'You look handsome in my colours,' she said.

'Wish me luck.'

'I do. Every time.'

Her dark eyes looked at him. There was something melting about them that was attractive and irritating at the same time.

'Hey,' said Petie, helping Duncan into the saddle. 'Don't be getting any ideas, you two.'

Duncan thought that was about right. Don't be getting ideas. Things were already complicated enough, what with him bedding the daughter of the racehorse owner he hated most in the world. He could do without getting involved with the daughter of the man who was giving him a fair crack of the whip. He shut down the idea. And with Duncan, when he wanted to shut down an idea, it stayed shut.

Duncan trotted Delacroix down to the start. The horse was strong, built powerfully at the front end, and Petie had warned that he would take some holding. One of the greatest delights to a jockey was that no two horses were alike. They could differ in temperament and ability in just the same way that human beings could, and each horse needed to be ridden differently. Petie had also warned that if Duncan held Delacroix back too much the horse could easily lose heart, lose the desire. It was a tricky call: risk him going too early, or risk him throwing in the towel through being held back too long.

Duncan was only over the second fence when he felt that desire begin to pull. It was immense. This was a horse that had to get to the front, but he was fighting to keep him back in fourth place. He followed his instinct and just let Delacroix go on. In most other cases he wouldn't have let the horse dictate in that way, but this was different. Delacroix jumped clean and keen, and by the time he'd cleared the fifth fence he had his nose in front. He progressed to a good length in front of the next horse and led them all home. A late rally from one of his competitors simply urged him to find a bit more at the run-in.

It was a great victory at a serious racetrack.

It was also an extraordinary feeling for Duncan, both

exhilarating and frustrating. He'd run the first race and his day was done. There were six more races still to come, including the Prince Dagobert Chase. He was pumped up after his victory and wanted to ride the full card. He was crackling with energy, but there was nowhere for it to go.

'I've seen something great there,' a jubilant Petie said to him before Duncan went off to the weigh-in. 'My time is coming up and you're meant to be there with me. When you come to see me on Monday, we'll talk. I'll make you an offer you can't refuse.'

An offer he couldn't refuse. It was a phrase from *The Godfather* film series. Duncan was in a dream. He had to pull himself together to answer Mandy Gleeson, who was there again in his face with her camera crew. He hadn't had time to get used to media attention, and here he was, not even sure he liked it. But he was a pro. He knew how to give them what they wanted.

After she'd cut the live feed, Mandy thanked him. He said, 'You haven't forgotten that tape, have you?'

'No. I haven't forgotten.'

'You're a good 'un, Mandy.'

'Oh I'm better than that. See you in the bar later?'

'You will.'

Duncan got a lot of slaps on the back from his fellow jockeys, and the evil eye from Sanderson, who had a fancied runner in the next race. He showered and got changed and made his way to the owners' bar. He'd arranged for Petie and Mike Ruddy to meet. Ruddy was a bit of a Champagne Charlie. He was already ordering fizz to celebrate the win on Delacroix. Duncan spoke in Petie's ear, telling him to go steady, and that Ruddy could ill afford it.

'I'll stand the drink,' Petie said.

'I didn't mean that.'

'No, it's fine.'

Ruddy certainly had the ability to talk to anyone. He would

often turn from a conversation he was having with one person to a complete stranger, and within minutes they would be like old friends. He would make introductions between people he'd only known for a couple of minutes. He could break into cosy little cliques. The odd thing was that no one found him annoying.

'I had a horse like that fella once,' Petie told Duncan. 'You couldn't keep him in a stable; he'd kick down the door. Then he'd be nice as pie. Here he comes again! Jeez, will you look at that!'

Ruddy came over again, sporting a fresh bottle of champagne like a trophy and with a tall, elegant blonde woman at his side. She had short, sculpted hair and was groomed like a model. Duncan put her in her mid to late thirties. She was stunning.

'I've decided I'm going into the model agency business instead,' Ruddy said. 'Christie here is going to be my first client.'

'It won't do you the slightest bit of good,' she said, smiling. 'I'm an ex-model. I've retired.' She shook hands, rather formally, with Petie and Duncan in turn. At five feet nine inches Duncan certainly wasn't one of the smaller jockeys in the business, but in her high heels Christie stood maybe five or six inches taller than him.

'Don't get ideas,' Ruddy said. 'She's a married woman. I already checked.'

They were distracted by the announcement of the start of the next race approaching. The jockeys were making their way to the start. As Christie and Ruddy looked away, Petie said to Duncan, 'I could get arrested just for the ideas she gives me.'

When she turned back, she said to Duncan, 'I had a bet on you for the first race. I bet one pound.'

'Did you get a good price?'

'I've no idea. I bet on the colours of the jockey's silks. My husband thinks I'm an idiot.'

'Does he own horses, your husband?' Petie wanted to know.

'Oh no. He just rides them. He's in this race. Sandy Sanderson.'

A detonating sound inside Duncan's brain went *boom*.

With the shouts of the crowd building to a climax outside, Petie and Ruddy stepped out on to the balcony. The bar was located more or less over the finishing post. Duncan was left alone with Christie.

'Don't you want to watch your husband in the race?'

'Nope.'

'You don't like horses?'

'I like horses well enough. Anyway, I know he's won it.'

'You can't ever be certain.'

'Not the big races maybe, but you can with a race like this one. When it's a smaller prize he won't ride unless he thinks he's going to win. That's what happens when you're Champion Jockey.' She lifted her champagne to her mouth and looked at Duncan across the top of her glass. 'You get to pick and choose.'

'What about you? Do you get to pick and choose?'

'Get me another glass of champagne.'

As Duncan was fetching Christie another glass, the people on the balcony decanted back into the bar. Ruddy and Petie came in. 'Sanderson by six lengths,' Ruddy said. 'Nothing more than poor-selling platers. They hardly turned up.'

Christie looked pointedly at Duncan.

'What?' said Ruddy. 'What?'

But Sanderson lost the big race of the day. The Prince Dagobert Chase was the second most prestigious chase in the country's National Hunt calendar. Three miles and eighteen fences, a thrilling race for four-year-olds and upwards. Duncan watched it from the balcony and he burned to be part of it. He didn't want to be up here taking tiny sips of champagne. He wanted to be out on the turf with the sound of hooves thundering in his ears and the mud flying. It was a matter of indifference to him

83

whether Sanderson won or lost the race: he had already won by being out on the turf when Duncan was stuck in the owners' bar.

As it was, Sanderson dropped in second. And the remarkable thing was that the old boy Aaron Palmer, now agented by Mike Ruddy and riding a less fancied 7–1 shot, was the man who squeezed him out.

In the roar of the crowd Ruddy was screaming himself hoarse and Petie was laughing at Ruddy. 'Come on, the Monk!' Ruddy shouted.

Somewhere within the uproar, whether to Duncan or to herself, Christie said, 'Now he'll be unbearable.'

Ruddy celebrated by stripping off his suit jacket and his shirt and flinging them across the bar, then throwing his hands into the air like a footballer at Wembley. His dark hairy chest was on show for everyone as he shouted, whooped, strutted around the bar like Mick Jagger on steroids, hands on hips, pumping his pelvis at anyone who made eye contact. One of the bar attendants remonstrated with him and warned him that he would be ejected if he didn't put his shirt back on. Petie found his shirt and jacket and Ruddy, still crowing, allowed himself to be dressed by Petie and Duncan.

'This is your agent?' Petie said.

'Somehow.'

'Lively company you keep.'

'It's 'cos I can't stop winning,' Ruddy shouted. 'And I haven't even started. Who knows it? Who knows it!' His hair was plastered to his head with sweat from his exertions. He cha-cha-cha-ed his way to the bar and called for more champagne.

Duncan made his way to the gents'. He didn't need to pee, so little had he drunk. But while he was there he wrote his telephone number on a scrap of paper and folded it into a small pellet. Back in the bar he said his goodbyes to Petie and Ruddy. He had to threaten to slap Ruddy to make him release him from a bear hug. Ruddy gave in and decided to introduce himself to some more people as the agent of the winning jockey. Duncan found Christie talking with a small group at the far end of the bar. He offered her a handshake with the pellet of paper in the palm of his hand. 'In case it gets too unbearable,' he said. He didn't even look at her to see if she'd taken the pellet or to gauge her reaction. He turned on his heel and made his way down to the Weighing Room.

There he found and congratulated a naked, red-faced and very happy Aaron Palmer. Sanderson wasn't around. Duncan walked to the car park, got into his Capri and drove back to his flat in Newbury.

When he got home, he took a very long, very hot bath. He sipped grapefruit juice and dozed as the bathwater cooled around him. The phone rang, waking him from his slumber. Instead of answering it, he ran some more hot water into the bath. After about fifteen minutes the phone rang again. He let it ring out.

Despite his win at a major event in the calendar, it had been an oddly unsatisfying day. He'd watched that Prince Dagobert Chase knowing that he was ready and that he was good enough to be in the running for the position of Champion Jockey if only he could get the rides. Ruddy had told him they would come, but he didn't have the patience.

In any case, Ruddy was a lunatic. Seeing him stalking the owners' bar bare-chested, he hadn't known whether to laugh or get away from the bloke as fast as possible. Here he was with an agent who was a madman and a trainer who was possibly funded by the IRA. The trouble was, he couldn't help liking both of them; but would they ultimately damage his career?

He got out of the bath and turned on the TV while drying himself. He watched *Robin's Nest*, even though he thought it was shit. When the phone went again, it was Charlie.

'Saw you on TV again,' he said.

'You should have come along, Dad. It was a great day out.'

'No, I'll not come.'

They talked in great detail about not just Duncan's race but the rest of the card, too. Charlie knew Aaron and was pleased for him.

After an hour, Duncan hung up and the telephone rang again almost immediately.

'She fancies you,' said a woman's voice.

'Oh. Who does?'

'That Mandy Gleeson. The ghastly bitch wants to get in your pants.'

'Now then, Lorna, what makes you say such a thing?'

'A woman knows. I can tell by the way she asks you questions. Your phone has been busy for over an hour. Who have you been talking to?'

'Well I'll come clean,' Duncan said. 'It was Mandy Gleeson.'

'Liar.'

'I thought a woman would know these things.'

'What are you doing?'

'I'm getting ready for an early night. I've got two rides tomorrow.'

'Can I come over?'

'No.'

'I'm lying on my bed, naked.'

'You should cover up. You might catch a chill.'

'I recorded you being interviewed. On the video. I'm watching you now while I play with myself. Are you sure I can't come over?'

'It's still a no. How was your Christmas?'

'Horrible. Listen, Daddy's got a horse running at Wetherby tomorrow. I've suddenly developed an interest. I told him I want to go with him.'

Duncan paused. 'Okay. We'd better not let on, though.'

'All right. But I won't take my eyes off you.'

'See you tomorrow.'

Wetherby the next day was a much less glamorous affair. There was no TV coverage, no media hoo-hah, and no glitter. It was back to the serious punters and racegoers and the steady day-to-day business of the turf. What there was instead of glamour was wind and rain.

Duncan often liked to walk the course before a race. Sometimes he walked it with another jockey, sometimes alone. Today he was alone. He was on the far side of the racecourse, on the opposite side from the grandstand, walking in light rain, when two men stepped from behind one of the birch fences. One wore a heavy serge overcoat, the other was a baldy with a sheepskin jacket. The one in the overcoat was smiling; the other wasn't. They were big men, with a heavy, maybe ex-military air. Security men.

'Hello, Duncan!' said the man in the overcoat. Midlands accent, maybe Birmingham. 'How's the course looking?'

Duncan stopped. He didn't know either of them. 'The course is looking fine.'

'Fancy it?'

'I always fancy it.'

'I'm 'aving a punt on you, anyroad. Cigarette?'

'I don't smoke.'

The man in the overcoat didn't offer his companion a cigarette, but lit up his own, squinting into the gusting wind. 'You know the Duke? Course you do. His daughter's got a crush on you. But you know that. Course you do. Anyway, the Duke ain't happy with that. I said you're too old for her. I said you wouldn't be interested. But the Duke asked me to have a word with you.'

'Right. You've had a word. Thanks.'

'Listen, Duncan, I'm a friendly sort of guy. Nice to be nice, ain't it? Take Bill here. He's not friendly. He'd break your legs soon as look at you.'

Duncan started walking again, but the two men swung in beside him.

'See, Duncan, natural for a father to be concerned about his daughter, isn't it?'

'I think the going is a bit softer than they're saying, don't you?' Duncan said.

The man stepped in front of him, impeding him. 'I'm tryin' to help you out here, Duncan. You wouldn't want Bill here to break your fingers, one at a time, would you? Snap snap snap. You see, it can all be avoided.'

They were at a stand-off. Eventually Duncan stepped around the man and carried on walking the course. The two thugs followed at his heels.

They came round the bend into full view of the grandstand. 'Mind how you go, boys,' Duncan said cheerily. 'Don't forget to get your bets on.'

They let him go on. Even though his back was turned, he could feel them staring after him.

Duncan had rides in the second and the fourth races. In the earlier race he was dumped from his horse at the fifth fence. He lay crumpled in the mud, breathless and hurting but then got up dazed and found his horse, which seemed fine. Duncan always showed more concern for his mount than for himself when he fell off. And there was another reason for getting up quick: you didn't want the track doctor to come over and find something wrong with you that would get you scratched from the next race.

Duncan's fall ratio was about one in twelve. In the past he'd got up from a fall and ridden with a broken wrist, a broken rib, a broken cheekbone and even a broken collarbone. Pain, he'd decided long ago, was just Nature's way of telling you that you were a fucking idiot for wanting to be a jockey. But jockeys were hard men and they always carried on until they actually had to be carried away in an ambulance.

What did those thugs think they could do to a jockey that he didn't already do to himself on a regular basis?

'That looked bad,' Petie said to him afterwards. 'Are you all right?'

'I'm fine.'

'You look a bit concussed.'

'That's my natural look, Petie.'

'You want me to get someone else for your next race? You look awfully pale.'

'Fuck off. That's my fucking ride.'

Duncan waved all attention away. He found a private spot to throw up, then wiped the vomit from his mouth and prepared himself for his next race half an hour later on a horse called Winklepicker. It was a maiden hurdle, over two miles and three furlongs. Winklepicker beat off twelve other horses to win at 7–2 to improve Duncan's strike rate.

After he'd dismounted in the winners' enclosure, Lorna rushed up to him, flung her arms around his neck and kissed him. When he managed to untangle himself from her, he took his saddle and the stable lad led Winklepicker away.

'Lorna, my darling,' he said. 'I've been dying to see you.'

'Really?'

'Burning for you. But it's not to be. Those heavies that came with your dad. They threatened to break my fingers and my legs. They said my career would be over if they saw me so much as speak to you again.'

'What?'

'I'm risking my life talking to you now. I can't take it, Lorna. I love you. But I just can't deal with that.'

'What?'

'I love you, Lorna. Goodbye for ever.'

89

He turned with his saddle, leaving her paralysed behind him. He had to work hard not to smile as he approached the Weighing Room door. He suspected that Duke Cadogan didn't really know very much about horses. About girls he knew absolutely nothing.

Duncan weighed in, stripped off and showered with the other lads. One threat, one fall, one win. It was a day's work.

'Are you having a drink with me?' Petie said afterwards.

'No. I want to get away.'

'So you're coming up to see us tomorrow?'

'In the morning.'

'You've only been up there a couple of times recently, what with things being so hectic. You know you're going to have to be spending a lot more time with us. You might want to move somewhere a bit nearer.'

'We'll have a talk.'

Petie looked at him oddly. 'You know I'm going to ask you to be my first-choice jockey, don't you?'

'We'll talk in the morning, Petie.'

He got up early and drove through the morning, past the ancient Rollright Stones in Oxfordshire and across the county border into Warwickshire. The fields were streaming with white mist and the grass shimmered with dew. When he pulled into the yard he saw Roisin coming across a field in boots and a long skirt, a scarf wrapped three times around her neck. With her long dark hair and the rose flush on her pale face she looked like she'd been dropped there with the dew. She waved and came across.

'We'll go in the house,' she said.

Duncan had never been in the house before. The few hours he'd had at the yard ahead of one or two of the races, he'd spent the time in the stables or on a horse's back. The house was an old cottage in need of renovation, while the yard itself was all modern blocks, newly built, clean as a whistle and orderly throughout.

When he got inside the kitchen he thought maybe the horses should live in the house and the people in the stables. It was a tip. Roisin put the kettle on for a cup of tea. She filled it from a tap on the end of a pipe that stood a foot away from the wall. The kettle itself was set on top of a metal plate in an open hearth, by means of an ancient swinging bracket and hook. The kitchen was full of spilling cupboards and boots and piles of racing forms and the sense that the whole thing stayed glued together by a resin or grime that was maybe three or four hundred years old. There was old braided electric flex poking from broken plaster in the walls. Duncan could see through to the lounge, where the floor was carpeted in uneven and various-coloured off-cuts.

'Do you live here?'

'What do you think I am?' said Roisin. 'I have a nice modern bungalow up in the village.'

'Cosy,' he said. He wondered if Petie were short of money after all.

She laughed, seeming to read his mind. 'You don't know my father. If I said "Daddy, I want a shiny Rolls-Royce, please", he'd say "Right you are, darlin'" and in the morning there'd be one sitting in the driveway; and if I said I wanted a new Cartier bracelet, well, he'd phone and have one delivered. But if I ask him why he doesn't get the builders to come and do something about this place, he'd say "Why do you want to be wasting all that money for nothing?"'

They both heard Petie coming up the path. 'I'm for a bacon sandwich,' he said.

'Well you'll have to wait for the kettle because we've only got the one hob,' she said, but to Duncan.

There was no *good morning, how are you, did you have a nice trip*

91

for Duncan. Instead Petie said, 'You wanting anything?'

'I'll have a slice of toast.'

Petie sniffed, rummaged inside a packet of white bread, brought out a slice and impaled it on a long fork, which he propped against the fire. They all sat looking at it. When the bread started to blacken, Petie turned it round on the fork and set the other side to toast. The kettle boiled, and when Roisin lifted it, Petie took a skillet, filled it with bacon slices, and put it down on the hob. Then he went to a dresser, found a knife and half a pound of butter and handed them to Duncan. The toast was done, so he picked up the fork and offered it to him as well.

'Give him a plate, for pity's sake,' said Roisin.

'What's he want a plate for?'

'Let's think why he might want one, shall we, Daddy?'

'What ye getting all posh for?' To Duncan he said, 'She's getting all posh since you're here.'

Roisin sighed, got up, found a plate and thrust it at Duncan.

With the bacon sizzling in the pan, Petie, now apparently mesmerised by its bubbling, said, 'So I want you to be my first-choice jockey. That means you have first choice of everything in my yard. But it also means that I have first call on you, above any other yard. For the rest of the jump season. And we sign to that effect. You know, a document. Then next season we look at it again. And if you want to walk away, you can; and if I think you're no use, the same.

'In the meantime, I'll not stop you riding for other trainers so long as it doesn't interfere with any of the fixtures that I have.

'You'll get the fixed rate per race, which wouldn't keep a horse in hay, so I'll add on a decent retainer, plus you'll get ten per cent of any prize money coming to you.' Petie's eyes, which he'd kept on the sizzling bacon in the pan, suddenly swivelled and he looked at Duncan. 'You're not saying very much.'

Duncan glanced at Roisin, who was stirring the tea.

'Oh don't mind her,' Petie said. 'She's the business head around here. She has to agree everything anyway. I keep no secrets from her. She's smarter than she looks.'

'No, you're fine,' Roisin said, sensing something afoot. 'Here's your tea. I'll leave you boys to it.'

She went out and closed the door behind her with a click.

'She's very smart,' Duncan said.

'I see. What is it? Speak.'

'Okay. Sandy Sanderson. He told me all your cash here comes from the IRA. He says you're money-laundering for terrorists.'

Petie leaned across the hearth, shook the pan and poked the bacon hither and thither. 'I see. And what about Duncan Claymore? What does he think?'

'I don't know anything. I just thought I'd ask you. Straight up, like.'

Petie took two slices of white bread and slapped all of the bacon between them. 'Have you seen the sauce anywhere?' he said.

There was a bottle of tomato ketchup on the table, so Duncan handed it to him and the Irishman gave himself a good helping. Then he took a great bite out of the sandwich. Duncan sat in silence. It was a few minutes before Petie finished eating. Then he took a great swig of his tea to wash it down. 'You know what, Duncan? Tea and a bacon sandwich. The two things go together, don't they? I mean, you could have coffee but it's never the same. No. Tea and bacon. Egg and chips. Beer and cigarettes. Some things go together. You know?'

'Yes.'

'Selling sand to Arabs. I was in building. When the petrol dollars started to flow in the Arab countries they wanted sports stadiums and horse tracks and all the rest of it and I got some jobs. I found out they couldn't make their tracks with all that sand they have. Too fine. It won't drain, you see. So I said I knew where there was some sand.

'Do you know how many sports stadiums and race tracks and athletics fields I built? That's where I got my interest in racehorses. The sand cost me almost nothing and the Arabs threw money at me. I had tankers of sand going out there every day at one point. I had boys shovelling sand over here and I almost needed to employ some lads to shovel the cash into my account, so much of it was there coming in. So then what? You can only eat three meals a day and you can only have one bacon sandwich for breakfast. There's more than I need. So I'm sixty-two and I'm retired from all that and now I've got my horses.

'My money is my own. It's not the RA's, or anyone's else's. Mine. Do you understand?'

Duncan nodded. 'I had to ask, Petie.'

'And I've answered.'

'You have.'

'Good. Now where's that girl? Roisin! ROISIN!'

Roisin appeared pretty quickly. She might have been eaves-dropping, but she'd changed into jodhpurs and was ready to ride out. 'Are you boys done?'

'We are. Get some papers drawn up so I can put my cross there and he can put his cross there, and we're away.'

'We'll ride out first,' Roisin said, showing no sign of wanting to be ordered around. 'Are you ready, Duncan?'

'I am.'

'Well then, why are you still sitting on your arse?'

8

Duncan had been waiting in the hotel restaurant for almost forty-five minutes. He thought she wasn't coming and the waiters were starting to look at him a little oddly as he took tiny sips of his lemon-flavoured water. At last she arrived, wearing a very short skirt and dark glasses.

'Are you in hiding?' he said. 'I mean, it's not sunny outside.'

'You never know who's watching,' she said as she sat down with the waiters fussing around her. They whisked away her coat and pulled back her chair a few inches. 'The Ritz. Very impressive. If you were *trying* to impress me, that is.' She took off her dark glasses, folded them and placed them on the crisp linen in a neat line with her cutlery.

Mandy Gleeson had beautiful eyes. It wasn't the nut-brown colour of them, nor the way her eyelids wrinkled, nor their almond shape. They seemed to be able to see through him. They would be difficult to lie to. So mesmerised was Duncan by Mandy's eyes that it made him smile.

'What?'

'Nothing. Would you like to order?'

She trawled the menu quickly and ordered a Caesar salad. He asked for the same but without the croutons. When the waiter had gone, she unclipped her handbag, took out a video cassette and laid it on the table. 'What are you going to do with it?'

'I'm just collecting tapes of my rides. For when I'm an old man. So's I can watch them from my armchair.'

'Bullshit!'

An elderly couple on the next table looked across at them.

'It's against the rules here at the Ritz,' Duncan said, 'to shout out your middle name.'

She smiled. She grazed her lower lip with her teeth. 'You think you're pretty cool, don't you?'

He took a sip of water by way of answer, but without taking his eyes from hers.

'Cool and confident. How confident are you? Let me guess. I know your sort so well. You've already booked a room upstairs, haven't you? Go on. Admit it.'

'You're joking, aren't you? Have you seen these prices?'

She shook her head. 'Liar. You thought I'd come here, have a nice lunch and then follow you upstairs. Just because you are ridiculously good-looking. Just because you are smart and witty and funny. Just because you have an outrageously sexy body. Admit it. Go on. You already reserved that room. I'd bet my horse-racing winnings on it. It's a cert.'

'There are no certs. And you'd be wrong. There's no way you would go upstairs with me right now.'

Her mood changed as she relaxed back into her chair. 'Well, you got that right.'

'Not on the first date anyway.'

'Oh, is this a date?'

That depends on what happens in the future. If we see each other again, it will have been. If we don't, it won't.'

Their food arrived. Mandy paused until the overattentive waiters had gone before speaking again. 'Okay, smarty. The quid pro quo. I want something from you in return. In return for the cassette, that is.'

'And what would that be?'

'Information.'

'Ha! Sorry! Everyone wants that. More than my jockey's licence is worth.'

'I'm not talking about betting information, you saddle sausage!'

'Saddle ... So what are you talking about?'

'We're doing an investigation into corruption. We think organised crime is behind a lot of it. We—'

'We?' said Duncan. 'Who's this *we*? Have you got a microphone in your knickers?'

'Do you take anything seriously? I mean the broadcasting company. We've got one or two good leads.'

'And I thought,' Duncan said, 'that it was my charm that got you to have lunch with me today. What a sad world it is when people have to use each other.' He turned and raised his glass to the old couple who were still staring at them from the next table. 'I said it's a sad world!' They looked away quickly.

Earlier in the season three jockeys had been banned from racing for their part in race-fixing. Lay-betting had recently grown in popularity: the practice of betting a horse to lose rather than backing it to win. This had been standard spreading practice for bookies since time immemorial, whenever they feared a result that might break them; but the recent interest had developed beyond the bookies. The three banned jockeys had been found guilty of not trying hard enough to win; 'failing to ensure a horse is ridden on its merits' was the exact phrase.

'Speaking of which,' Mandy said, reminding him of who was using whom, 'that tape won't do you much good. It doesn't show anything more than a bit of argy-bargy. Difficult to prove anything, if that's what you want it for.'

'It's just a souvenir. So let me get this straight. You want me to report on my colleagues in the workplace. To spy on them for you. Just because you are beautiful. Just because you're smart and witty. Just because you know that men admire you.'

'That's about it. And because I'm in television. Is that all you're going to eat?'

They talked a little longer, and when Mandy said she needed

to hurry away to a meeting, Duncan called for the bill. Mandy was strong on paying her share. 'I like to go Dutch.'

'No. This one is on me. Off you go and I'll take care of it.'

'Well. Next time I'm paying.'

They shook hands, all rather formal. 'One thing,' Duncan said. 'Saddle sausage. I'll get you for that.'

She smiled and moistened her lips with her tongue. Then she turned and left. Duncan watched her go. *Mandy Gleeson*, he thought, *you were sent to me by heaven*. He told the waiter he would take care of the bill at the hotel front desk. He did so by giving them Duke Cadogan's code word.

'Oh, and you can cancel the room,' he told the receptionist. 'I won't be needing it.'

Roisin made all the travel arrangements and they flew together to Punchestown for their last meeting of the year. It was the first time Duncan had ever ridden in Ireland. Punchestown was one of the great traditional Irish courses for National Hunt racing. Petie was a little jumpy himself, even without a horse. He was on his home turf and he wanted to do well. He'd brought just three horses over, but one of them was to be ridden by an old friend to whom he'd promised the ride.

Duncan rode a disappointing unplaced in his first race, a handicap steeplechase over two miles, his mount blowing up two furlongs from home. But he scraped home first in the valuable fixture race of the day on Cantabulous, much fancied by the punters at 2–1. Petie's other horse was placed, so although it wasn't a gala day for them, he was content.

Kerry turned up out of the blue and Duncan was overjoyed to see him. Kerry couldn't wait to get the plaster off his foot, and though he loved his family in Ireland, he said they were driving him crazy and he'd been glad to get away for a few hours. Duncan meanwhile introduced him to Petie and Roisin.

Petie had seen Kerry race in the past. He knew he was a damn good jockey, though he was shrewd enough in his evaluation to see that, good as he was, he wasn't quite on a par with Duncan. He needed another jockey in the frame, and maybe he calculated that having Duncan's buddy at the stables might be a cementing move. 'I'll be running more horses in different meetings come the new year,' he told Kerry. 'Let me know when you're back on your feet.'

'Be glad to,' Kerry said. 'Be very glad to.'

'How do you like my silks?' Roisin asked him.

'I like them well enough,' said Kerry.

Maybe Kerry held her gaze a moment too long, but Petie shook his head. Duncan had to fight back a smirk. *You're a condemned man*, he thought.

He got a chance to spend an hour or so alone with Kerry before leaving Ireland. They got on to the subject of Petie Quinn's money. Duncan had rung Kerry, and Kerry had a cousin who knew someone who knew someone and he'd found out what he could. 'What can I tell you, Duncan? He's a strong Irish nationalist, but then so am I. So is every Irish Catholic from here to Malin Head, so what does that tell you? Nothing in a pint pot. He might have been connected when he was much younger, that's all I could uncover. You have to be very careful who you ask, you know. Nobody likes those kind of questions these days.'

'That's good enough, Kerry. I appreciate it. Hey, that Roisin is a good-looking filly, isn't she?'

'Is she? I can't say I noticed.'

On the morning of New Year's Eve, Duncan was woken by a hammering on his door and the ringing of his bell. Whoever it was rang so persistently that the battery in the doorbell faded. Duncan eventually answered the door with a towel round his waist.

Lorna brushed past him. 'Why won't you answer your phone? Have you got someone else in here?'

'Cup of tea, Lorna?'

'No. Yes. I must have rung a hundred times. Why haven't you answered?'

'I've been away. Riding horses. It's what I do.'

'Liar! It either rings out or it's off the hook for ever.' Lorna went into his bedroom and immediately opened the wardrobe doors.

'She's in the bathroom, if you must know.'

Lorna checked out the bathroom but found it empty.

'Listen, Lorna. I told you. I was threatened by your dad's thugs. If I see you again, there are a couple of thick-necked Brummies who are going to break my bones one by one and make me watch Aston Villa on Saturday afternoons. I've been missing you badly. You don't need to look under the bed: I don't have another girlfriend. I want to see you, but I can't.'

'That's why I'm here. It's all fine.'

'Fine? What do you mean, it's fine?' Duncan knew perfectly well it would be fine. Cadogan was the sort of father who had given Lorna everything she'd asked for not because he loved her but because it was easier to get rid of her that way. He wouldn't know how to deal with a shrieking teenager on heat. 'How is it fine?'

She kicked off her shoes and took off her coat. 'I talked him round.'

'And just how did you talk him round?'

'I got his porn tapes out and showed them to his girlfriend. Then while they were shouting at each other I got his suits out of his wardrobe. He likes tailored Savile Row suits. So I laid them all out on the gravel driveway and I drove that yellow thingy car we borrowed—'

'The Lamborghini? You can't drive.'

'Yes, that one . . . No, I can't drive, but I can make it go forward and back, so I drove it over all of his suits and then I smashed the car into a tree and went back into the garage to get another one but he came out and stopped me so I tore my clothes off and went into the kitchen and the cook was in there with a defrosting bird – I think it was a pheasant – so I smeared the blood all over me and got the cook's knife and went back out—'

'Stop. I get the idea.'

'Well anyway, now I'm allowed to see you after all and you're invited to our New Year's Eve party at the house.'

'You're joking.'

If she was joking about these exploits, she didn't say.

'Party starts at eight.' She unbuckled her belt and stepped out of her jeans and knickers. Then she peeled off her turtleneck sweater, letting her large pink breasts swing free. 'Now fuck me.'

About a week after they found the nylon fishing line tied to one of their horses, an unfounded rumour swept the country's racing stables that strangles had got into Charlie's yard. Strangles was a highly infectious contagious disease caused by bacteria and spread to other horses by direct contact or contaminated food, water or equipment. It was a trainer's nightmare and isolation was the immediate next step.

There was no case of strangles at Charlie's yard. There wasn't even anything that looked like strangles. There was just a rumour, no more. But it was a very effectively placed rumour. Charlie had to field a lot of worried telephone calls. He also went to great expense to get a vet to give the yard a clean bill of health. He spent a long time returning the calls of everyone who had spoken to him about the matter, reassuring them and asking them to chase the rumour backwards by thinking about who had passed on the gossip. Of course, the lines of rumour were never forensic. But Charlie knew exactly where it would have started.

A couple of weeks after all that upset, a top jockey who had been riding successfully on a freelance basis for Charlie for almost a year suddenly announced that he wouldn't be riding for him any longer. No reason. No explanation. Yes, he was very sorry; no, Charlie hadn't done anything wrong, he just couldn't ride for him any more; sorry.

The owners stayed loyal to him. He lost only one horse during that period, and that was because of the strangles rumour. Of course he told as many people as he could what was going on. He had a word with George McEwan, the owner who'd brought him a dozen horses from Osborne's yard, triggering these issues in the first place.

'You want to go to the police?' McEwan said. He knew the Chief Constable for the county.

'Naw.'

'Well then, you've just got to tough it out. It'll pass. The bastards are smarting now but they'll get over it.'

They didn't get over it. They were still gunning for him. Charlie found himself summoned to an informal meeting of the Jockey Club subcommittee on insider information. This committee had been given a special commission to look into the problem of 'passing information for reward', and Charlie was asked to help with their inquiry. It took him two minutes to realise he was being implicated. He demanded to know on what evidence and because of whose testimony he'd been brought before the committee. He was outraged to find that they would not divulge names or reveal sources. Charlie pointed out that that meant that anyone with a grudge could simply point the finger at someone. He was told that the committee listened only to witnesses of integrity. Perhaps foolishly, Charlie got up and walked out. It was either that or say something he might regret. He subsequently received notification that although he was not being cautioned, he was under scrutiny.

On the surface, Charlie seemed to take it all in his stride. He was going to tough it out. He was not one to wear his heart on his sleeve, but the young Duncan knew how heavily it was weighing on him. Then, one afternoon at Newbury, it all came unglued.

Charlie had a much-fancied horse called Captain Pugwash, which was going well in the third race when one of William Osborne's jockeys stole his line while approaching a jump. Captain Pugwash landed badly and his jockey pulled him up before the next fence. Osborne's horse won the race. Afterwards Charlie was inspecting Captain Pugwash and he looked up to see Osborne in the winning enclosure, smirking at him. The sight of Osborne's grinning face was too much.

Charlie strode into the enclosure with his left hand held out in front of him. It looked as though he was offering to shake the hand of the winning trainer. Osborne, still smirking, accepted the handshake, but Charlie used the grip to pull Osborne's face on to his bunched fist. Charlie was no lightweight. The slap of knuckle on cheekbone could be heard across the paddock. Osborne fell at his winning horse's feet like a sack of wet sand. No one said anything, but plenty of people had seen what happened.

By contrast, no one had ever seen the veiled threats Osborne had made; nor the faked sore shins; nor the effect of the rumours of strangles; nor the trumped-up charges and the summons before the Jockey Club. All they saw was an old guy, purple in the face, who had lost it and attacked William Osborne, one of the leading trainers in the country.

Charlie left Newbury race track that day knowing that if he hadn't he would have been escorted off the grounds. Reports were made, and although Osborne chose not to press charges through the criminal courts, he did ask the Jockey Club to make its own investigations. The slow-grinding machinery of the Jockey Club went into action and Charlie was given a date on which he would have to appear before its disciplinary committee.

Privately he got a lot of support. A large number of people in the race game had been heartened to hear that Osborne had got his chops busted. One or two people who'd actually witnessed the blow called Charlie to tell him how much they'd enjoyed the spectacle. Charlie said little. He got his head down and prepared for some major races that were coming up.

Duncan lay with Lorna in the afterglow of sex, thinking about two things. One was how much actual weight loss was incurred through sex. The second was what to do about being invited to Duke Cadogan's New Year's Eve party.

He was being invited into the dragon's lair. That was, if Lorna was to be believed. He expressed his doubts and by way of response she picked up his phone and dialled a number. 'Can I speak to Daddy, please?' she said when she got an answer. 'Tell him it's urgent.'

She sat cross-legged on the bed, nude, pink, still perspiring. She held Duncan's gaze as she spoke. 'Daddy, he's with me right now. He doesn't believe he's invited to the party tonight. What? You can hardly blame him after you had your goons threaten him, can you? No, I don't care about that: you're going to have to tell him yourself. Tell him he's invited. And welcome.' She held the telephone receiver out for Duncan to take.

Duncan shook his head, but Lorna waggled the receiver at him until he took it. When she let go of the phone, she took Duncan's cock in her hand.

'Claymore?'

'Yes,' Duncan said.

'You'd better get yourself here tonight. I don't want any more breakages.'

'Okay.'

'It's black tie. You know what that is, don't you?'

'Yes.'

'Right then. Put the silly bitch back on.'

Duncan handed the phone back to Lorna. She had a short conversation with her father, all the while stroking Duncan's fattening cock. When she replaced the receiver on the cradle, she said, 'Believe me now?'

'This party? Will it be any good?'

'It'll be hideous. But you'll be there.'

Duncan wasn't sure he would be. He was planning to call round to see Charlie. He didn't want his dad to be alone on New Year's Eve, even though Charlie had told him he'd be fine and that he wanted Duncan to go out and enjoy himself. Not that New Year's Eve at the Cadogans' would be much of a knees-up. Most of the racing fraternity had meetings the next day to think about.

'What about this black tie business?' Duncan said. 'I've no suit.'

'We'll go into town this afternoon,' Lorna said. 'Daddy has an account. And you would look so sexy in a tuxedo.'

9

When Duncan pulled up at the Cadogan mansion at about eight thirty that evening, all the house lights were ablaze and he had to park his beat-up Capri next to some pretty fancy wheels. It looked like there were quite a few well-heeled guests. Two men in Crombie-style overcoats stood at the doorway, their breath rising in the cold evening air. Duncan recognised the bald-headed man from the pair who had tried to intimidate him while walking the course at Wetherby.

Baldy said something to his colleague from behind the back of his hand. Duncan passed them by without a word. No greeting, and no eye contact. He just walked in. Once inside, he heard music coming from deeper within the house and a formal butler addressed him as 'sir' and took his coat. At least the butler didn't know who he was, he thought.

Or who he wasn't.

He was led through to a crowded giant lounge with crystal chandeliers and a roaring log fire. All the men wore tuxedos and the women were mostly wearing long dresses. Duncan wasn't intimidated by the formality, but he didn't buy into it. There was an air of fancy dress about the party, as if the guests were acting, pretending to be old aristocracy or something. He recognised quite a few faces from the racing world, but not so many he would describe as friendly. Cadogan was extending his vice-like grip into racing. He'd bought his way in and continued to buy upwards, whether it was horses, contacts

106

or influence. There were two or three other racing dynasties around who could challenge him, but not everyone had his financial firepower.

Lorna spotted Duncan and raced to his side. She was wearing a low-cut shimmering oyster-grey dress with strappy sandals that made her slightly taller than him. 'Champagne for you, I think?' There were staff dressed like French maids bearing silver salvers. She beckoned one across and took a glass for each of them. 'Let me introduce you to some people.'

It was the kind of party where you got the feeling that those present didn't really have much affection for each other. Perhaps they were there to cement relationships or make connections. Duncan fell into light conversation with a man who described himself as a 'stress analyst'. Duncan thought he meant the kind of stress he was himself feeling at being at a party thrown by one of the men he most hated in the entire world; but in fact he meant things like metal fatigue. While the man was talking about ductile metals, Duncan looked over and saw Sandy Sanderson, along with his wife, on the other side of the room.

Near the fireplace with its crackling logs was a man he didn't recognise but who seemed to be holding court. His hair was cut almost Teddy boy style, short at the sides and with a bit of a quiff on top. He'd already loosened his dicky bow from his collar and was in the middle of telling a story to two men and a glamorous blonde. What struck Duncan as odd was that a fourth man stood just behind the storyteller, glancing around nervously and fingering his collar occasionally. He flexed his shoulders like a nightclub bouncer. *He's a minder*, Duncan thought.

Duncan tried to eavesdrop while pretending to listen to the man talking about ductile metals, but Lorna was already moving him on.

'Who is that man?' he asked before she had a chance to make another exciting introduction.

'Oh, him. George Pleasance. He has people beaten up.'

'What?'

'If you want someone beaten up, he's the man you go to.'

'Nice company your father keeps.'

'Oh, right. Yes. But he's also good if you want drugs.'

'I don't do drugs,' Duncan said firmly.

'Do you want to meet Shirley Devon? The singer?'

He was introduced to Shirley, who had had some pop chart success in the 1960s but whose star had waned. She was fun but was already well on her way to getting drunk. Duncan laughed with Shirley and Lorna, and fell easily into conversation with others. But he had to fight to keep his eyes from George Pleasance.

He knew a little bit about Pleasance. He was in the import business, and what he imported mostly came from Colombia. It was rumoured that he'd made his first fortune by importing cotton shirts. Thousands of them, each one starched with a white powder that had been dissolved in a giant vat through which the shirts were passed. At the end of the journey and safely through customs, the shirts were rinsed in another giant vat. The water in the vat was then condensed off, leaving a nice pile of top-grade Colombian marching powder. This was only a rumour, of course, and similarly Duncan had heard he had an interest in racing. He just hadn't known that he was a friend of Cadogan's.

It raised the question of what a rich, posh figure like Cadogan would be doing in the company of a man like George Pleasance.

Lorna stepped away for a while and Duncan was still thinking about George Pleasance when someone tapped him on the shoulder. It was Sanderson's wife, Christie.

'Surprised to see you here,' she said.

'Really? Why?'

'Oh, I don't know. I'd imagine you would have somewhere much more fun to go on New Year's Eve. Young jockey like you.'

She was stunning. She wore a white Grecian goddess dress

with gold trim, gathered to slender criss-cross straps exposing the sweeping tanned curve of her lovely back and the cup of her breasts.

'Does that mean you're not having fun yourself?'

She ignored his question. 'I just thought I'd tell you that you offended me. Passing me your telephone number like that. It's vulgar.'

'I apologise.'

'You're lucky I didn't tell my husband.'

'I am.'

'I might still tell him.'

'If you must do that,' Duncan said, 'here he is right now.'

Sanderson came up behind her, champagne in hand for himself and his wife. He looked a little sour. Christie took the glass and said, 'Sandy, this young man seems to think he can take what's yours. But I said he's going to have to show a lot more winning form before he can be Champion Jockey.'

'Claymore,' Sanderson scowled. 'I see you're trying to get your feet under the table.'

'What's that?' Christie said.

'He's not up to getting his rides through merit, so he's tupping Duke's daughter.'

'Is that what I'm doing?'

'I'd say so.'

Duncan looked round for Lorna and called her over. She hurried to his side. 'What was that you were saying?' Duncan said to Sanderson.

'Come on,' Sanderson said to his wife, already turning away. 'Let's find some people worth talking to.'

Christie turned to go, but not before focusing on Duncan for a moment. Then she smiled at Lorna and followed her husband.

'He's the top jockey. Champion,' Lorna said.

'Oh yes, he is.'

More guests arrived, amongst them a man Duncan had never

met but whom he felt he knew well. It was William Osborne. *Christ*, Duncan thought, *all three of them here under one roof.*

He emptied his glass of champagne. His hands were actually shaking. As his glass was refilled by a servant, it was trembling. He knew he was going to have to get a grip of himself. He took another drink and excused himself, finding his way to an enormous bathroom. There he looked at himself in the mirror and loosened his starched collar a little. He held his hand out in front of the mirror. His fingers still shook. Hatred was doing this to him, hatred of a passionate and thrilling kind. He was actually under the roof of one of his enemies, and was in the very same room as all three of them. He had an urge to trash things. He had to control himself, to save himself from committing some small act of vandalism, to bide his time. He had to disguise his feelings and shut his mouth, however bitter a game it was. He was going to have to ride covered up, as Petie Quinn would say.

He didn't get much time before he had a chance to practise. Just as he turned to lock the bathroom door it opened and Duke Cadogan swept in. But where Duncan expected hostility, Duke was utterly charming.

'Duncan!' he said, holding out a large manicured and beringed hand for shaking. 'You must think me so rude that I haven't had a chance to say hello yet. But honestly, I have so many guests here tonight – not all of them as interesting as racing people, but I have to be the good host to everyone equally – you know how it is, don't you.' He pumped Duncan's hand. 'Anyway, good to meet you finally.'

His accent was cut-glass. Duncan understood that he'd been educated at Eton before going on to Oxford. It was a different world, but Duke seemed very good at putting the jockey at ease.

'Is Lorna looking after you properly?'

'She is, thank you.'

Duke looked over his shoulder, as if someone else might

come in. He lowered his voice and touched Duncan's elbow. 'I'm sorry if we got off on the wrong foot. I'm a bit of an anxious fellow when it comes to my daughter, you know? I shouldn't have set those chaps on you. Bad form. Can you forgive an overprotective father?'

'Of course I can.'

'Splendid fellow! Now, I hope you're getting stuck into the Krug out there. Understand it's one of the few things a jockey can drink without putting on weight!'

'I'm doing my best with it.'

'Racing tomorrow?'

'Not for me.'

'Really? Perhaps you're not riding for the right people. We'll have to have a conversation about that. Anyway, I need the little boys' room, so I'll catch up with you later.'

Duncan left the bathroom feeling slightly dazed by the charm offensive. Surely Cadogan knew that he was Charlie's son? Was it just possible that he hadn't put the two things together? Or was he just good at doing that thing about keeping your enemies close?

He made his way through the guests to find Lorna. As he did so, Sanderson squeezed past him, putting his mouth close to Duncan's ear to say, 'Boom!'

Keep doing that, was Duncan's thought. *You're telling me what you fear most.*

Christie made her way behind Sanderson, with her nose in the air.

Duncan spent the evening watching people. Not so anyone would notice; but he took it all in. He could pretty much detect who was in Cadogan's inner circle, which of course included Sanderson and Osborne. There were a few minor celebs who shared jokes with them all, but even amongst those, he could tell who was intimate and who was just decoration. Midnight approached. One thing Duncan couldn't stomach was the idea of all the air-kissing that would happen.

He whispered in Lorna's ear: 'I'd like some fresh air. Let's take a bottle and sit outside to see the New Year in. Just me and you.'

Lorna's eyes glittered. She got up, grabbed a bottle of Krug and led Duncan by the hand. 'Bring two glasses. Let's get a coat.'

The two men on the door had given up their posts. The night was chilly and cloudless, and the stars were strong in the sky. The lawn in front of the house was floodlit. Lorna tottered on the gravel in her high heels and led Duncan around the corner, where they sat on a low wall. In the middle of the grass in front of them was a replica of the statue of Eros in Piccadilly Circus. They popped the Krug and filled the glasses.

Duncan looked at his watch. 'We've got ten minutes.'

Lorna hugged her coat around her shoulders and snuggled closer. She kissed him lightly. 'I wish you could love me a bit,' she said.

'I do love you a bit.'

'I wish you could love me a lot.'

'I don't have a lot.'

It was true. He had a chip of ice in his heart. He looked at Lorna gazing at him with doe eyes and he was worried she'd got it bad. He didn't hate her at all. In fact he was growing to like her more all the time. But he felt bad for using her.

'What do you think about? You always seem a bit elsewhere.'

'I was thinking about my dad. I went round to see him tonight before coming here. He's not doing too well.'

It was true. He'd called round before coming to the Cadogan party, ostensibly so they could both have a laugh about how Duncan looked in a tuxedo, but really to check that his dad had company. New Year's Eve triggered some unhappy memories for the old man. Duncan had offered to spend the evening with him, but Charlie wouldn't hear of it. Grey Gables was having its own knees-up and there was a rumour that one of the old

112

boys had been brewing illicit hooch. Charlie reckoned he had a chance of pulling one of the old birds. It wasn't a party for young folk, he had said, and added with crinkly eyes that Mrs Solanki was going to be there.

They'd had a drink together and toasted each other. Things had looked fine until Charlie got out of his chair and started looking for something in a file of papers he kept in a drawer. 'Before you go, Duncan, I want you to see this. It's a letter I've had. From the Jockey Club.'

Duncan's heart had sunk. That letter was almost five years old. He knew its contents. He also knew Charlie wouldn't find it because it had been torn to shreds years ago. He'd tried to settle his dad, but Charlie had become more and more agitated looking for the letter, until finally he'd exploded with frustration. 'Who the fuck are they anyway, the Jockey Club? Did I elect them into office? Did you? Did anyone? Self-appointed rich toffs living off the fat of the sport, chortling into their glasses of port and looking after each other. This fucking lord and that fucking duke. Clean up the game? It's like the Royal Navy trying to get rid of the queers on board; they'd have to start with the officers, wouldn't they? Well his lordship can come and lick the grey hairs off my arse before I'll go down there and sit in front of their committee.'

Charlie was reliving his old outrage, as he often did. It was like a thread from a woollen cardigan snagged on the barbed wire of a memory, and it pulled him out of shape. And the barbed-wire hook was the letter from the Jockey Club.

Duncan had managed to calm his father. He always did this by pouring a drink and getting Charlie to sit down. Then he would get on his knees, unlace his father's shoes and slip them off so that he could rub those old feet. It almost always worked. Foot-rubbing was something he'd done for Charlie since he was a small boy. He'd said to hell with the party, he'd stay here with his dad, see the new year in together. But Charlie wasn't having

113

that. Get along with you, he'd said. Find a girl and steal a kiss.

'I'd like to meet your dad,' Lorna said, snuggling up to him.

They heard the guests inside starting to count down from ten. Then there was a big cheer from indoors. Someone half a mile away fired a rocket into the air. Lorna leaned in for a kiss and Duncan felt suddenly protective towards her.

A voice in his head said, *Stop being a sap*.

She put her hand inside his trousers and they kissed some more. Then someone stumbled out of the front door, so she took her hand away. A figure in silhouette stepped round the corner and without seeing them lit up a cigar. He stood there puffing on his cigar, looking up into the cold night sky, then, as if an animal instinct told him he was being watched, turned and noticed them.

'Young lovers!' he said jovially.

It was George Pleasance, the importer and purveyor of high-quality cocaine. He came across and sat down next to them, tugging at the knees of his trousers as he positioned himself on the low wall. He leaned across and gave Lorna a peck on the cheek. 'Lorna, aren't you going to introduce me to this handsome young bloke?'

'This is Duncan. Duncan, meet George.'

They shook hands. 'And what does Duncan play in the band?'

'Duncan's a jockey.'

'A jockey! Well, we like jockeys.' He reached into his pocket. 'Have a cigar.'

'No thanks.'

Pleasance flicked his head, encouraging Duncan to take one anyway. He smiled and flicked his head again. Duncan relented and Pleasance struck a match for him, then puffed away on his own cigar, smiling at the younger man.

Duncan felt uncomfortable, so he said, 'Having a breather from the party?'

Pleasance said, 'A man can only take so much yak yak yak.'

For a man who didn't like the yak yak yak he asked Duncan quite a few questions about who he had ridden for in the past and who he was currently riding for. Then he complained about the cold and said he was going back inside, but not before telling Duncan that he should feel free to come to him for *anything*.

'Anything,' he said again. 'Anything at all.' He produced a business card and stuck it in Duncan's top pocket.

After he'd gone, Lorna said, 'Charming man, isn't he?'

'Yes. He is. Hard to resist.'

'That's how he gets them.'

'Gets who?'

'All of them. Jockeys. Trainers. Owners. Dancers. Pop stars. You should tear up that card.'

Duncan looked deep into her eyes. 'It's chilly. Shall we go back inside?'

Some of the guests were already preparing to leave, especially those who had a racing day ahead of them. Lorna and Duncan stood near the door as people said their tipsy goodbyes. William Osborne left without having said a word to Duncan all evening, and Duncan wondered whether he too had failed to make the connection. Sandy Sanderson also pushed his way past without a farewell, but Duncan knew that was a calculated snub.

Trailing a little behind her husband Christie Sanderson said, 'Nice to meet you again, Duncan.' She offered a kiss on the cheek and a handshake. Duncan felt a tiny pellet pressed into his hand, and under cover of the kiss she whispered, 'He's away for a week in Saudi.' Then she disappeared along with a group of other party guests.

'You know what?' Lorna said after they'd gone. 'I think Christie Sanderson has the hots for you.'

'You're joking. What makes you say that?'

'I saw her looking at you.'

'Really? But she's a married woman.'

'Ha!' said Lorna. 'Ha!'

10

Christie answered the door in a flimsy, floaty off-the-shoulder sleeveless dress that revealed her long naked arms and fell halfway to her delicate knees. Her short blond hair showed off her tanned shoulders and advertised her cornflower-blue eyes. She wore slingback heels that put her four inches taller than Duncan.

Duncan stepped inside and waited for her to close the door. She blinked at him, so for that provocation he pushed her against the wall and kissed her. She responded by slipping her tongue in his mouth. Still kissing her, he pinned her arms up over her head with one hand, pressing her hard against the wall and pulling the top of her dress down with his free hand. She wasn't wearing a bra, so her small, beautiful breasts were exposed. Her nipples were already erect. They were like brown berries. He stopped kissing her and shaped his mouth around her nipple instead, sucking hard.

'You don't hang around, do you?' she managed to say.

He answered by licking her other breast, then sucking the nipple until she gave a little squeal. Then he reached under her dress and swiftly yanked down her knickers. He fell to his knees, parting her legs slightly, and she helped him by stepping out of her knickers. Then she lifted the dress over her head and tossed it down the hallway. It had taken him twenty-five seconds to get her naked but for her shoes. He plunged his tongue deep inside her.

Christie wound her fingers into his hair as he licked at her. He drew back for breath, nibbling at the tawny inside of her thighs, sucking at her tanned skin.

'Don't mark me,' she said. 'Don't leave any marks.'

He stood, kissed her again and then swept her up in his arms. With her clinging to his neck, he carried her through to the lounge. A huge tan leather corner sofa dominated a room carpeted in white pile so deep it could have prompted air sickness. He laid her on the sofa. She looked slightly dazed. He kissed her again. The scent of her mixed with her perfume was almost enough to make him pass out.

She seemed to wake up and instantly yanked his pullover and T-shirt over his head in one movement. Duncan stood up so that she could unzip his jeans and work his trousers and underpants down. There was a moment of comedy when he couldn't get his shoes unlaced, until finally he tore them off and stood naked before her. She grabbed the bell-end of his hard cock and hungrily slipped it into her mouth.

He knew he should wait, be patient, savour her, take his time, but he couldn't stand it any longer. He stepped back from her and pressed her on to the sofa, parting her long legs. She was supple, like a dancer, and she spread her toned legs wide for him. Something about the fold in the back of her knee maddened him and he licked and bit at it. If this were a race, he would wait, but she was hot inside, and ready to come; it seemed too easy. The moment he reached down and stroked her with his fingers, she did come, noisily, gasping, shouting, pressing hard against the rolled curve of the sofa seat to push herself further on to him.

They were both soaked in sweat. Her tanned skin gleamed with tiny beads of perspiration and it made him want to lick her more. Then he looked up and realised that the walls of the room were decorated with blown-up photographs of Sandy Sanderson: Sandy jumping; Sandy with a trophy; Sandy

117

mud-splattered; Sandy mounting and Sandy dismounting. The entire room was like a religious shrine to the shit, and he hadn't even noticed. The images made him go soft for a moment; then he recovered and fucked Christie hard. She bucked and squealed under him.

Afterwards he lay on her, their sweat mingling and turning cold. At last he withdrew and lay on his back with the deep pile of the carpet tickling his sweaty back. He looked up at the ceiling, panting. She too lay breathing hard, gazing upwards.

They said nothing to each other for half an hour. They were paralysed and made speechless.

Finally it was Christie who was first to recover the faculty of speech. 'You can go now,' she said, still breathing hard. 'But come again the day after tomorrow.'

Kerry was back on the scene, fully recovered and racing again, though he'd lost some rides because of his injury. It was one of the harsh truths about racing. Kerry was freelance, the same as Duncan had been before Petie Quinn signed him up, and he would have to work hard to win back his position with some of the trainers. Petie, though, was willing to give him a chance in a couple of lower-grade races going off on the same day as Duncan was riding for him elsewhere. Now they were both wearing the sky-blue silk.

They were round at Duncan's flat one evening, watching *Blake's 7*, when Kerry said, 'How's that feckin' agent fellow working out for you? What's his name? Bloody Ruddy. Is he getting you the rides?'

'Do you know how many rides Bloody Ruddy has got me so far? One duck's egg.'

'One duck's egg? You should ask that Duke Cadogan. Get him on the case. You've got your feet under the table by all accounts.'

'I'm working on it.'

'Tupping the daughter. That's not the same as working on it. What you need to do is ...' Kerry scrambled to his feet and pointed at the television. 'Shoot the bastard! You've got a feckin' ray-gun, for feck's sake, why don't you use it?' He slumped back in his chair, looking disgusted. 'He's got a feckin' ray-gun in his hand. Why not feckin' well zap the bastard? That's what I'd do.' Kerry had a habit of responding to TV drama as if it was real life.

'They're on the same side, Kerry.'

'I've never liked the feckin' bloke. He's always up to something. I've never feckin' liked him since the first series. What were we talking about?'

'Mike. My agent. I was saying how useless he is.'

The phone went. Duncan got out of his chair and picked it up. 'Mike! What a coincidence! I was just telling Kerry here how fucking useless you are as my agent. What? Why?' He held the phone out for Kerry to take. 'Mike says he wants to speak to you.'

Kerry took the telephone. Duncan sat down again and pretended to pay attention to *Blake's 7*, though really he was eavesdropping.

'What's that?' Kerry said. 'Yes, he was just saying how useless you were. What? Fourteen rides? Fourteen? Right. Oh yes. Oh yes. Hang on.' He muffled the mouthpiece with his hand. 'He says he has fourteen rides lined up for you but you can fuck off and he wants me to take them all.'

Duncan snapped off the TV set. 'Give me that fuckin' phone.'

Mike – useless Mike – had somehow come through. He did indeed have fourteen rides. When Duncan managed to get him to shut up his high-octane babble, he wrote down the dates. Mike had said that if there were any conflicts then he felt sure that Kerry would be acceptable with the trainers. Kerry's strike rate as a young jockey was very similar to Duncan's.

Mike wanted another word with Kerry before he would end

119

the call. Somehow in that conversation he got Kerry to agree to him being his agent too.

'How did I agree to that?' Kerry moaned after putting the phone down. 'The fella ties you in knots.'

'He'll come good,' Duncan said. 'He's already coming good.'

'Do you know why he quit?'

'He just had enough of the game. That's what he told me.'

'There's more to it. According to what I heard.'

'What did you hear?'

'He was being asked to pull races all the time. Couldn't go along with it any more.'

'Where d'you hear that?'

'Ack, it's just Weighing Room tittle. Who knows. Listen, while we're on the subject of gossip, about Petie Quinn. I don't know whether to tell you this or not.'

'You'd better.'

'Well, it seems he was in deep with the IRA. But you should also know that it was a long time ago. I mean, back in the 1950s. When he was a young man. I'm told he's out of it now. If you're ever out of it; sometimes there is no *out of it*. I mean, there's so many splinter groups these days, you don't know if it's the officials, or the provvies, or just a group of hoods drunk on the street corner.'

'You think he's clear of it, though?'

'I do.'

'Right.'

Kerry leaned across and switched on the TV again. *Blake's 7* was still venturing out into the galaxy. 'No, no!' Kerry cried in anguish. 'I wouldn't let that fecker on my spaceship for all the tea in China!'

There were races at Leicester, Doncaster, Cheltenham and Ludlow all that week. Duncan was rising early to make the drive to Warwickshire, working the horses on Petie's gallops. Kerry went with him too, and Petie took a shine to him. Between the two of them, they were now taking care of all Petie's rides.

Every morning the routine was the same. Take the horses out in the morning mist, work them, go back to Petie's hovel of a cottage for a cup of tea and a bacon sandwich. Kerry at least, with a different metabolism, could join Petie in the bacon guzzling, while Duncan settled for a slice of toast dipped in bacon fat. Something was cooking too between Kerry and Roisin, leading Petie to speculate on how many times a fellow had to be measured up for his silk.

Roisin herself was a decent jockey. She'd started out in point-to-points and had competed in some serious races. But there came a time when she – and Petie – had to recognise that although she was pretty damned good, she wasn't outstanding. And in the jockey game, it wasn't enough to be good.

It came out that the jockey Duncan had replaced that day – the one who had supposedly fallen off the weighing machine – was Roisin. She hadn't fallen off the scales at all – that was just a cock-and-bull story so outrageous that no one would argue with it. Roisin and Petie had cooked it up. They'd been on the lookout for a young and hungry star-quality jockey. They'd watched Duncan win that earlier race and had simply nodded to each other. 'Go get him, Daddy,' Roisin had said.

And he had.

'I fell for it!' Duncan said. 'I believed every word.'

'So did the steward,' Petie said.

If Duncan had had any doubts about her ability, they were cleared when he saw Roisin working horses in the gallops. She knew her stock. She knew what was needed to bring them to fitness. She had an understanding that every horse was different. She understood that form wasn't a mystery presided over by strange forces, but that it could be manipulated to bring out the best. Petie's training accomplishments were 50–50 with Roisin.

One morning Petie and Kerry were leaning against the rail as Duncan and Roisin went thundering past. Duncan was up on Petie's prize four-year-old chestnut, Puckish Lad, while Roisin was ahead on a pacemaker.

They watched them take the turn, and then Petie said, 'Kerry, it's come to my notice that you've been asking certain questions about me.'

'Well?'

'It always gets back, you see.'

'Listen, Petie, I'm just looking after my man there. He's been a good pal to me, so he has. I'm just looking out for him.'

'Loyalty,' Petie said. 'A great thing in a changing world. I don't have any problem with loyalty. I admire it. But what do you think I'd find if I looked into your family?'

'You'd find plenty.'

'There you go. Kerry, you're a good man. And I look after those who are loyal to me.'

The two men gazed at each other with unblinking eyes. Then Roisin and Duncan came walking back over to them. Roisin's eyes sparkled. 'He's going great, Daddy!'

'What did you think, Duncan?' Petie asked him.

'This is the one,' Duncan said, patting the horse.

'All in the fullness of time,' Petie said.

Meanwhile, both Duncan and Kerry were bringing in prize money. They were getting noticed and the stable was getting noticed. Petie was asked to take on half a dozen horses from an owner who was dissatisfied with his current trainer. It all reminded Duncan of what had happened with Charlie, though Petie was in a different situation. He wasn't desperate for the income, so he could pick and choose.

After the incident at Newbury, where Charlie had stormed into the winners' enclosure to punch William Osborne in the mouth, Charlie found himself banned from that particular racetrack. That was bad enough, though Newbury was only one track amongst many. But the incident was reported further up the line and an investigation by the Jockey Club was triggered.

These things took time, and back at Charlie's stables it was business as usual. Then came a big meeting at the Cheltenham Festival in the middle of March, an event that was to jump racing what the FA Cup Final was to football or Wimbledon to tennis. Charlie had a number of horses entered across the three days of the Festival, but the great hope for the stable was a seven-year-old grey called Whistle And I'll Come, in the Queen Mother Silver Tassie. Two miles, twelve fences. Whistle And I'll Come was equal favourite in the early betting and a lot of money seemed to go on the horse very close to the off.

A huge amount of money.

Enough to arouse the suspicion of anyone who understood betting. Charlie and his lads had all had a good bet on their horse. They all fancied it. But they had no idea where all this 'clever' money had come from.

Whistle And I'll Come was on its toes in the paddock before the race. He was sweated up and spinning. It was the atmosphere of the Cheltenham Festival, Charlie said. It had that effect. The crowd were in an excited mood and it got to the handlers and the horses. Whistle And I'll Come was being ridden by an experienced jockey called Paddy Reid. Paddy had seen a lot of Cheltenham Festivals in his day. 'Let me canter him down to the start,' he said to Charlie. 'Burn off a bit of this froth.'

Charlie helped Paddy into the saddle, but Whistle And I'll Come was still circling, all the time with Charlie making soothing noises. At last Paddy was able to put his feet in the irons and they were off down to the start. He was followed by a couple of other jockeys on excitable mounts. One of them riding against him that day was a slightly younger Sandy Sanderson, equally fancied until the big money came in on Whistle And I'll Come.

Down at the starting tape it was touch and go as to whether Paddy was ever going to get Whistle And I'll Come to the line, and he seemed to have upset another horse, too. But at the last moment, after a warning from the starter, he trotted the heavily perspiring chestnut up to the line.

They were off.

Whistle And I'll Come leapt from the start like a thing possessed. Against all plans he jumped to the front, clearing every fence like they were just logs fallen across a path in the woods. He streaked home seven lengths clear. Nothing could touch him.

The horse was a favourite, and the crowd went wild. They cheered Whistle And I'll Come home and they cheered him in the winners' enclosure. Charlie went over to congratulate Paddy. He was thrilled at how easily the horse had won, but when he saw Paddy's face, his delight was short-lived. Paddy got down quickly and started to unbuckle the girth immediately. 'There's something wrong with him,' he said under his breath. 'Look at him.'

'What do you reckon?' Charlie said.

'A fuckin' army couldn't stop that horse today, Charlie.'

'Go get weighed in. I'll get this boy hosed down.'

Before the weigh-in was verified and announced so that the bookies could pay out, the words came across the tannoy. *Stewards' inquiry. Stewards' inquiry*

Both Paddy and Charlie were called to the stewards' room. They had to sit around for a while as the stewards told them they were collecting information. There were three stewards – two amateurs appointed like local magistrates and one stipendiary. One of the amateurs was a likeable drunk and the other was a puffed-up and self-important member of the local aristocracy, known to like spanking rent-boys. The stipendiary steward was a bluff and serious ex-military figure. He asked Charlie if he had any objection to a dope test.

Charlie had no objection; he knew they had the power to do a test anyway if they wanted to. But when he asked why it was thought necessary, the stipendiary steward said that one of the other jockeys had made a serious complaint about the condition of the horse. The drunk let slip that the complainant was Sandy Sanderson and that Whistle And I'll Come had tried to take a bite out of both 'poor old Sandy' and his horse at the starting line. Paddy admitted that the horse was overexcited but denied that it had caused problems for any jockey other than himself. It was a blatant lie, he said, and he couldn't think why Sanderson would say it.

Eventually the racetrack vet was called in and Paddy and Charlie were asked to go outside while he gave his evidence. After they were through with the vet, Sandy Sanderson was called in.

Finally Paddy and Charlie were recalled. The other witnesses had been released and the three stern-faced stewards sat behind a table. The vet had reported that the animal was in a hypertensive state, they said. He had taken a blood test but it would be forty-eight hours before the results were through. The minor aristocrat asked Charlie if he might have been minded to scratch him from the race after seeing him so overwrought. Charlie stated that the horse was behaving oddly but he'd seen it before at big races. Paddy said that he too had seen it before. The stewards repeated Sandy Sanderson's claims that the horse had tried to bite him and his own horse and Paddy reiterated that he was astonished to hear such claims.

The stipendiary steward said that both on- and off-course bookmakers had reported unusual amounts of money bet on Whistle And I'll Come just before the off, and asked if either of them knew anything about it. They suspected the horse had been got at, and added the phrase 'by persons unknown'. The question was whether to disqualify Whistle And I'll Come.

The implications of disqualification were enormous. Coming

right in the middle of the greatest jumping event in the racing calendar, it was unthinkable. Everyone in that room knew that the cowardly stewards would have to see with their own eyes the 'persons unknown' pushing a syringe into the chest of a racehorse or otherwise doping it before they would disqualify on such grounds. Charlie and Paddy, utterly crestfallen, waited with open mouths as the stipendiary steward announced that the result would stand but that they would recommend a full inquiry by the Jockey Club into the events surrounding the race.

A message was sent out and there was a huge cheer from the crowd as Whistle And I'll Come was confirmed as the winner. Charlie and Paddy were asked to say nothing whatsoever to the press. The matter would be handled privately by the Jockey Club without the need for negative media attention. Both of them undertook to keep their mouths shut.

11

Duncan lay face down in the deep-pile white carpet at Sandy Sanderson's home. Sweat caked his face and his back and made the carpet fibres stick to his skin in an uncomfortable way, but he couldn't move. He was paralysed all over again. Christie lay a few inches away, recovering her breath, staring at the ceiling. She was wearing nothing but a pair of black thigh-length high-heeled leather boots. She lay with her legs wide apart. She too was paralysed. All over again.

Whenever they fucked, it always left Duncan and Christie completely speechless. It took every fibre of them and sucked out every ounce of energy; so much so that after they'd both come, they had almost nothing left over. They lay stunned in each other's arms; then after several minutes they would find the superhuman strength required to just manage to roll away from each other, and that effort would cause them to lie in silence for another ten or fifteen minutes.

Duncan had never before been with anyone with whom he was so sexually compatible. She said the same. He reckoned that anyone who said that winning a horse race was better than sex had never had sex quite like this.

An hour earlier Christie had arrived at the door wearing a black leather minidress and those astonishing pirate black boots. She said she'd been given them after a modelling assignment but never got a chance to wear them; so she'd worn them for him. Duncan decided he was going to play things a lot cooler

127

this time around. He said he wanted to look round the house, and he did. There was a snooker room off the hallway, and a great curving staircase leading to the bedrooms. He wondered if he could make it an ambition to fuck Christie in each and every room, most of which had photographs and paintings of Sandy Sanderson gazing back with this or that trophy or champion horse.

He never got to the bedrooms. In fact he managed about three and a half minutes of staying cool. They got as far as the kitchen before he was dragging down her underwear with his teeth. The leather dress was pulled off completely, but not the black thigh-boots. The smell of soft new leather mixed with the bewitching smell of her in a way that he would always come to associate with Christie.

'Why can't I speak?' Christie said, still lying on her back.

'Me too. I mean, me neither. I mean . . .'

She sat up and looked around her, as if her own lounge was some place she'd been mysteriously dumped by an unknown force. 'Every time I fuck you, I feel like my brain has been scooped out.'

'Me too. I mean yes.'

She hauled herself to her feet. 'God. I'll make some coffee.'

Duncan waited a moment, then crawled across the room on his hands and knees, finding various items of his clothes. He pulled his trousers on, then got up and staggered into the kitchen to find his shirt. She was still nude except for the thigh-length pirate boots. She stood with her hands on her hips waiting for the kettle to boil, her tanned bottom resting against the rolled edge of the expensive marble worktop.

'Please put some clothes on,' Duncan said, 'or I'm going to have to do it all over again in five minutes' time.'

But she didn't. She stepped over towards him, with a model's slight sway of the hips, and kissed him passionately. When they broke off she said, 'God, this sex. It could drive you to crime.'

'Oh it could.'

She made the coffee in a pot, and while it stood, she went upstairs, reappearing after a minute or two in a bathrobe. They were about to take the coffee back into the lounge when the phone rang.

'Hi, darling!' she chimed like a little bell. She put a finger to her lips in warning. 'How are things in Saudi?'

Duncan picked up his coffee, left the kitchen and went through to the lounge. He was still amazed at what a shrine to Sanderson the house seemed to be. There were his photos on the walls, his trophies on very available surface, a couple of books about him on the otherwise empty bookcase and a rack of cassettes next to the video, hand-labelled recordings of his various triumphs, presumably so that he could spend hours on the sofa watching indisputable proof of his own sporting prowess.

He could hear Christie on the phone to him. She was utterly convincing. Casual, playful, sounding eager for him to come home. Duncan put down his coffee and found his coat, which had been flung to the floor shortly after his arrival. The cassette tape that Mandy Gleeson had given him was in his inside pocket. It was a pity he hadn't got the time to label it like all the others; instead he switched on the video, ejected a tape from inside the machine and replaced it with his own. For good measure he fast-forwarded it a little way.

He made his way through the hall to the bathroom. He could see Christie still chatting happily on the phone to Sanderson. On his way to the toilet, at the foot of the stairs but out of Christie's sight, he noticed an extension telephone. He decided to pick it up and listen.

Mostly Sanderson was just bragging. He was talking about Saudi princes and Saudi money and about how there were laws against drinking but you could get fine single malt whisky if you just knew who to ask and if you were important enough.

Duncan decided that even if you were his closest friend, you would have to conclude that Sandy Sanderson was the most self-adoring crashing bore in all of racing. He was about to put the receiver down again when he was seized by a wicked impulse.

He listened carefully to what was being said. Not to the words exactly, but to the rhythms of Sanderson's speech. It was almost like he was talking to himself. He waited until Sanderson drew breath and Christie began to talk, and right then he spoke a single word into the mouthpiece. He said it very quietly. It was barely a whisper. Just loud enough so that it could be registered but not quite loud enough to convince you that you'd really heard it.

What he said was: 'Boom!'

'What was that?' he heard Sanderson say, as if the Champion Jockey had suddenly woken from boring himself.

'What?' Christie replied.

'Did you just say something?'

'I was about to tell you that Duke rang here yesterday.'

'No, before that. Did you say something?'

'No, I didn't say anything.'

'Okay. Must be at this end. Arab phones. What did Duke want?'

The conversation was unimportant. Duncan listened in until they said their goodbyes, then put the receiver down at the same time that they did. Then he found his way to the bathroom.

'Everything okay?' he asked when he came back.

'Oh yes. He's had one glass of whisky since he's been out there, if you believe him. But he'll be whoring it.'

'Likes women, does he?'

'You could say that. He even liked me once upon a time.'

'I can't imagine anyone ever not liking you.'

'He has his women. I put up with it. To be honest, it bores me to have him around all the time.' She stood up and let her robe slip away from her. 'As for you, I don't know why you bothered to get dressed again. Because I'm not done with you yet.'

'Glad to hear it.'

'Boots on or off?'

'On. But this time I'm going to have to bend you over the table.'

Duncan had arranged to spend an hour in the sauna with Kerry that evening. He was already running late when he got back to his apartment. There was a large cardboard box outside the door. It seemed to have been hand-delivered. His name and address had been scribbled on the box lid with a felt pen.

The box was heavy. When he got the door open and the box inside, he found it contained a dozen bottles of champagne. There was a handwritten note inside, too. It just said: *Here's to a terrific new year, your pal, George Pleasance.*

'The thing is,' Duncan said in the sauna to Kerry, 'he's not my pal. I talked to him for maybe three or four minutes at that New Year's Eve party.'

'This is how it begins,' Kerry said. 'Watch your step.'

'Should I send it back?'

'Don't be a fuckin' idjit! We'll drink it and send the empty bottles back.'

'I mean, if I send it back it's like saying fuck you, isn't it? And if I keep it, he'll come again.'

'You can't send it back. Neither does it come free. This gift will be followed by another one. And then another.'

The sauna door opened and they both looked up. Kerry and Duncan often used the sauna to worry things out. They'd been doing it for years, to the point where if someone else came in, they resented it. A huge and flabby bald-headed chap stood at the door. He nodded briefly, then came and sat opposite them

131

and opened his legs as if to advertise the dimensions of his wedding tackle.

Kerry jumped up and turned the dial up another seven or eight degrees.

'I say!' protested the newcomer. 'It's already pretty toasty in here!'

'No, no,' Kerry said. 'This is Cabin A, which is the hot sauna; the milder one is Cabin B.'

'I've never heard anything about Cabin A and Cabin B.'

'Oh yes, sir. Very good for you, Cabin A. Stay in here with us. You'll be fine.'

The fat man harrumphed and sighed and wiped his brow with his towel. After a few minutes he went out.

'What would your old man say?' Kerry said.

'Charlie's a spirits man. He thinks champagne tastes like piss.'

'You know what I mean.'

'It's one of those subjects that's too near the knuckle, Kerry.'

'Right. On the other hand, you could mention it to Mike.'

'Mike?'

'Sure. If what I hear is right, and he got sick of being asked to pull races, then he might have something to say.'

'You know what?' Duncan said. 'It's too hot in here. Let's go and drink some of that champagne.'

The next day Duncan was riding at Lingfield. He was up against Aaron Palmer, the jockey who had also signed up with Mike. It was a Class 3 handicap hurdle for four-year-olds and upwards, over three miles, and Duncan fancied his chances. It was one of those races where no one wanted to take the lead, and when the starter let go the tape, nobody moved for about four or five seconds. Eventually somebody made the running.

There was little between Duncan's horse and Aaron's. They both hung back in third or fourth place until just before the last hurdle, when Duncan gave his horse the squeeze. But at the finish Aaron beat him into second place. Duncan knew experience and skill when he saw it raising the bar in front of him.

In the Weighing Room after the race he congratulated Aaron.

'You went two furlongs too early,' Aaron said. 'You'll see it next time.'

'Have a word in the bar after?'

'Sure.'

Mike had turned up to watch his two jockeys battle it out. He was waiting for them in the owners' bar. 'Fuckin' good race, lads. Duncan, you went a furlong too early.'

'Two,' said Aaron.

'What do you know about it?' Mike said.

It was Mike who had suggested that Duncan speak privately with Aaron about the champagne. Mike had confessed that the main reason he himself had jacked in the racing to become an agent had been because he was sick of being instructed to pull up horses. He'd already admitted to Duncan that he was second rate, and that meant that in order to get rides he'd become the kind of jockey who had had to have no greater ambition than that given him by the trainer. It hurt him to talk about it. But he told Duncan that he should speak with Aaron. 'Have a word with the Monk,' he'd said.

So in the owners' bar that afternoon at Lingfield, Duncan took the opportunity. 'Mike, will you give us a minute? I want to have a word with Aaron.'

'Not leaving me already, are you?' Mike said.

They didn't answer him. He bought the two jockeys drinks and left them at a table in the corner.

'Pardon me if I take the chair with my back to the wall,' Aaron said. 'I like to have a good swim, see everything.' He had a way of talking that was expressionless. If there was humour there you had to look hard into the criss-cross of lines in his leathery skin, and even then all you would see was two piercing blue eyes looking back at you. 'What's on your mind?'

'Ever been given gifts by someone with an interest?'

'Ha!'

'Well?'

'Would I tell you if I had?'

'Yes, you would.'

'Why's that now?'

'I've looked at all the pros. I've looked at the way different ones talk. I go around with my eyes open. Jockeys like to have their circle of mates. You're the most independent jockey I see. People respect you, but you've got no mates that I see; nor any hangers-on. That's how I want to be.'

Aaron took a sip of his white wine. He didn't blink or take his attention from Duncan. His Adam's apple worked hard in his throat to swallow the sip. 'That Kerry's a good mate of yours.'

'Yes. But he's not a hanger-on or a ligger.'

'Who sends you gifts?'

Duncan told him. 'It's just a crate of champagne.'

'This is how it starts. More will come.' The bar was filling up and the conversation level had grown. The older jockey carefully scanned the room as he spoke, as if looking for an eavesdropper. 'Starts with a bottle of this or a crate of that. Small stuff. Box of cigars. Then it's tickets to a big football match or a show. You think: I'll have that, why not. Then it's a night out at one of those discos in town, where the celebs hang out. Doesn't cost you a penny. I'll have that, why not? Then one night at those places there is a woman. High class. Kind of woman would make a bishop kick in a stained-glass window. She's yours for the night, doesn't cost a penny. I'll have that, why not? Then there's the golfing weekend in Spain with a lot of other lads, top footballers and the like. And then there's a car in the driveway for you, just on loan, like. Friendly.

'And then after all this, one day comes the question. And if you say no, they say, well what did you think it was all for? And what *did* you think it was for, for Christ's sake? Now there's a scratch on the car, you can't give it back. That night you had with the beautiful whore, you can't give it back.

'Somebody's got to take the fall for all that fun, Duncan. You or someone else. But you're the one on the end of the line, so it's going to be you.'

When Aaron talked about taking the fall, both men knew he meant the business of stopping a horse from winning. You could force an error and make a bad jump. You could pull up. You could ease up. You could literally fall off if you were crazy enough. You could do anything you wanted so long as you didn't win and the stewards couldn't prove a thing.

A horse owner Aaron had ridden for in the past came over and clapped him on the back and talked bullshit about the race. Aaron smiled and said little until the man was done. He moved away and left them alone.

'But you can't just send stuff back,' Duncan said. 'It's like giving him the finger.'

'Yes you can.'

'Did you ever send stuff back?'

'Did I agree to talk about me, or about the things I've done?'

When Aaron fixed him with his brilliant blue-eyed heart-stopping stare, Duncan understood why some of the other jockeys called him the Monk. He also knew why they never said it to his face. He felt like the older jockey could see to the bottom of his soul.

A weird intensity came over Aaron. He gripped Duncan by the wrist. 'You come to me for advice. You know the answer already. But I'll tell you this for nothing. I'm not a religious man. For me there's only one religion and that's the religion of getting over the jumps clean and true.'

He took another modest sip from his glass and stared out of the window. For a moment he seemed absorbed in his own

135

thoughts, his own world. He looked burdened. 'Take your father. Charlie is the sort of man who could have teamed up with any of those shady figures. He could easily have done those things he was accused of and got away with it because it would have suited them to protect him. But he didn't. Why? Because he was a man who was clean on the inside as well as on the outside. All they could do was rub some of their own dirt on to him; they knew what would stick and the people who would help them to make it stick.

'You see, people like Charlie are a big threat to them. You get one man brave enough to stay clean and the entire house of cards starts to fall in. I say thank God for men like Charlie.

'You know what I see when I go out there? A ray of golden light along the green turf, unbroken, between the starting tape and the finishing line. That's a jockey's life, that ray of light, and you're not riding the horse, you're riding that ray. Have you done your level best to win each and every race? Somebody comes to you and asks you, and so you pull up a horse, well, that ray of light is broken. It only has to be broken once, and you can win as many races afterwards as you like, but it's broken for ever. You can't put it back together. You've taken the fall; and after that, you're falling, always falling, for the rest of your jockey's life.'

Aaron let go of Duncan's wrist. Then he drained his glass, got up and left the table, leaving Duncan alone, wondering whether the old jockey was a loony or was truly inspired. After a moment Mike came and joined him.

'Heavy bloke, isn't he?' Mike said. 'But I do love the guy.'

'I need another drink,' Duncan said, 'and a fuckin' prayer book.'

12

The honeymoon between Duncan and Petie Quinn wobbled a little one morning in January. They were preparing a seven-year-old gelding called Round Robin as a possible for the Cheltenham Festival. Round Robin was lined up for the testing two-mile Queen Mabb's Championship Chase, a test of athleticism and speed with no margin for error.

Duncan arrived at the stables to find Petie in a tetchy mood, tearing a strip off one of the young stable lads. It wasn't anything Duncan hadn't experienced himself at six thirty in the morning from Tommy back at Penderton in the good old days. But even by Tommy's standards Petie was laying it on a bit thick. The red-faced kid who'd fastened a girth too tight or too loose or whatever was close to tears.

Duncan knew better than to interfere. He was going on the gallops with Roisin so he slipped away to get himself ready, but not before he saw Petie aim a good hard kick at the lad. Luckily the boy was quick and danced out of the way of the boot before disappearing like a rat across the yard. It was the first time Duncan had seen Petie lash out physically.

By the time Duncan had kitted up, he'd learned that one of the senior stable lads – a different lad – had had enough and had walked out that morning, leaving them short-handed. Then he heard the throaty exhaust of Kerry's clapped-out Hillman Avenger arriving. From behind the stables Duncan heard Kerry's car door open and close, followed by a loud exchange of words.

'Where the fuck have you been?'

Kerry said, 'Couldn't get the damn thing started, Petie. Bloody car needs an axe taking to it, you know?'

'If you can't be here on time, I don't want you here at all.'

'What?'

'You heard me well enough.'

'Jaysus! What's eatin' you today?'

'Have you come to do any work? Or just to jaw at me?'

Then Petie must have crossed the yard, because Duncan heard him roaring at someone else.

Roisin came by. She already had her riding helmet on. Maybe because of the mood her father was in.

'What gives?' Duncan said.

'Don't try to figure it out. He just goes into one now and again. It'll blow over.'

The plan had been for Roisin and Duncan to take Round Robin and another horse and gallop them up together, while Kerry and the rest of the gang went elsewhere. Petie had a change of plan. He wanted to work them, along with Kerry and Roisin and four or five other horses.

'The ground is soft and I want to see what that will do,' he said.

'It won't be as soft come March,' Duncan said, 'now will it?'

'I think it will be. We're in for a very wet spring.'

'How do you know that? Is this some kind of yokel farmer wisdom?' Duncan said, trying to make Roisin giggle. 'Did a swallow fly out of your boiled egg when you broke it open this morning?'

'What's that?'

'Did you find a sprig of green oak up the cow's arse?'

Petie glowered at him. Then he said, 'I want you to jump out in front today, and stay there.'

'This isn't the horse for that,' Duncan said.

'That's how you'll ride him,' Petie said.

By now, three or four of the stable hands and riders had gathered round. Maybe Duncan should have shut his mouth. 'This isn't how we've been working him, Petie.'

'No, we're changing that.'

'But we're only a few weeks away.'

'And it'll be soft and this horse has an engine and it will tire the competition early. That's it.'

'You don't know that! It doesn't make sense!'

Petie walked up close to Duncan. He was a few inches shorter than his jockey but he said, right in his face, 'How many times have I given you instructions? Never. So when I have instructions to give you, you'll take them.'

'I will if the instructions make sense.'

Duncan never saw it coming. Petie dug him a hard punch to the side of the mouth.

Some of the stable lads got between them, and within a second or two Petie was walking away back to his hovel of a cottage, with Roisin chasing after him shouting, 'Daddy! Daddy!'

Duncan was raging. He was all for going after the old man. But Kerry was there in his face. 'Let it go, will you? Let it go.' The group of riders and stable hands stood now in silence. One or two stared at the brushed concrete of the yard; others lit up cigarettes. But they all looked away from Duncan.

After a few minutes Petie came back out of the house with Roisin. By now Roisin was the one who looked furious. As the stable hands began to disperse, Petie called them all back together. He wanted them to listen. He walked towards Duncan with his head lowered. You could see the freckled bald spot in the middle of his thin brown hair like a bird's egg in a nest.

He drew himself to a stop, and without lifting his head muttered something. 'Ipogssse.'

'What was that?' Duncan said, looking to Roisin.

'Aye. Thassu. Mmm ipogsse.'

'Daddy!' Roisin yelled. 'You apologise properly now! Do it or else!'

Petie lifted his head to his daughter. 'What in hell do you want? Does a man have to lay himself across another man's boots? Does he have to lay down on the concrete, does he?'

'Daddy!'

Petie relented and looked Duncan in the eye. 'All right. I apologise. I was out of order. I shouldn't have done that. I'd take it back in a heartbeat if I could.'

'Forget it,' Duncan said. 'Let's get these horses away.'

'Ride as you see fit.'

'No. You're the trainer and the owner. We'll give it a go.'

'No, no. You're the jockey. You've proved it.'

'Hell, are we going to argue it the other way now?'

And the matter ended there. It was forgotten, so far as these things could ever be forgotten. Duncan followed Petie's instructions and jumped Round Robin to the front. In the soft going there was nothing that could come near him.

After returning from the gallops, Duncan and Kerry were invited into the cottage for the bacon sandwich ritual as if nothing had happened. Petie grunted a bit, moaned when he couldn't find the tomato ketchup and stared morosely into the fire as he ate and slurped from a giant mug of tea.

Duncan couldn't keep his mouth shut. 'Look, Petie, is anything on your mind right now?'

Petie didn't even look up from the fire. 'I'm not always a man to be around, you know?'

'Daddy has episodes,' Roisin said. 'He should take medication but he's too pig-headed.'

'What's an episode?' Kerry wanted to know.

'Most of the time he's all right. Another time he's like you see him now. Another time he works like a man possessed, or you

140

might catch him in a field in the middle of the night trying to ride a cow and he thinks it's Arkle.'

'That was just a bit o' fun,' Petie said flatly.

'Take your damn pills, why don't you?'

Petie still didn't look up from the fire. He picked up a poker and prodded a burning log. 'There is something I want to say. About your asking questions, Kerry. No one likes questions. But you were looking out for your man here, I understand that. I want you to know there *is* history, but it's long, long over. Things seem simple when you're a young man. It's over. I had to buy my way out of it, if you know what I mean. Twenty years ago.

'But listen to this, Duncan. I know what those bastards did to your old man. I know. And you want to know the only thing that stops them doing the same thing to me? They're scared of what they think I am, are you with me? Even though it's not true, they think it is. It stops them coming after me. And I like it like that. There. I don't mind if they keep thinking that way about me. It keeps them well away. That's the top and bottom of it.'

The others had gone quiet. Petie laid the poker down.

'Lads, I come good in the end. You ask my daughter here. Whatever faults I have as a man, I come good in the end. Now, shall we get some work done?'

The efforts of the Jockey Club to keep the issue of Whistle And I'll Come out of the media could not have been very strenuous. It was all over the tabloids that the horse had been doped. The dope in question was cocaine. Though the red-tops were careful to report only 'rumours' that traces of cocaine had been found in Whistle And I'll Come's bloodstream.

What blew the story up was the contribution of a bizarre ally that Charlie seemed to have found in a complete stranger who was a powerful figure in racing. Old Etonian Duke Cadogan went on record in every paper vouching for Charlie's character. CHARLIE'S NO CHARLIE USER SAYS DUKE ran one headline. CHARLIE'S MY DARLING chimed in another, as Duke Cadogan went out of his way to repeat, over and over, that Charlie was a respected trainer with an unblemished reputation. He would, he said, 'eat my hat' if the allegations against Charlie Claymore proved to have any substance.

This unasked-for support had Charlie rubbing his chin. He'd never met Cadogan; he'd never exchanged a single word with him; he'd never done any business with the man. Yet here was Cadogan speaking about him as if they were old friends. It didn't add up. Though, of course, this passionate declaration of support had the effect of inflating the story of a simple blood test – which might have been buried in the inside pages of the *Sporting Life* – to one that headlined the sports pages of every newspaper in the country. Anyone who had never heard of Charlie Claymore certainly had heard of him now.

Anyone who *had* heard of Charlie, and who thought of him as a reputable figure in racing, might now entertain doubts.

When the test results were returned, Whistle And I'll Come tested positive for cocaine. In addition, tiny traces of cocaine were found in samples taken from the horse's stable.

A bookmaker also came forward to prove that both Charlie and several of his stable staff had backed the horse heavily.

Charlie was called by the Jockey Club to give his account. He stated plainly that if there were traces of cocaine in the horse, then someone other than him or his staff had put it there; someone who wished him ill. When asked who that might be, Charlie named a couple of names and asked if they might also be investigated.

The chairman of the inquiry told him that he had no remit for such investigations.

'Remit?' Charlie asked. 'What's a remit? Is that the fancy word for a fat brown envelope stuffed with twenties?'

142

The chairman rubbed his finger under his nose and glanced away.

Three days later Duncan found his dad clutching a letter from the Jockey Club. The old man's face was ashen. He was trembling.

'What is it, Dad?'

But Charlie was unable to speak. Duncan gently prised the paper out of his father's hand.

The letter was very clear. Charlie had been warned off from racing for nine years. He was already sixty years old. His training days were done.

'Come on, Dad, sit down. I'll make you a cup of tea. There has to be a way we can fight this.'

Charlie allowed himself to be guided to the sofa, but he was still beyond speech. He seemed to be in a state of shock. Duncan made the tea and they sat in silence as it cooled before them untouched. Later, Duncan was able to identify the start of Charlie's decline to that very moment.

13

Another small gift arrived at Duncan's door. It was a bottle of fine single malt whisky. Duncan wasn't partial to whisky but he knew someone who was. He drove out across the Midlands to where his father used to have his stables.

Nothing was there of the old set-up. It was only a matter of five years and the entire thing had been knocked down. Charlie had sold up and the money was now paying for his stay at Grey Gables. The land had been divided into smaller lots, mostly used by people stabling and grazing leisure ponies.

There was one stretch of land of about an acre that Charlie hadn't sold off. It ran up against a tangled blackthorn hedgerow and a clear stream. In the corner of the plot a scruffy old caravan rotted into the deep grass. Dogs started barking as Duncan approached.

The caravan door opened a crack. A pair of hooded eyes looked out.

'George, it's me. It's Duncan.'

The door opened further. Two dogs ran out but they didn't bother Duncan. Gypsy George wore a white vest and dark tracksuit-type trousers. Duncan had visited him twice a year since the land was sold off, but the old boy had gone downhill a bit. His silver hair was close-cropped and his swarthy skin looked even more like leather. 'Oh, it's you!'

George let Duncan into the caravan. It was kept neat and tidy but it smelled a bit ripe, mainly of dog. Duncan set the whisky on the table without a word.

'I don't get many visitors,' George said.

'Never mind that,' Duncan said. 'George, I've found you a job.'

George had been Charlie's most loyal worker. After Charlie was warned off from racing and the racehorse owners had pulled all their horses from his stables, there was no money to pay the stable hands and they'd all been let go. It was George that Charlie had felt worst about. Not only did George know everything there was to be known about horses, he worked all hours and asked for little in return other than a spot of grass on which to rest his rust-bucket caravan. Not that Charlie had ever exploited George – always paying him the going rate – but he'd somehow become almost a family member. They went to each other for favours, and came to expect favours to be delivered.

When the stable hands had all gone from Charlie's yard, George was still there, still working, still cleaning up, still making himself useful long after Charlie had told him he had no more money to keep him.

Some evenings the three of them had sat up drinking and going over events, working out when the doping might have been done. The lad in charge of Whistle And I'll Come was a good 'un and hadn't left the horse's side. His name was Andy, and George was certain of him. But then Andy had told George that there had been a girl in the yard at the racetrack who had stopped by and admired Andy's plaiting. She'd been charged with the job of plaiting the mane and tail of another horse but admitted that she'd only pretended she was up to the job and was afraid of getting fired. Would he take five minutes to show her?

That was it. That was when it was done. Did he know the girl? No, never seen her before or since. What did she look like? Pretty. Well, she would be. He thought that maybe she had an accent.

Where from? Lancashire or Yorkshire maybe – oh and a head of red curls. It was hopeless. Did he recognise the other horse? No. It would only take a minute. Cocaine in solution. Syringe in the chest, probably. Job done. 'There's your answer,' George had said as he, Charlie and Duncan had sat drinking late into the night.

After Petie's recent bout of ill-temper had left him short-handed, Duncan had sung George's praises to the trainer. He'd seen a way to help both men. *If you can find him a spot of land for his caravan, Petie, you won't need a security officer. If a horse casts a shoe three fields away, George will hear it. Hard as nails, too.*

'It's just across the county border, George. In Warwickshire.'

'Warwickshire? Strange folk, they are.' George still had a strong Irish brogue.

'He's a rough diamond. Took a swipe at me. But he won't take a swipe at you.'

'Why's that then?'

'Come on, George. No one ever takes a swipe at you. They take one look at you.'

'Saying I'm ugly?'

'Your face will fit right in.'

He promised that George could still keep the deeds to this bit of land and said that Petie had offered to tow the caravan to its new site.

George scratched his head doubtfully. 'This caravan won't tow anywhere. It'll fall apart.'

'We'll work something out.'

'Has he got any rabbits on his land?' George was partial to rabbit stew.

'He's plagued with the things.'

George rubbed his chin.

It was all settled. Petie found George a new caravan, installed it on his land and piped water to it. The two men looked at each other without a word and yet the deal seemed to have been struck.

'That fellow's been around horses,' Petie said later to Duncan. 'Even if he does look like he's been kicked in the face by every one of them.'

'He's the reason my dad was doing so well,' said Duncan. 'Take him on a buying trip with you. You'll see.'

Privately Duncan was glad Petie had been in such a filthy mood the day he'd taken a swing at him. With George on the same team he felt his strength growing. It was another step on his way to making his move.

Lorna was complaining that she wasn't seeing enough of him. She didn't know about Christie Sanderson and Duncan was careful to keep it that way. He was genuinely busy training with Petie in Warwickshire, but when he did have some time off he asked if she could find out a day when her father would be at William Osborne's yard. He wanted her to arrange for him to have a look around.

'But that's boring!' Lorna said.

'After that we'll spend the day together. You'd better get Duke to square it with Osborne first.'

'Why?'

'I'm working for another stable. Don't want him to think I'm a spy.'

Before he went off to Osborne's place, he found that another small gift had arrived, in the form of an invitation. It was from Pleasance. A handwritten note, in the post, saying that he and some of the 'other boys' were having a night out at Tramp nightclub. Duncan's name would be 'on the door'. Don't bring Lorna, the note suggested, since this was a boys' night out. Duncan looked at the date offered. Saturday night, no racing the next day. There was no request to reply.

Duncan thought of Aaron the Monk. He placed the invitation under the transistor radio in his kitchen.

William Osborne's set-up was modern, well-regimented, clean and efficient. It dwarfed Petie Quinn's stables, and somehow made the Irishman's efforts look a little amateurish. Osborne stabled over a hundred horses with the staff list to match. They had so many young jockeys and stable lads and lasses that they ran a kind of hostel in the grounds where everyone was fed, lodged, counselled and, it was said, supplied with condoms after the local doctors complained that the place was an incubator for venereal disease.

Duncan and Lorna watched an ambulance leave the grounds. One of the young jockeys had been thrown over a hurdle when his mount stopped dead as if to say, no, you go over, I'm staying here. The lad had landed badly and had broken an arm.

'You're all mad,' Lorna said, squeezing up to him. She'd been guiding him on a tour of the place when the accident happened several fields away.

Duncan didn't need telling what a dangerous sport jump racing was. He was about to reply when someone came up behind them.

'Spying on us, are you, Duncan?'

Duncan turned. It was Duke Cadogan, in a cloth cap, muffler and green wellingtons. Osborne was there too, in a waxed Barbour coat. 'That's right. I'm taking notes on how fast the ambulance got here.'

'Bad break,' said Duke.

'What happened?' Duncan asked.

'Three-year-old gelding we're trying to get ready. But he's perfected this trick of running at a hurdle and stopping on a sixpence. You think he's taking the hurdle, and ... well.'

'He wouldn't do that with me,' Duncan said.

'I wouldn't be too sure. Better jockeys than that lad crying in the ambulance have parted company with him.'

So far Osborne hadn't said anything. He looked a little sour. Whether that was because of the accident or because Duncan was on his turf, it was impossible to tell. *They both know who I am and yet they say nothing. What sort of men can do that?*

'It's just bad training,' Duncan said, 'and bad riding, too.'

Osborne looked at him coolly. His mouth was twisted in a suppressed smile, but he couldn't keep the contempt out of his face either. Duncan had laid down a challenge knowing exactly how the man would react. 'You've got a lip on you, haven't you, son? Prepared to back that up?'

The fact was, that was exactly why Duncan had come. He had arrived on the lookout for anything that might get him into his jockey gear. Anything. He just hadn't expected it to arrive so early. He would have carried his boots and hat except that would have displayed his hand. 'Where can I get my gear on?'

'No!' Lorna shouted. 'We're supposed to be spending the day together!'

'Follow me.' Osborne was already leading him across the yard.

'Daddy, don't you dare let him get on that creature!'

'Looks like it's out of my hands,' said Duke.

'Tack room is over here,' said Osborne.

Within half an hour Duncan was changed and being shown the horse – a flighty liver chestnut called Parisa – and Osborne and Duke seemed to have assembled a small audience of stable hands eager to see a big mouth get his comeuppance. They probably sniggered too when the already frothed-up Parisa tried to take a bite out of Duncan before he was in the saddle.

Duncan took Parisa on a canter before he tried the jump that had caused the problem. He wanted the horse to get a feel of him in the saddle as much as the other way round. He cantered and stopped. Cantered and stopped. Went through a few changes of pace and direction.

He decided Parisa was a fine horse.

Then he turned and galloped the horse wildly towards the hurdle where the accident had occurred. Parisa's ears pricked up. He made for the centre of the jump. But about four lengths ahead of the hurdle, Duncan wheeled him round and out of the jump, cantering him away. Maybe those watching thought he had bottled it, but he didn't care about them. He wasn't there to entertain them. He did the same thing again: put Parisa at the jump but called him round the moment he felt the horse's excitement.

He did it again. And again. And again.

Charlie had told him that lots of horses refused jumps, in different ways. There was the ditcher, who dropped his shoulders and swung away at the last moment, ditching you into the fence. There was the ditherer, who showed he was scared early on, and was just no way going over that fence. There was the dirt-sprayer, who ran full pelt at the fence then somehow locked his foreleg in the dirt, spraying up mud and sending you clattering over the top. There was the drifter, who came off the jump line and simply tried to bypass the jump altogether. Then there was the ding-dong, Charlie had said, and that was a horse who had decided it was fun just to fuck you up.

Parisa was a ding-dong, and Duncan knew it. It was all about who was going to be in control at the crucial moment of take-off. Parisa was a smart horse who had learned to pretend to go into the jump with all engines, only to stop dead, and then to peer over the hurdle at the dumped rider as if to say, 'Everything all right?'

This time Duncan galloped Parisa at the hurdle, knowing that he would stop, and simply reined him back before the jump-off point. The horse stood at the hurdle, possibly surprised at still finding the jockey on his back. Duncan repeated the exercise, and held him there, looking at the hurdle. Then he went back to turning the horse away from the jump. Then standing. Then turning.

If the horse was confused, that was all part of the programme. Parisa had to know that Duncan was calling the shots. This entire process went on for some time. Duncan wasn't interested in an early spectacle; he was out to make a point. A few of the spectators drifted away, cheated of their chance to gloat. Not until Duncan was good and ready did he pat the horse and say, 'Come on. Now we go.'

Parisa took the jump beautifully. Duncan cantered him back and took the same hurdle again. He took the jump five times before going off on a gentle canter to jump several flights of hurdles. By the time he took the horse back to Cadogan and Osborne, the two men were standing with Lorna, all the other hands having drifted away.

'Nothing wrong with this horse,' Duncan said. 'Though I wouldn't try that unless you know what you're doing. Could make him worse.'

'You bored him to death,' Osborne said.

'No charge for fixing him, in that case,' Duncan said.

Lorna sniggered. 'Perhaps you should get Duncan to ride for you. Get a few more winners.'

Cadogan turned a pair of bulbous blue eyes on his daughter. Osborne looked away.

The entrance to Tramp nightclub was framed by a simple awning squeezed between the rows of classy tailors on Jermyn Street. There were a few people waiting outside in a line, so Duncan decided to push his luck and simply walk down the steps. At the desk he gave his name and said he was with George Pleasance. It did the trick.

The place looked like a gentlemen's club, with wood-panelled walls, as if some old buffer had had a disco and lights put in as an afterthought. But the atmosphere was excitable. The age range was very mixed and some people were dancing badly on the disco floor. There were lots of women in tiny skirts, and before he'd gone three yards he'd spotted an ageing film star, three footballers and a well-known politician. There was no VIP room. The entire club seemed to be offering itself as a VIP room.

Someone beckoned him from a table in the corner. A hairy paw with a big gold ring and a lighted cigar was waving at him. It was Pleasance. He was sitting next to three stunning women and a bald-headed man. One of the girls disappeared and Duncan was given her seat. Pleasance waved at a waiter and a glass on the table was filled with bubbling champagne.

Pleasance puffed on his cigar, smiling broadly at Duncan, as if he were fascinated by him. Duncan took a sip of the champagne. Still way overfocused on Duncan, Pleasance took his hand and shook it as if they'd never met before. 'Didn't think you'd come. Very happy you have. This place needs cheering up.'

Duncan glanced at the girls. 'Looks like you have plenty of cheer.'

The girls were smiling at him as if waiting for an introduction, but they didn't get one. The bald man just looked bored. Duncan saw that the next table was full of jockeys he knew either personally or at least in passing. On the far side, Sandy Sanderson sat entangled with a leggy brunette. Her long manicured fingers seemed to be stroking his thigh. Either he hadn't noticed Duncan's arrival or he was ignoring him.

'You know all those,' Pleasance said. 'Good lads.' He indicated the bald man. 'This is Norman.'

There was a slight nod from Norman, and a blink.

'I'm Judith,' said one of the girls brightly. She seemed to be able to make her eyes sparkle at will.

'I'm Selina,' said the other, an elegant blonde with a Mediterranean suntan.

'There, that's got that all sorted,' Pleasance said. 'Anything you want, the waiter will set it on my tab. Now I've got to take care of some things. Enjoy yourself.' He got up to go and Norman followed him, leaving Duncan alone with the two girls.

'So,' Selina said, 'are you a jockey too?'

Pretty soon he was mingling with the jockeys from the next table. They drank champagne. They danced with the girls. Other girls came and joined their table, then left. Occasionally there was a stir when this or that celebrity came in or when one got up on the dance floor. Duncan was surprised by how much bad dancing there was amongst the rich and famous. He got drawn into running a bet on who was the worst dancer in the room, the outcome to be decided by asking six pretty girls.

Pleasance returned with Norman, only to clap Duncan on the back and ask him if he was enjoying himself. Beyond that, he had little to say to him. 'So long as you're having a good time,' he said, 'that's all I want.'

While the other jockeys were getting sweaty drunk, Duncan paced himself. The only member of the company who didn't speak to him was Sanderson. Sometime just before midnight he saw Sanderson slipping out of the packed club, hand in hand with the leggy brunette.

Emerging from the toilets, he fell into conversation with a young man his own age. They talked about the number of first-division footballers that were in the club. It was only after they went their separate ways that he realised the young man was the movie star Trevor Buckingham.

Someone tapped him on the shoulder. He turned round to find Mandy Gleeson done up to the nines in high heels and a golden dress. In the lights she looked so lovely he had to gulp. He recovered to say, 'Didn't know this was your kind of hang-out, Mandy.'

'It's not. I'm working.'

He looked her up and down. 'Undercover?'

'Interesting company you're keeping these days.'

'Oh,' said Duncan, 'I'm a regular here. It's the low prices that bring me back.'

'I meant George Pleasance. I see you're well in at his table.'

'I knew what you meant.'

The DJ played a slow number. 'Dance with me?' she said.

They stepped on to the busy dance floor. On one side of him was maybe one of the Rolling Stones smooching with a tiny Asiatic beauty; on the other side someone who looked like a retired colonel was trying to quickstep one of the cast of *Coronation Street*. Mandy put her head against his collar and he gave in to the scent of her hair. She smelled wonderful. He thought maybe it was worth coming just for this dance.

'I hope you're not getting mixed up with him,' she said.

It pulled him out of his trance. 'Pleasance? No. I'm just checking out the lie of the land.'

'Why?'

'I have my reasons. But no, I'm not getting drawn in.'

'You say that now. He's got a lot of people in his pocket.'

Duncan looked up from Mandy and saw someone subtly motioning him from the edge of the dance floor. It was Norman, Pleasance's bald-headed minder. Norman tapped the side of his nose and nodded meaningfully. Duncan let him know he'd seen him but went on with the dance.

Mandy tipped her head back to look at him. 'He's not just a playboy,' she said.

'I know that.'

'Do you? He's got a lot of jockeys at his table, hasn't he?'

The dance came to an end. She leaned forward and kissed him on the cheek. 'I hope you know what you're doing,' she said. Then she melted away from the dance floor.

Duncan made his way back and Norman collared him. 'Fuckin' kiss-and-tell merchant,' he said. 'Find yourself in the *News of the World* if you ain't careful. Stick with these gals over here.'

'Right,' Duncan said. 'Thanks for the heads-up.'

By 'these gals over here' Norman meant Selina and Judith and three or four other high-energy beauties who danced in and out of their company. Judith was showing a lot of interest in Duncan. She was smart and funny and she repeatedly touched his knee with her fingertips. She smiled a lot and licked her lips whenever he had anything to say. The club was a high-class grope tent. He'd never seen so many people with their arms under the table. In the noise and the bustle of the crowded club, it all seemed to go unnoticed. Except by him. Though he had his collar torn open with the rest of them, he was watching.

Meanwhile, someone was watching him.

Pleasance sat down next to him, put an arm around his shoulder. 'If you want to take her home,' he said, 'it's all sorted.' Then he stood up. 'Got enough to drink here, Judith?'

Judith wasn't how Duncan imagined a whore. The plain fact was, he'd never been up close to a whore in his life. Judith seemed too smart, too fragrant, too fresh. She just seemed like a pretty girl who was out for a good time. It occurred to him that George Pleasance had a string of women like some rich men owned a string of racehorses. He had to bring himself to his senses.

Then Mandy Gleeson walked by. She'd spotted that he was holding hands with Judith under the table. She winked and carried on.

'Who's that?' Judith asked.

'One of those girls who gets you into bed and then sells the story to the papers,' he said. 'Apparently.'

'Oh,' Judith said, 'they are so despicable.'

At some point in the small hours, Duncan left and he left alone. The other jockeys were pairing up with the girls and he knew if he didn't go right then he'd be compromised. There was no sign of Pleasance so he said a quick goodbye to the surprised Judith. The staff at the door brought his coat quickly, just as if it had a ticket attached. He skipped up the steps and the cold London air was like a shave from an icy razor. He waited a moment to get his bearings.

Someone followed him out. At first he thought it was Judith. It was Mandy Gleeson. 'Leaving all alone? People will gossip.'

'Oh, it's you. Yeah, I wanted to get myself a reputation.'

'Too late to buy a girl a coffee?'

Duncan thought he could do with sobering up. 'Now that sounds like a good idea.'

She slipped her arm inside his and he got a whiff again of that delicious perfume. They walked down Jermyn Street to a place she knew, but when they got there it was closed. They walked to another place but it was shut too.

'Look,' she said, 'I live just across the river. I have coffee. But it's not an invitation.'

'Okay.'

'I mean it. If that's what you want right now, you should go back inside Tramp.'

'Coffee at yours sounds good.' He smiled innocently.

'Walking or cab? It's twenty minutes.'

'Walking.'

London at two a.m. wasn't asleep but it was chilled and relaxed. They walked the streets of Mayfair together and he liked the way she pressed up to him in her heavy coat. Cigar smoke and perfume hung in the air. He saw a rat run in the gutter. They came upon the river and crossed Westminster Bridge. She had an apartment up towards Waterloo.

It was good to get into the warmth of the apartment. She made coffee and brought out cake, but he just took the coffee.

'I forgot,' she said. 'What it must be to be always hungry but to have to turn everything down. So what's with George Pleasance?'

156

'I've got nothing to tell you about him if that's why you brought me here.'

'Steady, Mr Crocodile. No, it wasn't why I brought you here. But there are things that I can tell *you*.'

'How do you know I won't spill the beans to George? Him being so generous towards me.'

'Because unless I'm a really bad judge of character, it's just not you. Which makes me curious about what you are up to exactly.'

'Just sampling the good life.'

'Didn't your dad tell you not to take sweeties from strange men?'

How smart of her, he thought, *how smart of her to mention Dad.*

'He did. How much information have you got for your TV programme?'

'We've got lots. But it's not George Pleasance we're after. It's the Jockey Club.'

She laid it all out for him. George Pleasance was a cocaine smuggler on a big scale. The police and customs knew that; they just couldn't get him. He was too clever and his followers were too loyal. That wasn't the business of the journalists. What they wanted was to expose the Jockey Club, who were doing nothing about Pleasance using horse racing to launder huge sums of money from his drugs enterprise. Just as the police knew about Pleasance's cocaine exploits, the Jockey Club knew about his laundering activities. Pleasance operated with two basic methods, prepared to take a loss here and there so long as his percentages were high. She said he was smart enough to see betting losses as a tax. Sometime he would bet favourites, having interfered with the contenders either by getting to the jockeys or slowing the horses through difficult-to-trace doping, but his favourite method was to lay bets against a horse winning, since in that scenario the variables were easier to control.

157

'Or rather, the jockeys are easier to control that way,' said Duncan.

'You've got it. Now I know this; you know this; the Jockey Club know this. So why won't they do anything about it?'

Mandy said that getting proof was the killer – not getting proof that this or that jockey had held up a horse, because you would never get that kind of proof, even in the most fishy-looking circumstances. A horse would have to run backwards. But getting proof that the Jockey Club was sitting on information it knew would discredit the sport. The security team at the Jockey Club was a joke; their internal investigations were amateurish; they covered for each other and always had.

'Brown envelopes stuffed with cash?' Duncan said.

'That would help. We know the story but we've got nothing. No evidence. We're going round in circles.'

'Like I say, I can't help you. I don't know anything.'

'Better keep it that way. I do hope you know that Mr Nice Guy George Pleasance is not a nice guy behind the smiles.'

'I figured that out.'

'The police told me he's a killer. He doesn't dirty his hands but he has his executioners. Bag of cash, get rid of this one for me, but at this time, on Friday please, while I'm at the casino rolling it out on CCTV.'

'You know he mixes with Cadogan and Osborne?'

'Oh, we know who he's in bed with.' She stifled a yawn. 'Speaking of bed, there's your couch. I'll get you a pillow and a blanket. Don't look at me like that. I did make it clear. Well, didn't I?'

14

'You're riding for who?' said his best friend Kerry.
'You're riding for who?' said his trainer Petie.
'You're riding for fucking who?' said his agent Mike.

Gypsy George, now working steadily at Petie's yard, said nothing at all. He just gave Duncan a look that was as old as time. But it was still a look that said, *You're riding for who?*

The only person Duncan hadn't told was his dad, Charlie. That was going to be the most tricky.

'What are you going to say to your da?' Kerry said. 'How the hell are you going to let him know? He watches racing on the television every day. You can't keep it from him.'

'I know,' Duncan said. 'I'm still thinking about how to break it to him.'

'Well,' Petie said, 'I said I'd not stand in your way where there's no conflict with my horses, but I'm surprised to see you go that way. Not fixing to jump ship on me, are you?'

'No,' Duncan said. 'I promise you not.'

'I'm your agent,' said Mike. 'I know you've got a plan. You need to let me in on it.'

'It's just this ride,' Duncan said. 'Or one or two.'

'Or one or fucking two,' Mike said, shaking his head.

He was to ride at a minor meeting at Ludlow for Duke Cadogan. Lorna had pulled it off for him. It was only a Class 4 chase for five-year-olds and upwards over two miles: the Pinkland Insurance Handicap Chase. The horse was the

159

stubborn Parisa. As it happened, he was riding in Petie's colours in two other races on the same card, in the fourth race and the last.

'I hope to fuck you know what you're doing,' Kerry said.

The night before the meeting at Ludlow, Duncan went to see Charlie at Grey Gables. Mrs Solanki let him in, led him to Charlie's room and closed the door after him with a gentle click.

He'd brought Charlie a bottle of wine. There was a plate of Mrs Solanki's samosas on the table. They sipped wine and Duncan nibbled round the edge of a samosa, and they talked horses. Duncan told Charlie that George had settled in well at Petie's place and Charlie was overjoyed to hear it.

'I'm glad you've been able to do something for Gypsy George,' he said.

They talked in detail about Petie's horses and his training methods. Like Charlie, Petie was dedicated to fitness and diet, and Charlie liked to hear what he was up to in fine detail.

'He's keen to meet you,' Duncan said. 'He said he'd love you to look over his place.'

'He can come here any time he likes,' said Charlie.

'I think he would like to ask your advice about one or two things. He'd love for you to go down. Says he'll send a car to collect you if you're willing.'

'I'll not, son. The old back has been playing me up a bit. It's a long time sitting in the car.'

'He mentioned a troublesome mare. You should have a look at her for him.'

'You tell Petie he's welcome at my door any day of the week.'

'He can hardly bring his mare to Grey Gables, now can he?'

'Switch that radio on, would you, Duncan? Get a bit of evening news.'

With Charlie, Duncan felt like he was bringing a horse to a

birch fence. But this time there was no way of getting him to jump over it. He switched the radio on. The Ayatollah Khomeini had seized power in Iran. For some reason Charlie found it amusing to just say the words *Ayatollah Khomeini.* He said he'd once trained a horse called The Ayatollah.

'Really?' Duncan said.

'All right,' Charlie said. 'Out with it.'

'What?'

'What? He says *what.* I know you too well, son. Come on now: either piss or get off the potty.'

'I don't know if I can.'

'Well, I can't make you speak.'

'How much do you trust me?'

'Trust you?' He extended his arm in front of him. 'If you asked me for that hand I'd give it you. What are you talking about, trust?'

'If I said to you I was riding a horse owned by Cadogan and trained by Osborne, would you trust my reasons?'

Charlie glazed over at the naming of his enemies. He gazed beadily at his son. Then he reached over for a samosa and bit it in a clean snap.

Ludlow wasn't all fun. Duncan came second in the fourth race for Petie on an expected winner. Maybe he'd been distracted by the Pinkland Insurance Handicap Chase and all that went with it. It wasn't that it was a big race: it wasn't. Fourth rate, with ten runners of mixed ability, it should have been bread and butter to him.

But he had to find a private spot before the race to go and vomit.

William Osborne didn't help. He hadn't wanted Duncan on his horse, and though he didn't actually say so, his face made it plain. He wouldn't even look Duncan in the eye, in the paddock or anywhere else. Cadogan had overridden his objections.

Osborne, his face as hard as new saddle leather, bustled around in the paddock, barging Duncan out of the way. The show of public disrespect was obvious to anyone who happened to have been watching. *Bite your tongue*, Duncan said to himself, *bite your tongue*. Finally, pretending to check the horse's girth and still without looking him in the eye, Osborne said, 'This goes one way and one way only, and that's on the inside. All the way. You hang inside, I don't care what happens. That's what Parisa does and that's what you'll do.'

Duncan heard himself saying, 'Maybe we should have a cup of tea and a chat about it?'

Osborne looked at him for the first time. His eyes were boiling. He turned and walked away. One of the stable hands helped Duncan into the saddle.

Duncan cantered down to the start feeling the adrenalin start to pump. His muscles were unusually tense and he felt Parisa pick up his anxiety. The horse spooked at a passing spectator and bucked twice. Duncan cursed. He knew he should be relaxing the animal and showing his authority, but he felt his experience draining away. *Get a grip*, he told himself, *get a grip*.

Parisa hung back at the opening of the race and Duncan in his anxiety failed to push him on to get a good position. He would have liked to have tucked in about third or fourth, but the pack had settled on the inside and he was pretty much boxed in most of the way round. But he felt that Parisa had the strength to muscle through, come the ask, if only he could stay focused. *You're riding like an amateur*, he thought. He was travelling in a thicket of jockeys. He knew he had to get out, make space, make daylight. Twice he did see daylight, but on the outside rather than the inner. He would have gone for it, but he needed to stick to Osborne's instructions if he was going to be allowed to ride for Cadogan again. While his instincts screamed at him to chase the daylight, he hung on the inside.

He was getting jostled and he knew it was time to do the jostling himself. He had to find the strength to make it happen. Trying to press forward, he was nudged by a muscular grey. Parisa stumbled on a divot and lost his advantage. Duncan knew the error was his own but he cursed Parisa on.

With two fences to go, he was still boxed in. Parisa cleared the birch nicely, showing no sign of his tricks or hesitation. But there was no way through unless Duncan took him out wide. Approaching the last fence, he gave Parisa a squeeze. It should have been impossible, but the brave horse surged forward and pushed its way between two other runners. Duncan's heart leapt: suddenly he could see that beam of light again. Coming into the final jump, he battled again for space and landed sweetly on the other side. It was all going to be on the run-in. Parisa was giving everything, the crowd was roaring, but he just didn't have enough to take him past the two lead horses and came in third.

Duncan was pissed off. He knew Parisa was a fine animal and could have won that race on the bridle. Osborne's instructions had held him back. The question was: could Duncan keep his mouth shut?

He knew exactly what was coming.

Osborne was waiting in the paddock. 'You fucked the start. You lost it from the off.'

'A good trainer would sort that out,' Duncan said mildly.

The argument was bullshit both ways, and Duncan knew it. Any horse could get off to a slow start and you couldn't always figure why. He got down off Parisa, gave him a good pat and held his head to show he was happy with him. He took the saddle off him and went off to the Weighing Room without another word to Osborne.

Petie sidled up to him. 'You should have gone wide.'

163

'Don't I know it.'

'So why didn't ye?'

Duncan gave him the look.

'Ha!' Petie said. 'Fuckin' trainers, eh? Ha ha. Well, get those colours off your back and mine on.'

But the final race of the day was a crash. Three quarters of the way round, the girth snapped and Duncan had to pull up.

It was disappointing all round. But he'd ridden for Cadogan, he'd ridden as he'd been asked and – more less – he'd kept his wild mouth shut.

Mission accomplished.

Duncan and Kerry found a decent flat to share in Banbury. It was close enough to Petie's yard across the border in Warwickshire and it was a good central point from which to get to most race-tracks. It was located in the centre of town, close to the pubs and shops. It was also just a few doors away from a Chinese takeaway called Two Lucky. Kerry, a great fan of Chinese food, couldn't stop going on about how they wouldn't even have to cook. They could live out of silver-foil containers for the rest of their days.

The very first time they went into Two Lucky, they were recognised by the owner. He was an avid gambler and he'd seen their faces on TV. Mr Lee's lips were pulled back in what seemed to be a permanent smile. 'You two jockey!' he shouted at them with glee.

'Well, yes.'

Mr Lee had just a few strands of black hair combed back over his head, and black-framed spectacles with thick lenses. Behind the lenses his dark eyes swam with happiness. 'You no pay!' he shouted.

'Yes, we pay,' Kerry said.

'No, you no pay! You gimme gootip!'

Despite their protests, Mr Lee gave them their chow mein and beef in black bean sauce – and a lot other things they hadn't ordered besides – and wouldn't accept a penny. The same thing happened every time they went in.

'We're going to have to give him a lead sooner or later,' Kerry said.

'We can tell him this or that horse I'm riding has a good chance,' Duncan said. 'Jeez, this black bean sauce is good.'

'One chow mein,' Kerry taunted, 'and you're in Mr Lee's pocket.'

They were in the Banbury Cross one evening, eyeing up the local talent. 'What's going on with Roisin, then?' Duncan wanted to know.

'She's a grand lass.'

'I know that. But I think she's gone a bit sweet on you, Kerry.'

'Never mind sweet. What about yourself with this Lorna Cadogan? You keep buying her presents. A silk scarf here. A bracelet there. I've seen the way she looks at you with those puppy eyes. She wants your little jockey babies, so she does.'

'I like the girl.'

'I know you like the girl. You're not after fucking her around, though, are you? Just to pick up those rides?'

'I told you: I like her.'

'Only that wouldn't be good, now would it, Duncan? If that's what you were doing?'

'Hey! We were talking about you and Roisin! How did you switch it to me?'

'Look now,' said Kerry. 'What do you think of those two at the bar? We've got to christen this new pad, haven't we?'

Maybe girls thought they would get something exciting in the saddle; or maybe it was just the novelty. But being able to say you were a top-flight jockey was good pulling power. Kerry went up to get another couple of drinks and happened to fall into conversation with the two girls at the bar. He had the

165

ability to make a girl laugh in the first two minutes of talking to her.

He brought the pair of them back to the table and introduced them to Duncan. The boys shot the perfectly true line that they were new to the area and needed to hear about where to go. Then they let slip that they'd like to stay away from places that might have paparazzi around, since they were both top jockeys and needed to keep their names and faces out of the newspaper. Even if they'd already figured that the paparazzi were as likely in Banbury as titties on a bull.

'Champagne!' said one of the girls, a willowy brunette with giant eyelashes and pink lipstick.

'It's slimming,' Duncan said.

'I never knew that,' the other girl said, heavier built but very pretty, with a scoop blond haircut like a wave under her chin.

'It's just what we tell people,' Kerry said, smiling. 'Would you like a glass or shall we just talk about it till it goes flat?'

'Where do you girls work?' Duncan wanted to know.

'Electrical goods,' said one.

'Electrical goods,' said the other.

'Ah! Vibrators!' said Kerry, and for some reason the brunette snarfed champagne bubbles down her nose.

Right, at least you're in then, Kerry, thought Duncan.

When the girls went off to the pub toilets together, clutching their handbags, Kerry said, 'Mine's the brunette. Yours is good-looking too.'

'You're joking,' Duncan said. 'She's got more chins than a Chinese telephone directory!'

'You've got shit in your eye from that last race! She's beautiful. We can't all be whip-thin. Come on, we're on for christening our new flat.'

'I dunno, Kerry, I'm not up for it.'

'Up for it or not, you better play my wingman. Look, here they come again.'

166

It wasn't long before Kerry had invited the girls to come and look over their new pad, where he promised there was more bubbly and music on his shiny new Bang & Olufsen stereo system. The flat was about ten minutes' walk from the pub. Back there they popped a new bottle, talked for a bit and danced a little. Pretty soon Kerry had manoeuvred his brunette into his bedroom.

Duncan and the other girl chatted for a while, until she started looking at her watch.

'You want me to call you a taxi?' he said.

'That would be great. Will my friend be okay?'

'I'll vouch for Kerry.'

After the girl had gone, Duncan got ready for bed. Kerry and his new girl were whipping up a storm in Kerry's bedroom. The girl was giggling and laughing. Whatever was happening, they were having a lot of fun in there. The sort of fun Duncan had just denied himself.

There was a reason why he hadn't wanted to be with that girl, and that reason had surprised him. It was Lorna. He hadn't wanted to be unfaithful to her. Christie, on the other hand, had barely crossed his mind. He was screwing Christie to get back at Sandy Sanderson, pure and simple. With Lorna it had started out that way too: a way of getting at Cadogan. But something had changed along the way. In a process that he could never have predicted, he had started to get real feelings for Lorna. She was fun and she was clever, but there was also a wild streak to her, and at the moment she was pouring all that wild energy into her relationship with Duncan.

He stood in the bathroom, watching himself in the mirror as he brushed his teeth. *Oh quit being so bloody wet*, he said to himself.

*

The next morning being a Sunday, with no race meetings or work, Duncan was enjoying a lie-in until he heard the phone ringing in the hall. He got out of bed draped in a sheet and answered the call. It was Roisin. She'd gone to the supermarket, she said, and she guessed they'd have nothing in the new flat so had bought a whole mess of bacon and bread and ketchup and she thought to drop round and they could christen the flat with bacon sandwiches.

'Christen the flat,' Duncan repeated dumbly. 'With bacon sandwiches.'

'Sure,' Roisin said cheerily. 'I'll be half an hour. Tops.'

'Okay,' Duncan said. 'Okay.'

He put the phone down and knew he was going to have to wake Kerry. Roisin's relationship with Kerry had become semi-serious. He knew for a fact they were having sex. If Roisin got there to find a girl in his bed, there would be fireworks.

He pulled on his jeans and gently opened Kerry's bedroom door. The occupants slept, Kerry snoring lightly. An empty champagne bottle lay on its side at the foot of the bed. Duncan tiptoed to the bed and tried to rouse Kerry. Kerry didn't stir, so Duncan pinched his nose. Kerry snorked and opened his eyes. Duncan pressed a finger to his lips and beckoned his flatmate out of the room.

'You've got twenty-five minutes before Roisin gets here,' he told the buck-naked Irishman.

Kerry's eyes flared wide open. 'Holy Mother of God! Jesus, Mary and Joseph! Roisin will string me up by the balls! Look, you'll have to get in bed with the girl!'

'That won't work.'

'What am I going to do?'

'Okay, don't panic. Here's an idea.'

Five minutes later, Kerry was dressed in full jockey kit. White poloneck undershirt, jodhpurs, boots, gloves, helmet, set of goggles hanging from his throat. He even held a riding whip as he shook the girl awake.

'Huh?' she said as she blinked at him.

'I'm off to work,' Kerry said.

'It's a Sunday.'

'Oh, we jockeys don't take a day off, didn't you know that? Now if you're quick out of bed I'll give you a ride home in the car. To wherever you live.'

'No breakfast?'

'Breakfast? Ha ha! We jockeys don't go in for breakfast. I'll have to hurry you, though, my darlin', because I'm already a wee bit late. For the first race. Training. Gallops. You know.' He slapped the side of his riding boot with his stick for emphasis.

From the hall Duncan shouted, 'You'd better get a move on, Kerry. You know what that bastard is like if you're late!'

The girl swung her legs out of bed, frowned and found her bra and knickers. Within five minutes Kerry was driving her across town.

When he got back, Roisin was already in the flat, cooking breakfast. Kerry marched in and kissed her warmly. At least he'd taken his helmet and goggles off.

'What the hell are you kitted up for?' Roisin said.

'New stuff. You know. Just giving it a stretch. Awfully tight.' He held aloft a jar of instant coffee. 'Plus I nipped out for coffee. Thought you might forget it.'

Roisin wrinkled her nose and turned back to the lean bacon sizzling in the pan.

'It's beautiful!' Lorna said when she opened the package. She held the scarf to the light so it could shimmer on the mulberry silk.

'It's silk,' Duncan said.

'It's not just silk! It's the design. This is a Daniel Hanson silk scarf. I've seen them in Harrods. They cost a fortune!'

'I'm not much good at picking out gifts for women. No practice.'

This was true. Duncan's mother had never been around for him to buy gifts for at Christmas or on birthdays. But that was something they had in common. Lorna had been brought up by Cadogan and a series of nannies. Cadogan had never remarried, though he'd had a series of girlfriends, some of whom Lorna even called Mummy. The absence of a close mother had shaped Duncan and Lorna in similar ways.

'It's way too expensive. You can't afford this. I've got all the fancy things I want. It doesn't mean anything.'

'You don't want it?'

'No, I love it! It's gorgeous. But what I'm saying is that an hour in your company is more to me than anything you could buy me. I mean that.'

It was Sunday afternoon and they were going out for a hack on two quiet mares that Cadogan stabled near the house. The sun had broken out and it was perfect hacking weather. Along the way Duncan broke the story of Kerry in his full racing kit. Lorna laughed. She asked him if he too had had someone in his bed, and when he said no, she accepted it, and he liked that she did. In return she told him a couple of stories about her father being caught with his pants down by potential stepmothers.

It was a fine afternoon. When they were unsaddling the mares afterwards, Lorna said, 'This has been the best day of my life.'

'Don't say that!' said Duncan.

She told him that Cadogan kept a yacht moored in Brighton Marina. She suggested they go down there for a couple of days when he had a space in his calendar. He said they would.

*

But it wasn't to be Lorna with whom Duncan took his next break; it was George Pleasance.

George called him up one night. 'Got your passport in order?'

'Yes.'

'How's your golf swing?'

'Well. It's okay. Not great. Why?'

'Got your suntan lotion?'

'What?'

George had a big place in Marbella. Swimming pool, tennis court, all that. Close to the golf course. He and a bunch of his buddies were off there for a couple of nights' rest and relaxation. Mostly jockeys, but a couple of other friends too. George had already checked on Duncan's schedule and had established that he was free. All taken care of: car to the airport, flight, accommodation at the house, golf club membership, nightlife.

'The most strenuous thing you'll have to do,' George said, 'is put on your sunglasses. Are you in?'

'Sure,' Duncan said. 'I'm in.'

'Ask your friend along too. Kerry. The more the merrier.'

'Will do.'

Duncan put down the phone and walked back into the lounge, where Kerry was watching *Blake's 7* again. 'Who was that?' he asked.

'Just Lorna.'

'Checking up on you?'

'Something like that.'

'Jesus!' Kerry shouted at the TV screen. 'Did you see that studio set wobble!'

He called Lorna to tell her he was going.

'Don't go,' she said.

'It's just a couple of nights.'

'Duncan, it's not the whores I care about. If you want to run

171

around with whores, nothing I think or say about that is going to make any difference. It's Pleasance.'

'What about Pleasance?'

'He pulls you into his world. Once you're in, you can't get out. I've seen how he works.'

'I'm a big lad, Lorna.'

'No you're not. You think you're smarter and you can ride everything that comes along. But he's in a different league. Look at Daddy. You think he's a major player, but he's frightened of Pleasance. He hates him. Pleasance has Daddy in his pocket in ways I don't understand.'

Lorna had told Duncan that George Pleasance had entered her father's life when Cadogan had run short of money. Cadogan had made his money in the City, mainly in the futures market. But he had made some disastrous decisions. Whereas most men would have sold off their car collection, their impressive artworks, their fine racehorses, Cadogan couldn't bear to lose face. He simply had to hang on to the pretence that his stock hadn't changed. Enter George Pleasance. Just as Lorna was trying to warn Duncan, once Pleasance had sunk his claws into you, there was no way he could be shaken off.

'I'll be careful, Lorna, I promise.'

'You know what they call him? What people call George Pleasance? The Tailor.'

'The Tailor?'

'Because he's always got the measure of you. And everyone else. He'll stitch you up.'

'I'll remember that.'

'But no one says it to his face.'

'Right.'

'I'm trying to protect you, Duncan.'

'I appreciate it.'

'You're out of your depth. These are bad people. Daddy included. I love you, Duncan.'

He wasn't sure he wanted to hear her say that. He had spent so long building an impenetrable shell around himself that now he didn't even know his own feelings. Those three words were enough to make him doubt what he was doing. At first he had thought that Lorna was nothing more than a silly girl who ran around spending Daddy's money. The truth was, he had come to admire her more and more. She'd been damaged by Cadogan's remoteness and complete lack of interest in her. Despite that, she was a brave, witty and forceful girl. She was also very beautiful. What more could a man want?

There was silence on the telephone.

'I'll see you in a couple of days,' he said.

He hung up.

George Pleasance's spread in Marbella was stunning. A great white wedding cake of a building amid sprinkler-fed green lawns and with a large kidney-shaped swimming pool into which a white statue of a urinating cherub pissed three streams of sparkling water. The Mediterranean spring sunshine was hot and the sky a brilliant blue. Duncan was given a cool tiled room in the shadows at the rear of the house. Four other jockeys had been invited, two of whom he recognised from his night out at Tramp. Three other men, friends of Pleasance's, made up the party: two men who wore lightweight suits even in the Mediterranean sunshine, plus a braying figure in shorts and a polo shirt who was introduced to him as a stockbroker.

There were girls around, too. And if anyone wanted a break from the beer and the wine and the whores and the silver dishes of cocaine that stood on the table in the hall, there was golf on offer. There was no pressure to join in. Duncan lay by the pool, he swam. He pretty much kept himself to himself.

On the last afternoon he was alone in the pool. He swam a few lengths at high speed, and when he stopped, he closed his eyes and leaned his head against the cool concrete lip under the pissing cherub. That was when he felt someone else slip into the water next to him.

15

Of Petie's best horses, Duncan and Petie were working on Wellbeing and The Buckler. Wellbeing was the mare who had hacked up easily as a 20–1 winner in a competitive Conditions Chase at Lingfield just before Christmas. The Buckler was the strong-minded gelding Duncan had run up second against Sandy Sanderson's dirty tricks. Both horses had had trouble-free preparation since, and they were both in fine form. Petie had worked hard to get them into condition for the upcoming Cheltenham Festival; he'd also worked hard to try not to let anyone outside the stable see just how good the two horses were.

'Spies are everywhere,' he said.

Duncan knew from his days as a lad at Penderton that that was true. Information was big business. There were men hiding behind trees with powerful binoculars. There were characters in pubs always willing to stand rounds for the stable hands. Successful bookmaking was about having access to information about the health and form of a horse: did a horse have a cough; had it got a bruised foot; had it missed any work through lameness; how was it performing in the gallops; how was its breathing; why was a trainer like Petie getting up at five o'clock in the morning to put a horse through a gallop? On and on it went. Detail after detail, all of which could be converted into cash. Information increased the bookies' profits and decreased their losses.

Wellbeing and The Buckler were queen and king of Petie's stables. The average punter hadn't worked this out yet. But certain people inside the business were sniffing round. Petie asked his staff to stay away from the local pubs, where snoopers had been asking questions. He asked them to drink further afield. He also increased security. He astonished everyone by having – at great expense – closed-circuit cameras installed. They were the sort of thing you only saw at airports, military bases and high-security depots. For the first few days the stable hands would stop and wave at the cameras, until the novelty wore off.

Petie liked to bet, and he liked good odds. He was determined to keep the information at home.

Kerry had adopted Wellbeing. The Buckler was Duncan's pride. They were both going to be entered for the Cheltenham Festival in March. Those morning gallops in February at the crack of dawn were things of beauty. The light would be grey and then a flake of pink sunrise would appear as they pounded the turf, the horses' breath steaming in the air, Roisin in a cape with her stopwatch, Petie huddled in a long coat and with his leathery face set in a grin of satisfaction.

Glory days, preparing for the Cheltenham Festival.

But before that, there were plenty of everyday races to be run. Duncan had been noticed. His dream of being Champion Jockey was a long way away, but he'd been gathering enough winners for his name to become a serious contender. His strike rate put him in with the runners. He was a major prospect for upcoming seasons. His name was mentioned in the racing columns as the kind of young jockey who might be looking for bigger stables than Petie Quinn's next season.

Petie showed him the article.

'No one has asked me anything about that,' Duncan said. 'They've just gone ahead and printed it.'

'You'll leave me or you won't,' Petie said.

*

Of course there were rules against jockeys betting, but no rules to stop owners and trainers betting on their own horses. And no rules to stop jockeys' mothers, grandmothers or maiden aunts betting on or against a jockey's chances.

'Can you be sure?' Lorna asked him.

'You can never be sure,' Duncan told her. 'Racing is sometimes rigged but it's rarely fixed.'

It was an evening when they had the entire Cadogan spread to themselves. Duke was away for a couple of days with his latest girlfriend and only the domestic staff and groundsmen were around. Duncan would stay over on these occasions. They might take one of Duke's vintage motors from his car pool and drive it up to one of the pubs in the local villages, or to a restaurant.

They lay sprawled on a giant white leather sofa in Duke's lounge, with the lights dimmed and the expensive artworks on the walls lit by carefully trained low-level spotlights. 'Explain the difference,' she said.

'A fixed race is where the winner is already sorted before the race. A rigged race is one where the chances have been shortened or lengthened in some way. To fix a race you would have to get all the jockeys to agree who is going to win. You'll never do that. There are too many honest jockeys around. I've even met one or two. But for a rigged race you might get one or two jockeys to agree to lose. That might give another horse more of a chance. But it's not quite fixed.'

The conversation had all come about when Duncan had been discussing a horse he was riding for Petie the following day at Leicester. It was only a Class 4 race but the horse, he said, was certain to win. It was another almost unknown horse called Standard Contract. Through bad luck it had been pulled up, fallen or faltered in its most recent outings, but it was running way below its league, and Duncan was riding it. He was so confident, Lorna asked him if the race had been fixed.

'We don't fix our races,' he said. 'You think because the Duke and George Pleasance are into rigging races that the whole industry works like that, but you're wrong.'

'I don't know how you can be so certain that it will win, then,' she said.

'There's no certainty,' he said again. 'There's no certainty a dead bird won't drop out of that big fireplace in the next five minutes. But I know it won't. And I know this horse will win.'

Lorna looked at the fireplace. Then she got up and went across the room to the big polished mahogany desk. There was a Rolodex on the desk and she flipped it open. She picked up the phone and dialled a number. When someone answered she said, 'Hello, I want to place a bet on the Duke Cadogan account, please.'

She listened, then cupped the phone and said to Duncan, 'What's the name of the horse again?'

'Standard Contract. What are you doing?'

'He says, where is it running?'

'Leicester, three fifteen.'

She repeated the details into the phone. 'He said the odds are six to one.'

'That's as good as you'll get.'

'Five hundred pounds to win,' Lorna said into the phone.

'No!' Duncan shouted, hauling himself off the sofa. 'That's way too much!'

She shushed him. 'Five hundred to win,' she repeated into the phone.

Duncan stood over her as she completed the transaction. She hung on to the phone for a while, and then, as if in answer to a question, she said, 'Red Rum.'

There was some further instruction on the other end before she put down the phone.

'That's a fucking crazy bet, even if I'm certain, and I'm riding the thing,' said Duncan.

'I've got faith in you.'

'But Lorna! The horse might have a cough in the morning, or go lame. Or have a bad journey up to Leicester. Or another stable might have a surprise. And this isn't flat racing, this is jumps. Anyone can get unseated or brought down.'

'Where's all your confidence gone? You didn't tell me all this before I put the bet on.'

'No. But I didn't know you were going to lay out five hundred quid on me. And what sort of bookie is open for business at this time of night?'

'That's daddy's special bookie. They'll take bets any time, anywhere, about anything.'

'And what was all that about Red Rum?'

'Oh that was just Daddy's code to activate the bet.'

'Does he have a code for everything? Five hundred quid! You'd better hope I'm in good form tomorrow.'

'You mean I'd better not wear you out in bed.'

'You've got some trunk, Lorna, I'll give you that. Speaking of bed, why don't you rustle up some cold things and some drinks from the kitchen and let's take them upstairs. Don't bother the staff.'

Lorna was happy to oblige. 'Okay!' She shimmied away.

Duncan waited a beat and then went across to the open Rolodex on the desk. He found a pen and made a note of the number Lorna had just dialled. Then he waited quietly for her to come back from the kitchen.

Duncan was riding three horses at the Leicester meeting. Two for Petie, one for Cadogan and Osborne. Or rather, one for Cadogan and Osborne at the orders of George Pleasance. It seemed that if George Pleasance said he wanted something, he got it. And what he wanted was for Duncan to ride the favourite, Supernatural, in the fifth race of the day.

Kerry was also there riding for Petie. He spotted George Pleasance early in the proceedings. 'Hey,' he said to Duncan in the Weighing Room, 'you still haven't told me much about what went on in Marbella.'

'Very little. I swam in the pool. Slept on sunloungers. Stayed away from the whores.'

'I'll bet.'

Duncan flicked a towel at him. 'It's all in your feverish Paddy imagination.'

'I'll bet.'

Duncan looked up, and as luck would have it, there across the Weighing Room, gazing back at him with what was maybe half a smile, or half a frown, was the Monk. Aaron nodded briefly at him. He seemed to be able to look right into Duncan's heart.

'You look distracted this morning,' Roisin said to him in the paddock, as he was preparing for a two-mile novices' handicap chase. 'Are you okay?'

'I think I ate something that disagreed with me.'

'When Petie came along she said, 'He's got the scutters, Da.'

'No,' said Duncan, 'I'll be all right once I get going.'

'It's that foreign food. I told you to be careful what ye was eating and the water ye drank.'

'Let me get down to the start. I'll be fine.'

He saddled up and cantered down to the start line, trying to concentrate on the race ahead. But he wasn't properly focused. He didn't ride a bad race, but came in fourth on Standard Contract when he felt he could have given a much better account. Petie seemed reasonably happy. He was more interested in the progress of Lemontree in the fourth, whereas the previous race had been just an outing.

Duncan stuck by the story of having a dicky tummy. He locked himself in the cubicle in the Weighing Room so he could have time to himself. His face was too readable. It was better if they thought he was nursing a bad gut rather than a bad conscience.

In the fourth race he was up against the Monk. Aaron never acknowledged him before the off; he never acknowledged anyone. He was in the zone. It was his own crystal-clear place. There were no other riders. Duncan admired that. He tried to clear his head of all thoughts before the race. He sat behind Aaron all the way round, as if he was in the older jockey's slipstream. Then, when he felt Aaron go, he gave Lemontree a squeeze, too. It was enough. Aaron's horse went out into the front with only one fence to jump. But Lemontree had an extra set of burners. She jumped well at the last and left Aaron at a standstill. The last thing Duncan remembered was Aaron turning slightly and squinting at him through muddied goggles. There was the nearest thing to a smile on the Monk's face. Not really a smile. But nearly. Lemontree hacked up six lengths clear.

Petie was very happy; Roisin ecstatic, since the horse had been one of her purchases; Kerry was pleased for him.

All he had to do now to complete the day was *not* win the fifth race for Cadogan on Supernatural.

He weighed in from the previous race, then found the valet, who had his change of colours ready for him. He would be riding in the scarlet with white star and red chevrons of Osborne's stables. When he came out, George Pleasance, showing off his great mane of silver-and-jet hair, was there to wish him luck.

Out in the paddock, Osborne was waiting with his usual face. No eye contact, and this time no instructions either on how to ride Supernatural. Cadogan was there too, smiling broadly, fedora pulled down low over his eyes. 'We're letting you go on one of our favourites today,' he said. 'Don't let us down.'

Duncan wondered whether Cadogan and Osborne were in on it. Were they in on everything? Perhaps yes, perhaps not. George Pleasance made no appearance in the paddock. It wouldn't do to have a known cocaine smuggler consorting openly with Cadogan and Osborne, even if the police and the Jockey Club and the betting authorities all knew about it. What would the punters do? Duncan thought. He fixed his goggles and cantered down to the starting line.

The fifth race was the biggest race of the day. Supernatural was odds-on favourite to win the Class 3 Novices' Hurdle for four-year-olds over two miles and four furlongs. The starter was having a problem with one or two horses and he was having to circle them. Duncan stood unaffected, trying again to clear his thoughts.

But in his mind he was in a warm and quiet swimming pool, under a setting sun. There was a slight ripple as he felt someone else slide into the pool beside him. It was George Pleasance. No one else was around. George had his back to the sun, so that his face was almost in silhouette. Duncan had had to squint to see the whites of his eyes and his row of white teeth.

Then the horses were away like a flock of birds. Herd instinct. Duncan took a clear central position behind four leaders and rode steadily, keeping pace, keeping plenty in hand. Supernatural was a decent ride, rightfully favourite in this class of race. The track had turned muddy and there was a lot of earth being kicked up by the leaders. She cleared the first hurdle neatly and the flying mud slapped at his goggles and his helmet and the drumming of hooves shut out the sound of everything else.

Was he about to surrender that unbroken beam of light? He thought of the Monk's face turning to him as he'd galloped past him in the last race. It only had to happen once. Take a fall and you fall for ever. But did it count if your reason for throwing a race was not cash, not corruption, but pure revenge? If it was just one move in a larger plan?

He held his position and Supernatural was jumping beautifully. The mare was enjoying the race. Her ears were pricked forward, waiting for the word, the squeeze, the nudge. Sometimes you could tell a horse knew it was going to streak out in front. You could feel the swell of nerve and muscle. This was a winning race.

But he had to gain trust. He had to worm his way in, to a place where they would begin to rely on him. There was no other way. He had to change his face when he was with them; make them think he was one of them; make them believe he was just like them. He had to deceive them all. This was the price he would have to pay.

George Pleasance had slipped into the pool, all smiles in the golden light of the setting sun. 'You know what I'm proud of?' he'd said. 'I've never once asked a jockey to take a fall for me. Never once said: pull up, don't try, don't win. I've never had to. I don't believe in it. I much prefer to give a jockey a win–win. No repercussions. Never.'

'Why are you telling me this?'

'There's a horse I want you to ride. She's called Supernatural. Good one for you to win on. You're a future champion, you are, Duncan. Not this year, no, but in the future I see it and I want to be there with you. So there it is. My gift to you. Win on it and there will be more, I promise.

'But I'm going to have a good bet against you, Duncan. I'm going to lay a bet for Supernatural to lose. I always tell the jockey. Then if he wants to please me, that's his business. I give a man a choice. But if it's not a fair choice, a difficult choice, then it's not a choice, is it, Duncan? There you have it. I've taken a shine to you. Win or lose, it's all right by me, son.' And with that George Pleasance had hauled himself out of the pool, grabbed a towel and walked away across the warm tiles.

Duncan hadn't seen Pleasance after that until today's races.

The front-runners were beginning to tire as they reached the third last. He could hear the swelling cries of the crowd in the grandstand, mostly urging on the favourite.

No, he decided, it was too much to surrender. There was still that beam of light between him and winning the race, and he couldn't break it. His revenge was going to have find another way. He gave Supernatural a squeeze and the mare responded, picking up the pace now. But in that moment he thought of his father, Charlie, broken by those bastards. Where was their conscience? They hadn't cared about trampling a good man into the mud. Why should he care if he had to throw a race or two before getting the justice he wanted above everything else?

He was a torn man. He rode inside the bubble of noise kicked up by the hooves of the charging horses. He had two fences left and the last stretch in which to make his call. Supernatural was bursting to go. As the second-last fence came up, he saw a gap on his right and he made for it. But as he did so, he felt a bump as another rider went for exactly the same spot. Their stirrups clashed. The weight of the two animals impacted equally. Supernatural flew the hurdle, but she was on her forehand, and when she cleared it her nose dived and touched the turf.

At first Duncan thought he was going to stay on her back. He flew forward and felt his feet dig into the stirrups. But then the horse stumbled again as she tried to right herself and Duncan was spun off to the left. He was pelted with mud as he flew through the air and he landed heavily on his shoulder. He had his wits about him enough to crouch into a ball as the horses coming up behind him took the jump, landed and then leapt over him. A hoof caught him on the hip. Then the drumming retreated and he was left in the dirt. He looked up but couldn't see Supernatural anywhere.

He got to his feet, still holding his whip. He pulled off his goggles and walked to the side of the track in a daze. First-aiders were running in his direction. 'I'm fine,' he told them. 'Is the horse all right?'

'Still running,' said one of the first-aiders. 'Here, let's have you sat down a minute.'

'I'm fine.'

'Don't be an arsehole. Sit down!'

'It was taken out of my hands,' Duncan said.

'What was?'

'Decision.'

'He's concussed,' one of the first-aiders said.

'No I'm not.'

After the first-aiders were satisfied that he was neither concussed nor had broken any bones, he made his way back to the paddock. Supernatural had already been unsaddled and taken back to her stable.

Osborne was still there. 'There's an inquiry,' he said gruffly.

That would mean Duncan would have to give evidence to the stewards about what had happened. No doubt some of the punters would feel that he'd been unfairly impeded. Not that it would make any difference now to the result as far as he was concerned.

Cadogan was there. He clapped Duncan on the back. He didn't seem too upset. 'Jolly bad luck. Glad to see you're okay.'

Petie and Roisin had come into the paddock. They were just relieved to see that he was unhurt. 'Not hiding anything, are you?' Petie said. He always said that. He knew jockeys too well; knew that most of them were not above hiding a cracked rib or two, or worse, just so they could hang in for whatever fixture lay ahead of them.

Still in his silks, Duncan made his way up to the stewards' room. As was the way, the room was hastily arranged into a makeshift courtroom, even though the 'inquiry' was a bit of a joke. The stewards were just finishing talking to the winner, a jockey called Mike Nation. Duncan knew him a little from the Weighing Room. He was a fine fellow. On his way out, he asked Duncan if he was okay.

They asked Duncan a few questions about what had happened at the second-last fence. Duncan said it exactly as he saw it. 'I saw a gap and I went for it. Mike saw the same gap and

185

went for it at the same time. We clipped each other. My horse stumbled on landing and her nose brushed the grass.'

You didn't think it was interference?'

'Mike did nothing wrong. Nothing I could have done, or he could have done differently. He went on to win it fair and square.'

Some papers were shuffled. One of the stewards said the result would stand. The announcement was quickly made over the public address system, echoing round the track. It was all over.

Later, in the owners' bar, Duncan found Petie, Roisin and Kerry. They were having a drink with Mike and Aaron. George Pleasance was across the other side of the room, drinking with Osborne, Cadogan and a couple of others. Duncan tried to avoid eye contact. Pleasance seemed to be doing the same thing.

'Well,' said Aaron at last, 'that was a bit of bad luck you had there, Duncan.'

'Right.'

'But you came through unscathed. So was it a bit of good luck?'

Duncan looked up. The Monk's face, gazing back at him, was completely unreadable. What did he mean by that? He couldn't possibly be in with George Pleasance. On the other hand, Mike might have told him that Cadogan had come to him with the ride and that he as an agent hadn't gone looking for it. The Monk was beginning to unnerve him. It was like he knew everything.

Or maybe he had just meant that it was good luck to fall off without injury. For sure, there were a dozen ways to slow up a horse and lose a race, and falling off wasn't exactly first choice. You'd have to be an idiot. It was too damned dangerous.

'Let's call it good luck,' said Mike Ruddy. 'It ain't been a bad day.'

16

Christie had been calling him. He'd neglected her. His damned conscience had been getting the better of him again. What was it about Lorna that made him want to keep away from other women? Maybe he should talk to a priest or something; find out what the hell was going wrong. Sometimes he wished he were a Catholic like Kerry. That way he could go up to the confessional box and say, *Help me out here, Father, I've gone right off sinning.*

Sandy Sanderson obviously didn't have a problem. He was as horny as a three-balled rabbit. Any and every Thursday night, you're safe, Christie had told Duncan. Somehow Sandy had come to an arrangement with his mistress that he would always be with her on a Thursday night, whatever was happening the next day. Christie wasn't supposed to know. Officially it was his regular boys' night out, but it had been clear to her for a long time. She wanted to see Duncan that Thursday. That meant lying to Lorna, and he didn't like doing that.

He was going to have to find a way of extricating himself from Christie. Screwing the Champion Jockey's wife had limited satisfaction. It had been fun planting tiny clues around the house for Sanderson to find, but it just wasn't deep-down satisfying. When revenge came, it was going to have to be much more far-reaching.

Christie opened the door. She wore something that made her look like a Greek goddess. It was a loose-fitting, low-cut pleated white minidress. It revealed the beautiful curve of her elegant shoulders and her long, long legs. There was a gold sash at her waist and she wore high-heeled gold-leaf sandals with wraparound strands climbing up her tanned calves.

'Are we fancy dress?' Duncan said.

'Get in here,' she said, pulling him in and closing the door behind him. She grabbed his belt buckle and led him through the house towards the kitchen, where as before she had champagne chilling. As she led him, he noticed the light was on in the dedicated snooker room.

She poured champagne. 'You've been avoiding me,' she said.

'No. I've been very busy. You should know that, with Cheltenham coming up.'

The Cheltenham Festival, with its Gold Cup and other landmark races, was just a couple of weeks away. A kind of fever started to take over all major stables in the build-up to the Festival.

'I know that. But I told you: Thursdays are always clear. Where were you last week?'

'I do have a girlfriend, you know.'

'You're not telling me it's serious. I thought you were just after getting a few races.'

'Think what you want.'

'Let's not fight.'

Duncan felt a little sorry for Christie. She was surely one of the most stunningly beautiful women he'd ever met in his life. And yet here she was on a Thursday evening playing second fiddle to Sanderson's mistress, whoever that was; and having to complain about playing second fiddle to her lover's girlfriend, namely Lorna. She had wealth and beauty in great store and yet she was desperately lonely for company.

'Kiss me, Duncan,' she said.

'Wait. Have you been playing snooker?'

'Yes. While I was waiting for you.'

'Can you play?'

'I could wipe the floor with you. Before I married Sandy, I went out with Tony Swinton.'

'Tony the Terminator? You're joking.'

She shook her head. 'Want to try me?'

They spent the next hour not having sex but playing snooker. She took a frame; he took a frame. Then, with Christie poised to win the third, Duncan broke the rules. It was the sight of her bent across the table, the green baize shining under the overhead lamp and the catchlight winking on the snooker balls. He reached around her waist and slid her knickers down to her ankles.

'This means I win,' she said.

'Yes.'

He stuck three fingers inside her and she gasped and rocked against the table. She drew herself erect and let her snooker cue rattle to the floor. Then she slipped off her sandals, one after the other, before climbing on to the snooker table itself. She got on her hands and knees on the green baize and spread her buttocks open, swaying slightly, waiting for him to join her.

He undressed quickly and climbed up on the snooker table with her. He was already aching hard but he knew how he wanted her. He pushed her so she was belly down on the baize and spread her arms and legs towards the corner pockets of the table. Then he kneeled astride her legs, pulling her ankles up either side of his hips and rocking her back on to him, pushing deep inside her.

She groaned and clawed at the baize, threatening to tear it as he rocked back and forth on her. In turn he raked her tanned back. Her fingers found her way around a pair of the Crystalite snooker balls and she hung on to them as if they were a way of staying attached to the table. At last he lifted up her buttocks and she raised herself to her hands and knees so that he could push deeper and deeper inside her.

He felt her flood. He turned her over so that she was lying on her back, now blinking at him, her eyes seeming to dissolve in the light from the overhead lamp. When he was beyond the point of no return, he shouted out her name. Just as he was coming, she grabbed his balls a little too enthusiastically. Duncan shot up in the air like a rocket. He hit the fringed canopy lamp overhead so hard that it shattered and, fittings and all, tumbled down around them on to the baize of the snooker table.

The excitement was growing at Petie's yard as they counted down the days to the Cheltenham Festival. The Festival was the pinnacle of jump racing, three days in which a year's preparation, anticipation, hope and action was played out at a superb venue. It was a mix of showground and sporting event in which the very best horses and the bravest jockeys got to compete. Here you needed that little bit of extra luck and that little bit of extra heart. It was a place where reputations were forged in the heat of the race and where owners, trainers, jockeys, stable hands, bookies and punters came together in a carnival atmosphere that also dragged in with it crooks, freaks, con men and fortune-hunters. There was music and shopping tents and pageantry aplenty.

It was a theatre of dreams. For those centrally involved in the sport it could provide glory of the kind that would last a lifetime in the memory. It was the thing Charlie Claymore was aiming for before his dreams were shattered by the conspiracies of Duke Cadogan, Sandy Sanderson and William Osborne. Duncan could taste glory weeks ahead of the event. He wanted it for himself; but most of all he wanted it for Charlie.

Three great days; every race momentous. The Festival kicked off with Champion Hurdle Day. The second day, the one on which Petie was planning to make his mark, was Champion Chase Day. The final day saw competition for the Cheltenham

Gold Cup, a long and punishing race over three miles, two and a half furlongs, on a track gone heavy.

It was time for the big boys to show their muscles. Though Petie was not quite in the same league as trainers like William Osborne, Alan Bonsor or Dick Sommers at Penderton, he was bubbling under. He was thereabouts. Unlike those others, he wasn't anywhere near Champion Trainer capacity, but his presence was a threatening one. He'd proved he could pull off surprises and upset the big-time boys on more than one occasion.

Mandy Gleeson had persuaded Duncan to set up an interview with the shy Irishman for a journalist friend. The newspapers had identified Quinn's stable as a presence to watch for at the Festival. They'd assembled a photograph in which Petie, scruffy as ever, peered into the camera flanked by Duncan and Kerry in their brilliant silks.

'Talk about crucified between two thieves,' Petie had said, scowling at the newspaper.

'Bit of attention won't hurt, Daddy,' Roisin had said.

It was true. The Cheltenham Festival was all about glamour, and the news boys wanted their stories. They wanted Davids and Goliaths; they wanted fairy tales; they wanted talk of dark horses and piebald ponies. The punter running his eye down a page of form might let his finger come to rest at Quinn's name a little more often.

Meanwhile, the training at Petie's yard was becoming intense. Fitness, health and diet. Petie was a revolutionary in thinking about horses and how they raced. Of course everyone knew you had to have a fit horse, but they hadn't quite figured out the fine tuning for a super-healthy animal that would lead to maximum fitness. He experimented with their diet all the time. He had a food scientist set up a kind of laboratory in the grounds. The scientist wore a white coat around the stables. He took samples of the horses' blood. Some people thought Petie was crazy, that he was going over the top.

'Listen,' Petie said to Duncan one day. 'If you're not feeling well, you can tell me. But that horse over there can't tell me, can she? She can't say: look here, Petie, I'm feelin' a bit under the weather, you know? But if we look at her blood, we can see if she's right, and if she's not right we can try to get her right.'

But as well as these modern ideas, he was old-school, too. He was still inviting Charlie down to see the set-up and Charlie was still refusing. So Petie went to him and consulted him about using a tongue-tie on a horse that had been doing well but occasionally when tongue-tied would give up and lose heart. There was no rhyme or reason to it. Charlie asked what he was using for the tongue-tie and when Petie said leather, Charlie said: to hell with that, make a new one out of an old pair of tights. Petie scratched his head and said he'd give it a go. Duncan thought he was just humouring the old man.

Petie told Charlie he had a box at Cheltenham and wanted him to be his guest. Charlie declined again, and Petie told him, well, the place was there anyway.

Gifts continued to arrive from an appreciative George Pleasance. A crate of champagne. A box of Havana cigars. A pair of tickets to watch Nottingham Forest in the quarter-finals of the European Cup. As far as George Pleasance was concerned, Duncan had taken the fall. Duncan wanted him to keep thinking that.

There were some repercussions. Mandy Gleeson invited him to have lunch with her in Soho.

'Is that all you're going to eat?' she said to him when his lunch arrived. He was fretting about his weight and taking pee pills in the run-up to Cheltenham. 'We could have made it a picnic on the banks of the Thames. I could have brought you a lettuce leaf in my handbag.'

'Do I detect a hostile note?'

'I'll be honest with you, Duncan. The talk around our investigation is that you've gone over to the dark side.'

'On what evidence?'

'We know George Pleasance made a huge lay bet against Supernatural. I honestly thought you were different.'

'Have you ever fallen off a horse, Mandy?'

'Once or twice.'

'In the middle of a race? Jumping a fence at thirty miles per hour or more? You'd have to be fucking crazy. If a jockey wants to hold back, he will run out or pull up or gear down.'

'Unless he wants to keep his reputation intact. Unless he wants to make it look really good.'

'You're full of shit,' Duncan said. 'You think you know all about it. But you can't see over the fence.'

'Give me some information, then.'

'You've got the information. Now you're like a six-year-old, filling in the pictures with coloured crayons.'

'What are we supposed to conclude? You suddenly start hanging around with George Pleasance. You ride one of Cadogan's horses. It's a stonewall favourite and it happens to have a calamity fall.'

'Do you know what *I've* concluded, Mandy? That everyone will already have made up their minds one way or the other, mostly shaded by what they read or hear in the media. What was that about the journalist and the whore? Something about power without responsibility?'

'That's a bit rich from someone who enjoys Mediterranean nights. Marbella, wasn't it?'

'You sound angry. I suppose you're still not going to let me fuck you.'

Mandy stood up and fumbled inside her handbag. She flung a couple of banknotes on the table. 'No, but I'll pay for your lettuce.'

'Sit down, Mandy. Come on. We said we would help each other. Let's tell each other what we know.'

He persuaded her to sit down again. The idea had been for him to hear what she knew; where her investigations had led her. He apologised and told her what he could: about the un-solicited gifts from George Pleasance. He told her the truth, which was that he'd been under no direct pressure from Pleasance to take a fall, and that Pleasance's clever technique was to let jockeys recruit themselves into his schemes. He also told her she would just have to believe him when he said that his fall from Supernatural was unplanned.

In return she told him something that her team of journalists had recently uncovered. 'Rah-ho-tep,' she said.

Duncan sat up. Rah-ho-tep was one of Cadogan's horses. It was running at Cheltenham on Gold Cup day. Not in the Gold Cup itself but in the Grand Annual Handicap Chase, the last race of the day and of the Festival.

'It's showing favourite already and it's being ridden by—'

'By Sandy Sanderson,' said Duncan.

'Correct. Now my information is that George Pleasance – or rather his cronies – are already laundering drugs money by spreading small lay bets against Rah-ho-tep.'

'He'd have to do that. You can't lay in huge bets because as soon as the bookies get a whiff they'll close down. But if he spreads it around the country, and if Rah-ho-tep stays in place as firm favourite, then he'll get some pretty cool odds.'

'He's overseen a massive shipment lately. He's got a lot of cash to rinse.'

'If you know this, how come the police don't?'

'They will. But our story will break first. After the Gold Cup.'

Duncan nodded, trying to take in the implications. How typical of George Pleasance. He would want to be there on Gold Cup day, larging it. Obviously he would stay away from rigging the trophy title itself, but he would so much want to be there on the day. His vanity was his weak point.

Mandy narrowed her eyes at him. 'You're around Cadogan's place a lot these days,' she said knowingly. 'You'll let me know if you hear anything?'

'Sure.'

'Anything at all.'

They finished lunch. After she'd gone, Duncan sat in the restaurant a while. His half-eaten salad lay in front of him. He decided to smoke a cigarette instead of finishing it.

It wasn't just Mandy Gleeson with whom his relationship was a little fraught. Everyone around the yard was getting keyed up. Petie was becoming more exacting in his demands. Even though the training was going well, he wanted to micro-control everything. He even bawled out Roisin for saying she wanted to use the toilet at a moment that wasn't convenient to him.

Duncan thought he'd chosen his moment carefully to broach something, but his timing wasn't good after all. He mentioned that there was an off chance Cadogan might also want him to ride a race or two at Cheltenham. It wasn't even necessarily true. Duncan had been hoping to nudge Lorna to help him pick up a ride.

'No,' Petie said.

'I'm not talking about a clash of fixtures. Just if I happen to be free one of the days.'

'I said no.'

'We had an agreement. If I was clear, I could ride for who the hell I wanted.'

'I don't care about no fuckin' agreement. I want your head straight and settled on my fuckin' rides. No distractions. This is Cheltenham we're talking about. It's not Toytown Races.'

Petie looked at him with a shining, defiant face. Duncan took a step towards him. They were almost eyeball to eyeball. Duncan was about to speak when he felt a huge paw grab his collar and drag him away.

It was Gypsy George. 'Come up to my caravan for a spell,' he said.

'I want to sort this out.'

George's arm was round Duncan's shoulder. It was half friendly uncle, half neck-lock. George marched him out of the stable yard and over to his caravan. The door was propped open, as always, and George led him inside.

'Now then,' he said. 'What are you planning?'

'What? I'm not planning anything.'

George's leathery skin seemed to break into a thousand wrinkles. 'Duncan, did I put you on your first horse?'

'Yes.'

'Well fuck yourself, then.' George was still smiling.

'All right,' Duncan said.

'And how many horses have I seen just before a race?' George said. 'Their coat shines. They're on their toes. Ears pricked up. Maybe ready to take a nip at one of the other horses. Sharp, you might say. But too sharp, you might also say. Using up too much energy. Sure you want them to be ready. Muscled up. Alert. Nice coat. But not too sharp. Not grinding their teeth.'

'You made your point, George.'

'I did. And maybe you'll make yours. But whatever it is you're planning, you can't do it on your own.'

'I have to.'

'You can't. You need to get your lieutenants gathered around you. And take them into your trust.'

'I don't know 'bout that, George.'

George squinted at him and lowered his voice. 'Maybe this is other folks' fight and not just your own. Have you thought of that?'

Duncan looked hard at the older man. They heard footsteps approaching George's caravan.

'Knock knock feckin' knock.' It was Roisin. 'Well, Daddy wants to know if there's any chance of getting any work out of anyone today. And don't shoot me: I'm just the messenger.'

17

But there were a few less glamorous races to be concerned with before Cheltenham. While Petie was holding back his top horses, he was still intent on bringing on some of his novices and younger horses for next season. These lower-class races were also seen as a chance for Duncan and Kerry to get themselves into peak condition and readiness for Cheltenham.

Hexham in the north-east was set in beautiful surroundings but was one of the more unfashionable tracks, struggling to make itself pay. But with top jockeys and major trainers counting the number of winning races to get their respective trophies they didn't have too much trouble in attracting big names, even if the cameras were unlikely to show up. There was always bread-and-butter jockey work to be done whenever the bright flags were flying elsewhere. Both Duncan and Kerry were riding at Hexham and they found themselves in the Weighing Room with Duncan's old friend Sandy Sanderson.

Sanderson was out to mop up a few lower-grade races, including a Class 4 Hurdle for five-year-olds and upwards over two and a half miles, in which he was up against Kerry. As soon as Duncan realised this, he wanted to Kerry to swap, to let him ride against Sanderson. Kerry wasn't having any of that, and neither was Petie.

Ahead of the race, Kerry was pushing things as far as he could go. 'I shall have to keep my eye out for that Sandy Sanderson,' he said in an overloud voice that made all the other jockeys wag their ears.

Sanderson, who was pulling on his boots, just sneered.

'I mean, wasn't it you telling me, Duncan, how Sandy likes to cuddle up close and get his boot over your stirrup?'

'I'm sure I never said that,' Duncan said.

'Oh yes. An old trick, that one. What you don't want is to be squeezed in between him and another horse. Or you'd be *snookered*.'

Duncan looked away. Sanderson glanced up at Kerry.

'That'd be a good way of putting it, wouldn't it? Snookered. I mean, like when you're caught on the snooker table with, say, a pink ball between your white ball and the one you're trying to pot. Well, you know, one jockey pushing up close so you can't see a gap there. *Snookered*. That's what I'd call it, Duncan. Wouldn't you?'

'If you like.'

Sanderson stared hard at Kerry. But he said nothing. Then the jockeys were called out to the parade ring.

'I'll try not to get snookered!' Kerry called out cheerily as he pulled his helmet on and went out on to the track.

'That Kerry speaks in riddles,' Duncan's valet said.

'He does,' Duncan said. 'He rides a bit close to the edge, too.'

Whether or not he rode too close to the edge, Kerry won the race. Afterwards he said he might have had Sanderson rattled. Duncan thought not; he thought Sanderson was too much of a pro to be unsettled by Weighing Room banter.

Duncan anyway had his own race to think about. It was the Hexham Silver Bell Novices' Chase, and he was expecting a winner. It was another Class 4 and there were only six runners in it over a two-mile course. Duncan was even-money favourite on a mare Petie was bringing on for next year called Because I Said So. The opposition was patchy, though there was a mare called In Plain English from his old stables at Penderton that was also well fancied.

He got off to a good start and tucked in, letting one of the less experienced jockeys set a pace he would be unable to keep up. The ground was heavy and they were all going to tire. One of the runners went down at the first fence; Duncan looked behind him and saw the jockey sprawling and his mount running out wide. He recognised the pink cap and white silk of the Penderton stables and he thought, *Well, that's this one in the pocket.* But the mud was deep and then the leader went crashing into the fourth fence, unseating his jockey.

There was still plenty of time for Duncan to wait out on the inside when disaster struck at the sixth. A jockey in front of him swerved into the fence. The horse jumped clear but went down, and Because I Said So clipped his heels and was brought down also. Duncan thought he felt a crack as he hit the earth, but as he knew there was nothing behind him he was up quickly. Because I Said So was up quickly too, and stood waiting, looking at Duncan as if to say: what the hell happened there?

Duncan was mightily pissed off. That might have been one of his easiest races. He was winded, sure enough, and his breath was short, but he felt okay. Then he pressed his ribs and felt a stinging pain. He thought it possible he might have cracked a rib. The emergency care staff were already running across to him. He knew both of them from two previous falls at the same track: Beverley Fillingham and James Cockerill. They were like old friends.

'I'm fine,' he said to James. 'Go and look at that other fellow.'

He walked over to Because I Said So and took the reins. Then he heard a strange noise.

It was coming from the grandstand. It wasn't anything like the sound the crowd usually made. You could be a quarter-mile away and you could tell the difference between the crowd roaring in a favourite and the crowd applauding an outsider. This sound wasn't like either of those two things. It was confusion and hilarity and anxiety all mixed. Then he heard Beverley shouting to him. He was holding his rib and couldn't understand what she was saying.

'Go ahead, Duncan!'

'What's that?'

'Get back on! There are no runners.'

'What?'

'Don't stand there discussing it! They've all refused ahead of you.'

'Refused?'

Duncan leapt back up on Because I Said So. He took a steady canter up to the next fence. He had a clear run and was over it easily. Still looking around him in disbelief, he passed one of the horses that had refused and who showed no signs of getting back into the race.

He had nine more fences to clear and he took them steadily. This time the noise from the grandstand switched back to a familiar sound. It was the roar of punters welcoming in the favourite; and the cheers of even those who'd bet against him. He was the only finisher.

He held his hand across his mouth, almost embarrassed by the win, as he walked Because I Said So into the winners' enclosure. For once in his life he was speechless. *If anyone wants to discuss fixed racing*, he thought, *they can start with this race.*

In the winners' enclosure there was jubilation on his behalf at such an outrageous win. In the Weighing Room afterwards, everyone was laughing and smiling and clapping him on the back. Except for Sandy Sanderson.

Lorna got Duncan invited to join in pigeon shooting on Cadogan's grounds. They were set up for shooting the clay type and the grey type too. Cadogan was also well stocked and organised for grouse and pheasant shooting and was fond of having his friends over for a session.

It was something George Pleasance enjoyed too, though it was March, and grouse and pheasant shooting was out of season. But then again, cocaine smugglers and horse-race fixers were not always likely to be strict adherents to the rules of rough shooting, and if a pheasant sometimes got confused with a pigeon, the world didn't end. George Pleasance was pleased to see Duncan there. His way of demonstrating it was to pat him on the cheek with a leathery hand. No mention whatsoever was made of recent racing events.

Duncan didn't have much in the way of kit, so Lorna had fixed him up in the 'uniform'. Waxed Barbour coat; green wellingtons; cloth cap. It was impossible to distinguish him from everyone else out shooting that day. Though the truth was, he felt a chump. He felt like someone in disguise.

Lorna, on the other hand, had been born to the sport. She was familiar and handy with swinging the over-and-under double-ejector multi-choke, and she was a pretty good instructor.

'What did I just say to you, Duncan?'

'Uh?'

'This isn't a toy. I said keep your finger off the trigger until you're ready to shoot. What did I just say?'

'You said keep your finger off the trigger until you're ready to shoot.'

'So why have you still got your finger on the trigger?'

'Uh.'

On the clay shoot, he got the hang of things quickly, though she noticed him wince once or twice at the recoil. She asked him about it.

'Nothing much. I bruised a rib or two in the fall at Hexham.' The truth was, that 'bruise' was hurting like hell. He was sure he'd cracked a couple of ribs. But he wasn't going to let anyone

202

know in case it might in some way threaten his rides at the Cheltenham Festival.

After a while Lorna asked him if he wanted to go into the woods and try for the real thing. He said he was ready. There was strict protocol to observe in the woods to make sure everyone was safe, especially from beginners like Duncan, but Lorna talked him through it. He liked to see her taking charge. He was softening to her all the time.

A wood pigeon flew up. Duncan aimed and missed. Then a pheasant whirred up out the bush. It was so slow and heavy and noisy in its flight, Duncan didn't even make the effort to track it.

'It's okay,' Lorna said. 'They're out of season.'

'They're too easy,' Duncan said.

'They are. Wait for a pigeon. They're a little faster.'

Pretty soon another pigeon flew up, a white collared dove. Duncan aimed and fired. It dropped like a stone into the bush.

'Bravo!' shouted Lorna. 'Well done you!'

But Duncan didn't think it was well done. Neither did he think it was brave, if that was what was meant by *bravo*. As sporting activity went, he didn't think there was much bravery in it compared to leaping fences at forty miles an hour amongst a galloping herd of horses. It felt cheap.

'What's the matter?' Lorna said.

'Let's sit down a minute. Here, under this tree. Put the guns down. There's something I've got to tell you.'

They sat under the tree. 'What is it?' Lorna said, looking pale.

'All of this. It isn't me. I've been faking it, Lorna.'

'What do you mean, faking it?'

'It just isn't me. Stalking the woods in a cloth cap and green wellingtons. Wearing a tuxedo at new year's parties where people don't like each other. Getting pissed and snorting cocaine. None of it is me. I can't keep pretending. I do it to be

203

close to you. But the fact is, if you and I are going to be together – I mean, if we're going to be something like serious – I can't keep faking like this. I'm a jockey. All I want to do is ride horses. I want to become Champion Jockey and I've no interest in this lifestyle. It would just get in the way. It's nothing to do with riding – not for me it isn't, anyway. If you want to be with me, you have to know that.'

'Duncan, why do you think it is that I am drawn to you? It's because you are so different to my father. I don't think he loves me and the truth is I don't think I love him. I feel like all these years I've just been an inconvenience to him and he has used his money to buy me off whenever I have made demands. I've had lots of goodies but no good love.'

'It doesn't have to be like that, Lorna. I can give you good love but not many goodies. Maybe when a few more successes come my way—'

Lorna put a finger to his lips to shut him up. 'What if I said I could help you become Champion Jockey? Not this year, maybe not next, but in the future?'

'What? I'd say let's get rid of these guns and go back up to the house to your bedroom.'

'Right. Come here.'

'Ow!'

'What is it?'

'Bruised ribs,' he said, laughing. 'Go easy on a man, will you?'

Cheltenham was all anyone could talk about. The training was all done, the form was in and there was little more to be added in practical terms. Except for the endless talk about this one's chances and the other's prospects. At Petie's yard they took the horses over the gallops, but steadily, dreading the idea of any of the yard bruising a hoof or picking up a small or silly injury.

The stable runners had been finalised. Duncan and Kerry

each had two rides on day one, Champion Hurdle Day. On Champion Chase Day, Duncan was booked for three rides and Kerry two. On Gold Cup Day, the last day, they had one ride apiece. None of Petie's jockeys were riding in the Gold Cup itself. 'Next year,' he said, waving away all questions. 'That'll be ours next year.'

This left both Duncan and Kerry hungry to get their names in more races. Petie just wasn't the man to stick a horse in a race for the hell of it. He regarded running a horse out of its class as no experience at all, and unlike some of the main movers and shakers in the business, his stable was too small to have a stake in every race going.

Duncan was still hoping for an offer from Cadogan, but it was looking less likely. Kerry too was fishing around. Mike Ruddy said he was 'working on it', but it was a tall order. Duncan wasn't above pressing Lorna to ask for him. Her answer was a shrug. 'Osborne hates your guts,' she said. 'Daddy's not your biggest fan either.'

No, Duncan thought, *but George Pleasance thinks the sun shines out of my leathery jockey arse right now.*

The big surprise was that Roisin was going to have two rides on Champion Chase Day. One of these races was for women jockeys only. The other was open to both sexes. There was a feeling that women-only races were just a novelty, and that female jockeys had been struggling to prove that they could compete at the top level.

'I dunno,' Kerry said. 'It can cut up rough amongst the men. What if she gets hurt?'

'On a better horse I'd back her against you any day,' Duncan said.

'What does that prove? And didn't she fall off the weighing machine?'

Roisin, who had to listen to this, said, 'You dog, Kerry! You know damned well we made up that story so that we could pull

205

in Duncan on the day. The stewards won't agree a last-minute switch for nothing.'

'So it wasn't true?'

'Where did I put that whip, you wee shite!'

Then he got a rub. Cadogan asked him to ride in the first race on day one of the Festival. The Tipping Point had little chance and would be well served to end up in the first four. Cadogan had gone through Mike Ruddy.

'Take it,' Mike had shouted down the phone, not knowing that Duncan had every intention of taking it.

'What about Petie? He's put his foot down.'

'You leave Petie to me. I'm your agent. You pay me so that everyone can think I'm a shit and you're the nice guy. So you just be nice to Petie while he and I have a talk.'

'He's no pushover.'

'Look, Duncan. You made a deal with him. Free to ride, free to choose. That was the agreement and he's not changing it now. Besides, with the form you've been in, he's not going to want to lose you next season. Don't you worry about it. He'll shout at me and I'll shout at him and then we'll all do things my way. Your way. You know what I mean.'

Duncan put down the phone. He didn't like setting other people to fight his battles. Then again, as he thought about, it did have its uses.

At least with The Tipping Point no one was likely to ask him not to try.

18

'I heard them talking,' Lorna said. It was a few days before Cheltenham. 'It was one of those discussions that sounded like it wanted to be an argument. But George Pleasance always gets his way. They were talking about one of Daddy's horses called Rah-ho-tep.'

They were at Cadogan's place. Duncan had taken every opportunity to be up there with Lorna lately, and that afternoon – apart from the staff and groundsmen – they had the whole place to themselves. Before he'd gone into the house, Duncan had parked his old Capri and gone to have a look at the great hangar of cars. By now he knew how to access the garage from the main house. It seemed but a short while since he'd first walked into that garage, cursing Cadogan and picking out the Lamborghini for the day, never guessing that he might fall for Lorna.

As he went in, the sensor flickered on a row of lights one after the other to reveal once again Cadogan's enormous collection of silent motors. He looked over the cars for a moment before he left them to their silence and their dust.

He spent the afternoon with Lorna, most of the time naked and having sex on the giant leather sofas. It was Lorna who had prevailed on Cadogan to give Duncan at least one ride at Cheltenham. She was expecting her father back in the evening, so Duncan sent her upstairs to get showered and changed, telling her to come back wearing something that wouldn't make Duncan want to change his mind.

He gave her a couple of minutes, then followed her upstairs to make sure she had actually got into the shower. Then he crept back down to Cadogan's lounge. He already had the number from the Rolodex Lorna had used to place a bet, and he picked up the onyx-handled receiver and dialled the number.

He remembered exactly the words Lorna had used, and when he got an answer he said, 'Hello, I'd like to place a bet on the Duke Cadogan account, please.'

'Certainly. Can I have the race venue, time and name of runner, please.'

'Cheltenham, last day, four forty-five.'

'And the runner?'

'Rah-ho-tep, to win.'

'And the stake, sir?'

Duncan named a figure and the line went quiet. Then the voice said, 'I'll just have to verify the number you are calling from, sir. Is it all right if I phone you back immediately?'

Duncan agreed and put down the phone. He wondered how Lorna was doing with her shower upstairs. He strained his ears for the sound of running water. He needed to stay by the phone. He couldn't afford to have any of Cadogan's staff answering.

After a moment the phone rang and Duncan whisked the receiver off its cradle immediately.

'Thank you, sir,' said a new voice. 'I'm just going to confirm the bet you are making with us. Rah-ho-tep, to win at Cheltenham, four forty-five, last race of the final day.'

'That's correct,' said Duncan.

The new voice repeated the figure.

'Correct,' said Duncan.

'Can you give me the gateway code, sir?'

'That's Red Rum.'

'Thank you. It's such a large bet, I'm just going to have to get approval upstairs. Can you hold on?'

'Yes.'

Duncan hung on to the phone, straining his ears once more to make sure Lorna hadn't finished in the shower. The voice at the other end of the line took an age to return. He thought he was going to have to hang up. He heard someone coming.

It was one of the maids. She bustled into the room, and then seeing him she backed out smartly. She couldn't possibly know who he was speaking to.

At last the voice returned. 'Thank you, sir. Because of the extremely large character of the bet, I have to ask for a second gateway code. I hope you don't mind the security.'

Duncan froze. He didn't know another gateway code. The only other word he knew was the one he'd used at the Ritz. He took a deep breath and said, 'Oscar.'

There was a pause at the other end of the line. 'Thank you, sir, and I'm sorry for the extra security. Your bet is live.'

'Thank you.'

'Thank you, sir. Have a good evening.'

Duncan replaced the receiver. He sat back and waited. After a few moments Lorna came bounding down the stairs, showered and perfumed.

'Did I hear the telephone go?' she asked.

'Don't think so. Or maybe one of the staff took it.'

They heard the sound of a car drawing up outside.

'Just in time. Here's your dad.'

19

Downpour. For the three days before the Festival the heavens had opened and saturated the course. The waterlogging was so heavy that there was speculation about the Festival being postponed. But then the sun came out and the puddles disappeared and the superb ground staff started working miracles on the track.

The great thing about an event like Cheltenham was that everyone was there. It was like a gathering of the clans, but with stables instead of clansmen. The owners and trainers were like the chieftains, with their courts and their attendants; and the jockeys were the champions or gladiators sporting the colours of the court. Of course there were those you might not want to see as well as those who gladdened your heart. But everyone was there.

Sandy Sanderson happened to be one of the first jockeys Duncan spotted. He wore the same bitter half-smile as usual, treating everyone around with casual disdain. He'd been Champion Jockey an incredible nine years running, but this year his crown was under threat. He was still out there in front, and the matter wouldn't be settled until after Cheltenham, and probably still in his favour. But there were a lot of people in the game who had enjoyed seeing the crown wobble.

On the other hand, there were many people not connected with the inner circles of racing who seemed to love him. The punters. The media. Somehow this man was still as popular as ever with the general public.

Duncan got to catch up with the gang from Penderton, and many other friends from across the years. Of course some new acquaintances were there too, including Aaron Palmer. Mike Ruddy, suited and booted, was keen to exhibit his own little court. Things seemed to be going well for Ruddy in his new incarnation as agent, because he arrived in a neat Alfa Romeo with two glamorous 'personal assistants', tanned, leggy girls whose job seemed to be nothing more than following Ruddy around holding clipboards and rolled umbrellas.

'Are we paying you too much?' Duncan said.

Ruddy took him aside. 'Sshh. Car, girls and clipboards all hired by the day. I'll have ten new clients by the end of the Festival. Any more trouble with Petie?'

'None. What did you say to him?'

'He saw reason. Here, that daughter of his is a bit of all right, isn't she?'

Clever man, thought Duncan. He'd spotted that Roisin was and always would be a bridge to the old man.

Duncan was riding the first, third and fifth races on the opening day. The first race was in Osborne's colours on The Tipping Point. He would have preferred to open in Petie's silks, but that wasn't to be. As it was, Kerry would be opening for the Quinn stables in the second race on Brighton Taxi, the very first horse Duncan had ever ridden for Petie.

Duncan went into the paddock. Osborne was his usual cheery self. He bared his ginger-spotted teeth like an old nag.

'It's a great day for the races!' Duncan said brightly, deliberately trying to get up Osborne's nose.

'Nothing to do with me,' growled Osborne. 'One race and you're done. You're out of my hair.'

'Which hair would that be? No one's had a look under that sweaty old fedora for six years.'

Osborne had had enough. He walked away. 'Get this idiot legged up,' he said over his shoulder to one of the stable lads.

Duncan could exchange banter all day with someone like Osborne, and without ever looking ruffled. But there was someone in the paddock he didn't want to bandy words with. Someone who in the scowling game could make Osborne look like a rank amateur. He could still almost make Duncan's knees tremble.

'That's one thing as I never thought I'd see. Charlie's lad in Osborne's silks and on the back o' Cadogan's 'oss.'

It was Tommy, from the Penderton stable, still head lad.

'Good to see you, Tommy!' Duncan tried.

'Good to see you,' Tommy mimicked, withering. He stood and stared and shook his bony old close-cropped head.

Duncan felt a shaft of shame, but there was nothing he could say right then. He'd been through the same thing the night before. On visiting Charlie at Grey Gables at first his father hadn't wanted to see him. He'd got the sporting papers in his hand and had seen Duncan's name printed on the card against that of William Osborne and Duke Cadogan. He seemed to have forgotten everything that Duncan had said to him last time, and they'd had to go through all the shouting and tears and emotional recriminations again.

But even Charlie couldn't make him feel the way that Tommy could. Crusty old Tommy represented everything in the racing game that was right and true. And his last words to Duncan in the paddock before turning away were, 'That's right, son, you hang your head.'

It was almost enough to make him want to finish the game right there, before the Festival had even started.

He mounted The Tipping Point and groaned out loud as his cracked ribs squeezed.

'Hey, are you up for this?' said Osborne's stable lad. 'You've gone white.'

But it wasn't the pain in his ribs that had turned his face white. It was the stinging shame from Tommy's words. He turned his mount and trotted down to the starting line for the first race, a hotly contested Grade 1 curtain-raiser called the Brightstar Supreme Novices' Hurdle. It was just over two miles, run on the old track at Cheltenham, with just eight hurdles.

The starter had a reluctant horse to deal with, so he circled the pack a few times before calling them in. Then they were off. The 'Cheltenham roar' went up from the crowd, a traditional greeting for the first race. Even so, the reluctant horse stood as still as a statue as the others broke free, and stayed that way for several minutes.

The Tipping Point was good going forward, so Duncan decided to stay close to the two front-runners and see if he had the stamina for the run-in. The ground was heavy and loose and kicking up a lot of black mud. Some of the runners were clattering the stiff hurdles rather than jumping them, but The Tipping Point was clearing well and showing no sign of error. An idea stirred in Duncan that he might have a chance here after all.

He raced with the favourite, negotiating the left-hand track and sensing the growing murmur from the grandstand as they approached the third-last. When it came to making his challenge, the jockeys ahead of him saw him coming, gave a squeeze and he was left behind. The Tipping Point just tired. Duncan felt the horse might have finished closer, but he just didn't stay going. He fell away to sixth place on the run-in, with the crowd cheering home the favourite.

It was more than he had a right to expect – Osborne or Cadogan giving him a chance in the opener was never going to happen. He tried to remind himself what a great event this was, and that he'd been there and was part of the curtain-raiser; but it just wasn't him. He had no interest in making up the numbers. There was no satisfaction in riding an unfit horse into sixth place.

Mandy Gleeson was in the winners' enclosure, interviewing for TV. She signalled to him as he came in before turning away with the microphone for a few words from the favourite's trainer. She no doubt wanted to ask him on air how he felt about riding in the grand opener. But he was anxious to get out of Osborne's silks and back into Petie Quinn's sky blue. And that was what he was doing in the Weighing Room when someone slipped past him and said quite loudly in his ear, 'Boom! Boom!'

Sandy Sanderson was already on his way before Duncan could reply. He could have shouted after him. Something about exploding his overhead snooker lamp. But *no*, he thought, *I've other plans for you.*

He went out to watch Kerry in the second race, the most highly regarded minimum-distance novice chase in the calendar, named after the legendary steeplechaser The Poniard and attracting the best novice chasers around. After the joint favourites Kerry was amongst the pick on an Irish seven-year-old called King Solomon's Mines. He ran a good race too, and finished a staying-on third.

There were to be no big prizes that first day for Petie Quinn's cohort as Duncan and Kerry were outclassed in the remaining races. Duncan also claimed a third, and though there was no glitter to be had, it was felt that Quinn had announced himself on the big stage and that he was keeping his powder dry for deeper into the Festival.

Petie's big day was the second day, Champion Chase Day.

'Got all your Mad Micks and your Provo Paddies around you today, Claymore?' It was Sandy Sanderson in the Weighing Room. His hostility seemed to be growing. On the first day of the Festival he'd chalked up just one winner where he might normally have expected three or four.

'Oh they'll be around here somewhere,' Duncan said. 'Waiting for you.'

'I'm surprised you don't race in a black hood, son. That's how they do it up on the Falls Road, isn't it?'

'Oh, you don't see a lot of horse racing on the Falls Road,' Kerry chipped in.

But Sanderson was on his way out of the Weighing Room. That was his style: snipe and go.

Roisin it was who was first to sprinkle the glitter powder. The Amateur Riders Novices' Chase had been replaced this year – amid great controversy amongst the dinosaurs of the racing fraternity – by the women-jockeys-only event. Women jockeys were not new to the game, but not everyone thought they were up to it. As if to prove or disprove the point, one of the most gruelling races – four miles and twenty-four fences – had been given over to the event. To say it was well supported was an understatement. Every major stable was represented in the race.

Roisin had been working exclusively with Gypsy George to bring on a seven-year-old French grey she and George had bought amongst a bunch, called Drap D'Or. He wasn't exactly a handsome thing, with a wall eye and a tendency to dish. But he had a will of iron and a habit of doing everything he was asked. Duncan, who'd already ridden the old track on day one, was on hand with advice about the going; Kerry had advice about everything; and Petie kept telling her not to risk anything, especially in the tiring stages. Finally George scared everyone into staying away from Roisin, who was a sound jockey in her own right and not in need of an overload of instructions.

Drap D'Or was quite low down in the bookies' rankings, with a starting price of twelves. It was an agonising race to watch. Twenty horses ran. Two fell and three more unseated their jockeys before the twelfth fence. Roisin patiently tracked the leaders but blundered at the twentieth fence, just recovering.

215

She seemed to be outpaced and pushed back into third place after the third fence from home, but in this soul-sapping, arduous race with an uphill finish she rode hard, asking the wonderful and ugly Drap D'Or to find something. Drap D'Or answered, rallying on the flat to take a strong lead and make a glorious finish.

The Quinn camp was ecstatic. Roisin, splattered in mud from head to toe, walked Drap D'Or into the winners' enclosure talking into Mandy Gleeson's microphone about what a great big old heart the horse had; but probably every TV viewer was thinking the same thing about this slip of an Irish lass, her face streaked with mud and her eyes flashing inside the outline of where her goggles had been.

They all waited for Roisin to weigh in, Duncan hugging Petie, Kerry hugging Duncan and Gypsy George smiling but trying to ward off some of this excessive hugging. Then Mike Ruddy joined them, roaring his head off and shouting about how he was going to sign up Roisin and make her a household name.

Mandy Gleeson meanwhile was calling over to Petie for an interview alongside the winning jockey. Petie did his normal disappearing act, indicating that Gypsy George was the real trainer. Mandy stuck a microphone in front of George and quickly found that his idea of handling the media was to fold his arms and scowl a lot. But luckily it was Roisin the camera wanted, and that day she was the belle of the ball.

In the next race Kerry brought home a winner in the juvenile handicap hurdle. Two wins for a couple who seemed destined for the marital bed even before the Festival was over. In fact it began to look like such an event might even shape itself round the Festival.

'And a little bird tells me that you and Roisin Quinn may be an item?' Mandy Gleeson simpered into her microphone.

'I don't know where you've got such an idea!' Kerry said,

lifting his saddle off the winner. 'And if you say any more, you'll have her father to deal with.'

'Speaking of Petie Quinn, can you help us get him down here? He seems a little camera shy.'

'No, he loves the camera, he does. Look, there he is now just, shouldering through the crowds. Get him up here.'

But of course they couldn't.

As if not to be outdone, Duncan won the very next race, the Spookair Festival Trophy Chase, also a Grade 1, on his old friend Wellbeing, the gorgeous but misshapen little horse with the heart of a lion that had been one of his earliest rides for Petie. Three in a row for the Quinn stables was almost too much to hope for.

Duncan was pumped by the roar of the crowd as he streaked through to win by three clear lengths with plenty in hand. The smell of victory was in his nostrils now, and it was as if he'd suddenly remembered his entire reason for being there. From that moment on all he could think about was the next race; and then he would be thinking about the next race after that; and then the next.

The feature race of the day was the Sparkbet Stayers Hurdle. Three miles. This time around Duncan would have another chance to ride the brave-hearted The Buckler, up against Sanderson on the fancied A La Mode, a French gelding that had won all of his last four outings. But of course Petie hadn't managed to keep The Buckler's form a secret either, and Petie's fine liver chestnut gelding had attracted serious money from the punters and was 3–1.

Down at the start Duncan looked over at Sanderson, not as a mark of respect or recognition, but just to be sure of where he sat in the pack.

Then they were off, at a ridiculously sedate pace as no one

wanted to go out in front. For a while it was like an afternoon hack for elderly country gentlemen. Someone had to jump in front at the first and Duncan made sure it wasn't him. In fact he positioned himself at the rear. It was going to be a long slog in the mud, this three-miler, and there was no home for burnouts.

The Buckler was showing a little frustration at being held way back, but Duncan felt the heavy ground was going to test his stamina so he kept him well covered up. He had a suspicion that the field would thin just after the top of the hill. Someone up ahead had jumped into a three-length lead at the sixth, which would give them a moment of glory for the cameras, but for a race like this they were already spent. They were all still well bunched over the eighth, heavy traffic. Then a little daylight began to appear. Duncan squeezed up. Sanderson, no less crafty, was just ahead of him. But then suddenly at that hurdle there were fallers! Two down. Jockeys sprawling, horses' legs flailing. Duncan cleared the hurdle and swerved to avoid the mêlée, though the beautifully well-balanced The Buckler hardly seemed fazed.

Duncan giggled in the saddle. He had no idea where that giggle came from. The tremor of his laugh transmitted through the horse. The Buckler's ears pricked forward. He was enjoying this as much as Duncan was! The horse that had jumped out to the front was already tiring. It fell away like a rag in the wind as The Buckler surged on. Now it was only him and Sanderson out in front.

Duncan noticed that A La Mode had a slight drift to the left at every jump. Not that the drift lost any ground for the class horse, but Duncan thought he could use it. Make it pay. There was no way Sanderson was going to use any of his old tricks on him this time around.

He hit the pedals on The Buckler and took Sanderson on his right at the jump, preventing the other jockey from coming anywhere near him. They landed neck and neck. Sanderson scowled across through his goggles. He was having to urge every last ounce out of his horse. The stick was coming down hard, whereas Duncan knew that The Buckler had more. The Buckler pinged the last hurdle gaining such an advantage that the Cheltenham crowd roared to the heavens.

A La Mode pressed hard in the run-up to the finishing post. In the last few strides he looked to have caught Duncan. But he just didn't have enough. The Buckler was home and dry, with the crowd roaring in his ears. It was the sweetest of victories. Vindication. As far as Duncan was concerned, it didn't matter what happened for the rest of the Festival.

With the cheers still ringing out, Mandy Gleeson wanted to interview him. He paid tribute to his team and to the wonderful horse and he even said generous things about the way Sandy Sanderson had ridden the race, which he knew would stick right in the older jockey's craw.

He got off the horse and sent Gypsy George to drag Petie Quinn forcibly in front of the cameras. Quinn arrived rubbing his hands nervously and looking over his shoulder. 'Here's your man,' Duncan said. 'Everything is down to this wonderful man. Everything. And you'll be hearing a lot more of him, too.'

Petie looked like they'd already heard too much about him.

'Petie!' said Mandy Gleeson. 'You're a hard man to track down! Now I've got you, I'm not letting you go. You've burst on to the scene here at Cheltenham: Duncan here has just won the impressive World Hurdle; you're winning everything today and your daughter Roisin won the lady jockeys' race. Can it get any better?'

'Well, you know,' Petie said.

'A great Champion Chase Day showing for you, Petie.'

'Yes, yes. Very nice.'

Gleeson was a pro. 'But it's not like you're an overnight success. You've been in the game a while.'

'Yes. For a while.'

'So what was the best? Seeing The Buckler take this race, or seeing your daughter win?'

Petie put a finger in his ear as if there was a bit of loose wax rattling around. 'Both worth celebrating.'

She also knew when to back out. 'Well, congratulations to you and your team, Petie, and we'll let you go and celebrate.' She turned back to the camera. 'I'm sure that the name of Petie Quinn is going to turn up again and again at Cheltenham. We still have more races to come, and of course, the climax of to-morrow's Gold Cup.'

Mandy Gleeson pulled Duncan aside some time after the day's races. 'I've got something to tell you. One of our journalists on the team has been in George Pleasance's pocket.'

'What?' Duncan said. 'How long?'

'Nearly a year. No wonder he's been one jump ahead of any-thing we could get on him.'

Duncan made a quick calculation about whether this would affect him and anything he might have told Mandy.

'Don't worry,' she said, reading his mind. 'Anything you might have said to me never went any further.'

'What are you going to do about it?'

'We've only just found out. We're trying to think how we might use it to our advantage.'

'Good. Do you think you can keep it like that for another few days?'

'What's in your mind?'

'Oh, I don't know.'

That same evening, a rather distinguished-looking Chinese gentleman with a permanent smile entered the Ritz. He had just a few thin strands of black hair combed back across his head. His glasses had unusually thick lenses. He seemed to be enjoying a special air of privilege: perhaps it was the company of the extremely nubile young lady, around half his age, on his arm. They dined in lavish style in the restaurant. They ate foie gras and drank champagne.

At about nine o clock in the evening they finished their dinner and took the lift up to a room.

Mandy Gleeson, sitting in the lounge and to all intents reading a newspaper, was able to observe this gentleman and his companion. She was also able to establish, without too much difficulty, that his dinner and accommodation for the evening had been placed on the account of Duke Cadogan.

20

Sandy Sanderson whistled as he let himself out of his lover's cottage that Gold Cup morning. It was seven thirty and the day was beautiful. A golden sunlight was breaking through the mist. What was there not to like about the world? He'd left Jeannie sleeping and happy in the cottage that he owned; had his usual race-day breakfast of coffee and one thin slice of toast spread with honey; he was about to get into his sleek black Porsche parked discreetly at the rear of the property. And more than all of this it was Gold Cup day!

Life didn't get better than this.

He'd had nine years as Champion Jockey, and if he swept up a couple of end-of-season races, this would be his tenth. Undisputed champion. He'd taken five more winners at this festival alone, and today he was pretty certain of winning the Gold Cup itself. The challenge was there, of course; it was always there. But he knew he was riding the top horse of the hour for Osborne and Cadogan, and all he had to do was steer her home. There was that detail to take care of in the last race, on Ra-ho-tep, but that was nothing new; and anyway it was the kind of detail that had brought him the Porsche, the cottage hideaway in the Wiltshire hills and the sweet young thing snoozing blissfully upstairs.

The Cheltenham Festival was the time when he felt most alive, confident that no other jockey could touch him.

As he dropped the latch on the cottage door and turned to

cross the gravel driveway to where his Porsche lurked in the shadows, something made him draw up short. Something unfamiliar. Something not quite right.

It was a scent on the morning air. Just a tiny whiff. It made him stop.

He couldn't quite place the smell. He made his way across the driveway, crunching the gravel as he went. As he reached for the driver's door, three black-clad figures, all wearing balaclavas, seemed to unfold themselves from the shadows of the black Porsche. Sanderson very nearly shat himself.

Two of the three held small handguns levelled at him.

'Top o' the morning to you, Mr Sanderson,' said one of the figures in a strong Irish brogue.

Sanderson went to stammer a reply. 'Say nothing,' said a second Irish voice, gruff and unfriendly. 'Get into the back of the car.'

'What can ...' Sanderson began

The gruff figure waved his gun. 'If you want to get out with your kneecaps intact, you'll shut your mouth. That's the last I want to hear from you. Nod if you understand.'

Sanderson nodded.

'Take his keys,' said the gruff voice.

The third figure relieved him of his Porsche keys, and the keys to the house, and opened up the car. Sanderson walked stiffly to the vehicle and made to get into the passenger seat.

The figure with the more cheerful voice waved his gun. 'Oh no. It's the boot for you, laddie.' Sanderson scowled as the boot was opened. He climbed in. 'Just as well you're a wee jockey. Not much room else. Now settle down, 'cos we're going for a wee fun drive.'

The boot was closed over Sanderson's head.

*

When the boot was opened again, he shouted, 'I need to piss!'

'What?'

'I've taken a pee pill.'

'Is that legal?'

'Please!'

Sanderson realised he was in some sort of a barn. He thought he could smell cattle, and maybe sheep too, but there was no sign of any livestock. The barn was cobwebby and it looked like it hadn't been used for farming in a few years, though it still had all the trappings: grain feeders, hay bales, pitchforks, rat traps hanging on hooks. He had a bad feeling. He thought maybe he was about to be tortured. He looked up into the rafters of the barn. An old-style bicycle complete with pannier basket was suspended there, its shape plumped with black cobwebs.

He'd been disoriented by the drive. In the darkness of the boot he'd tried to identify any familiar sounds in case it would be useful for telling the police later. Now he had a nasty feeling that there might not be any later.

He was roughly pulled out of the boot by the three figures in balaclavas, who worked in silence. First they let him take a piss in the straw. When he'd finished, they blindfolded him, and tied his arms behind his back. Then they gagged him. After that they pulled off his shoes and socks and tied his ankles together. There was a dragging noise.

'Is it money you are after?' he shouted through his gag.

'Can't hear you wit' that gag on ye,' said the cheerful one.

He was pushed backwards and chopped at the back of the knees so that he fell into a chair. He was left there for some time and he thought perhaps the three had gone out of the barn. But after a while he heard them arguing in hushed tones.

'I say we just blow his fuckin' head off and dump his body up the lane.'

'No,' said the gruff voice. 'We stick with the plan. Blow his kneecaps off. That was the agreement.'

'He got a look at you when you put him in the boot. Your mask slipped and now he's seen your face. He's a dead man.'

'I didn't see anyone!' Sanderson screamed, muffled through his gag. 'Nothing! I swear to you!'

'What did he say?' asked one of the men.

As the first of the six races of day three of the Cheltenham Festival got closer, the rumour swept the racing fraternity that Sandy Sanderson had failed to turn up. It seemed unthinkable: Gold Cup day and no sign of the Champion Jockey. So far the news hadn't got out to the punters, but because everyone behind the scenes had already been told, it was only a matter of moments before the information leaked out.

There were a lot of croaky voices around after winners and happy owners and trainers had spent the night lashed to the bar, and so there were a lot of jokes about how Sandy Sanderson had been unable to find his way home; or about how he'd slept in a ditch; or about how he'd been ensnared by one of the cigarette-promotions models or the Guinness girls. Jokes became rumours and rumours became stories. Maybe with this or that jockey the stories might have been credible, too, but not with Sanderson. Whatever he was, he was a pro through and through. He never failed to turn up.

He was scheduled for three races on the last day, and the first race of the day – the Triumph Hurdle – was one of them. Of course everyone knew that his big race was the fourth, the Gold Cup itself. The fact that he was running in the Grade 3 curtain-closer was seen as a signature farewell to the Festival rather than a major race for him, a little flourish and a swish of the tail. In the same way the opening race was his calling card, an announcement of his intention for the Gold Cup. But right then he looked like weighing in for none of them.

Cadogan was in the stewards' office with Osborne, where

he'd been allowed access to the telephone to make some calls. The two of them had had a discussion about whether they should first call Christie, knowing perfectly well that Sanderson would have been with his mistress in Wiltshire.

'Just call the tart!' Osborne had said.

'But I won't be able to tell Christie I called her first!' Cadogan complained.

'All right, call Christie first, but get off the blower damned quick and then call his tart.'

Cadogan went through the motions of speaking to Christie, who knew perfectly well that Cadogan was fully informed about Sandy's Thursday-night arrangements. She was cool, icy even, but no, she had no idea where the Champion Jockey might be.

Cadogan was about to hang up, but then Christie cut up rough. 'Surely,' she said, 'you have his number.'

'Number? This is his number, Christie.'

'You know exactly what I mean.'

'I'm sure I don't.'

'I mean his Thursday-night number. He told me you had it, in case I ever needed it in emergencies.'

'Really? I'm sure he didn't ... I mean, if he did, I must have forgotten it. Or if he did—'

'Forget it, you shit.' Christie hung up.

'JUST CALL THE TART!' Osborne screamed when Cadogan had finished.

Of course when Cadogan called Sanderson's mistress, she had nothing to offer. She'd woken up with Sandy, heard him pottering about making breakfast and heard him leaving the cottage. She'd even heard the Porsche leave the driveway before she'd turned over and gone back to sleep.

No, he hadn't said anything about going anywhere other than Cheltenham.

No, he hadn't said anything unusual at all. Where was Sandy right now? she wanted to know.

As did a lot of people.

There was half an hour to go before the Triumph Hurdle. Cadogan and Osborne discussed the matter with the stewards, who were prepared to allow Tim McPhee, one of Osborne's team, to take Sanderson's place at the last minute. Nothing needed to be said until the Gold Cup came around, by which time Sanderson might have shown his face.

Duncan only had one ride on Gold Cup day, and that was in the first race. He would have been up against Sanderson, and he was on Lemontree, the horse he'd ridden so well against the Monk a while back. With the news that Sanderson was no longer riding, the odds changed and Lemontree became the favourite.

Petie, though he'd already had a great Festival, was jumpy and mad keen for Lemontree. 'Where the hell is Roisin? This is her horse, after all.'

'I'm here, Daddy, standing right behind you, if you'll only stop working up a sweat.'

'George, get Duncan up, will you? I don't know what the matter is with you all this morning. You're never where I want you. You're at sixes and sevens.'

'We're all right,' George growled. 'This is our race.'

'Get yourself down to the start,' Petie said a little sharply, 'and look like you're ready to ride.'

Duncan said nothing. Maybe after all this time he was managing to curb his lip. He trotted Lemontree off to the start.

At the barn, Sandy Sanderson was beginning to wonder if he'd been abandoned. The three hooded figures seemed to go out, then come back in, then go out again. He'd heard the door creak open another time but wasn't certain whether there was anyone there.

'Hello,' he croaked from behind his gag.

There was no answer.

'Hello.'

He strained to listen. There was no sound. Then came a slight rustling across the floor. He thought maybe they'd left him and that he could hear a rat moving in the barn. He pulled at his bindings but it was hopeless. Then out of nowhere he felt a piece of straw pushed in his ear.

He roared.

'What's the matter with ye, ye wee shite?' said a voice. He recognised it as the cheerful one.

'Water,' said Sanderson. 'A drink.'

He felt the gag being unbound and a water bottle was put to his lips. He drank and some of the water spilled down his front.

'Don't waste it now; that's all there is.'

'Where are the others?' Sanderson said.

'Others?'

'There were three of you.'

'Oh, they're up at the house.'

'House?'

'Yes, up at the big house. Talking with the big boss about what to do with you.'

'What to do with me?'

'Yes. They're discussing it now. With the big boss.'

'Why me?' Sanderson pleaded. 'What the hell has all this got to do with me?'

'Oh, that's because of allegations.'

'Allegations?'

'Yes. Hints and allegations. And implications. And suggestions. And assertions.'

'I don't know what that means!'

'Sure you do. Making hints. About certain organisations.'

'Has this got something to do with Claymore?'

'Who?'

'Duncan Claymore?'

'There you go again. I wouldn't be making any more implications and suggestions and allegations if you know what's good for you.'

'I meant nothing by it.'

'Who is Duncan Claymore?'

'No one. Nothing. Listen to me. I should talk to your boss.'

'Oh, why is that now?'

'I can tell you how to make some money. Either for yourselves or your organisation.'

'Organisation? Are you saying we're part of an organisation now, is it?'

'No no no, that's not what I meant!'

'Sounds to me that's what you meant. What organisation would that be?'

'No, I don't know anything about that. I'm sorry I said it. Listen, you can make some money.'

'How would I do that?'

'Do you know what a lay bet is?'

'Of course I know what a lay bet is. D'ye think I'm fuckin' well thick because I'm Irish? Is that it?'

'No no no. Please listen. Listen to me.' Sanderson was almost in tears. 'You don't have to hurt me. You could make yourself some good money. Today.'

Duncan caused a slight delay in the off as he got Lemontree to take a last look at the hurdle. The starter circled them and they were off. The Cheltenham roar went up and it was spine-tingling. The opening pace was very fast. Duncan had to nudge Lemontree not to get caught napping. The horse in front took up a two-length lead with the second out wide.

Duncan told himself to be patient; to hang in tight at about third place.

Lemontree jumped nicely, making a little ground at each

hurdle but there were still plenty of runners in with a chance. No one slacking. There was still danger on the rail, and it was such a fast race it surely was going to be a test of stamina in the end. The Osborne horse was in front and extended his lead three out. Lemontree leapt like a salmon and at two out the leader began to tire. *Have you got it?* Duncan asked Lemontree, and the beautiful animal responded by stretching his neck out, and cruising into the lead.

The answer was yes. Duncan felt the thrilling knock of blood in the brain, the surge of adrenalin that always came when he knew victory was possible. The stamina of the creature was astonishing. But it wasn't over yet. He saw a flash of the Osborne silk over his shoulder, and on the other side a third horse was making a late rally, steaming up behind him. The final hurdle seemed to come up at him with great speed.

The last jump was an exhibition in itself, heart-winning to the crowd. Duncan didn't even feel the horse touch down. The Osborne horse lost a whole length and he had only the third horse to battle back at the finish. With the crowd roaring him on, Lemontree found another gear. The third horse tired. They romped home with plenty to spare and Duncan not only knew he'd won the Triumph Hurdle, but also that Petie had found himself a horse that was going to be a trailblazer for the next few seasons.

After the hugs and the tears of joy and the weigh-in, Duncan went in search of Lorna. She threw her arms around him.

'Listen,' he said to her. 'I hear Sandy Sanderson went missing. Mention it to your dad that I'm around and willing, will you?'

'They've already settled on another jockey for the Gold Cup.'

'I know that. I'm not interested in the Gold Cup. There are other races. Like the last one of the day.'

'Would you jump in Sanderson's grave as quick?'

'Yes, if it had a set of stirrups. Just tell him I'm available, will you?'

Kerry wound up the Festival for the Quinn stables riding in the Grade 2 handicap hurdle, coming in a respectable third, but there was enough elation from the previous day to carry over. By then it was plain that there was no Sandy Sanderson for the Gold Cup either, and probably for the rest of the day. By now it had just become a piece of added intrigue, a media talking point. It took nothing away from the breathtaking excitement of the Gold Cup race itself.

It was, after all, the race everyone had been waiting for, Champion Jockey or no Champion Jockey, its history studded with the legendary names of the racing world, including Arkle, and Golden Miller – who won it five times in a row in the 1930s. It was the pinnacle of jump racing.

And yet it was not the race that interested Duncan the most.

For all its glamour, Duncan was more focused on what was happening in the last race of the day. He watched the Gold Cup event itself along with Kerry and Petie and George and Roisin, but he had to fake his enthusiasm. True, he was very happy to see the grand prize won by the favourite, Canned Heat, from his old Penderton stables. It was one of Tommy's, sure enough, and his jockey showed balls of steel. Canned Heat was produced to hit the front on the line itself. He was going to have to go and look Tommy in the eye and congratulate the Penderton team. But he still had more important things on his mind.

At last Duncan was sought out by Duke Cadogan. He asked him to meet out by the horse boxes. They found a quiet place.

'Why all the cloak and dagger?' Duncan wanted to know.

'Osborne won't have anything to do with you,' Cadogan said smoothly, tipping forward his fedora, 'but George Pleasance asked me to have a word with you.'

'Oh?'

'There might be a place for you on Ra-ho-tep in the last race.'

231

'Only if you need me.' Duncan managed to make it sound as if he didn't mind whether he did or he didn't.

Cadogan looked all round, to make sure no one was within earshot. 'You have to understand this, Duncan. It's not Ra-ho-tep's day.'

Duncan blinked.

'You got it?'

Duncan shrugged.

Cadogan's eyes bulged wide. He leaned in to Duncan. 'No, you have to be clear. Today is not Tep's day.'

'I get it.'

Cadogan stared at him for a long time. Finally he said, 'I'll tell the stewards.'

The Gold Cup had already been run when the figure returned to the barn and removed Sanderson's blindfold. From behind his balaclava he said, 'Mr Sanderson of this parish, I've done a bit of negotiating on your behalf with the big boss.'

'I told you there's big money in it—'

'Shut it!'

'Yes. Yes, sir.'

'We're going to let you off with your brains and your knee-caps intact if you can follow certain instructions.'

'Just tell me what to do.'

'You wait here till dusk. I'll loosen your bonds. At dusk you slip out of the back of the barn. You can't go before dusk because you can be seen from the big house, front and back. You can't be caught; you won't get a second chance, so don't risk it. You make your way home. You make up a cock-and-bull story about how someone must have spiked your drink last night. Anything. Say anything. Something about a Chinese syndicate maybe. You know, the sort of thing you'd tell a priest.

'More important, you don't say anything about us. It's

clear you know who we are. If you make any references to any organisation, army, provisional, official or otherwise, or if you give any description of us, we'll come back for you and blow your fucking head off. Now can I be any clearer than that, Mr Sanderson?'

'No, that's clear,' said Sanderson.

'It's your lucky day, Mr Sanderson.'

'Yes. Thank you, sir.'

'I'll just loosen your ropes now and I'll be going back up to the big house. You keep your head down. Like I told you.'

'Yes, yes.'

Sanderson, grateful to have his arms and legs free, settled down to wait for dusk. He was almost too stiff to move, so he lay back on the old straw. He strained his ears for signs of activity from the house, terrified that someone up there might have a change of mind. A bird settled on the roof of the barn. Beyond that he heard nothing.

After another couple of hours he thought he sensed a change in the light. He crawled towards the rotting wood of the barn wall, where he found a knothole to peer out of. All he could see was open fields. He got up and went to the back of the barn, but there seemed to be no way of escape there. He made a stealthy crawl to the front door. He looked up the overgrown and briar-tangled driveway but couldn't see the big house.

Finally he inched his way around the front of the barn, careful not to be seen. Only then did he realise that there was no house, big or otherwise. The barn stood alone in acres of open countryside.

The last race of the day was something of a sideshow. Parties were taking place in the bars and in the owners' bar, where champagne flowed and Buck's Fizz spilled. New business contacts were already being made, friendships cemented and one or two choice remarks might already be cementing into feuds. The stewards were roundly lambasted, as they were every year, as know-nothing idiots. Duncan glimpsed, up there on the owners' balcony, the lion-haired figure of George Pleasance, bottle of champagne in one hand and cigar in the other. His face, as ever, was wreathed in generous smiles

But while all that was happening, the Grand Annual Handicap Chase was still to be run. It was a Grade 3 race run over two miles and 110 yards, and for that at least the jockeys and the horses were still sober. It was an odd race in some ways, attracting both professional and amateur jockeys, and the last few years had seen riders come in at 40–1, 20–1 and 16–1. But to confuse the punters it was also a race that plenty of previous winners won. It was a course where form was essential, and Ra-ho-tep had won here previously at 3–1 and on the same heavy ground.

Petie came out to the paddock to wish him luck, even though it wasn't his formality. Roisin was there too.

'I don't know where he goes before a race,' Petie said to his daughter, 'but he's in a zone and you just can't get there.'

'Leave him to it, Daddy. In fifteen minutes it will be all over.'

Duncan was just about to mount when something made him look across the crowd. Many people were gazing at him, which was unsurprising since he was favourite to win the race. But there amongst them, leaning on the white-painted rail and gazing at him with a blank expression, was the Monk. What the hell was he doing there? Duncan was legged up into the saddle and walked Ra-ho-tep across to the rail. But the Monk was gone. He scanned the crowd looking for those piercing blue eyes, hard jaw and expressionless face. Maybe he had imagined it.

Trying to shake off the image, he cantered Ra-ho-tep down to the start, where he waited in his silks of scarlet with white star and red chevrons. He was the punters' even-money favourite. If he could be said to be in the zone, he was absolutely there

234

as his own man. But a huge knot of anxiety was swelling in his stomach. He was still the jockey of the unbroken beam of light. So far he had never willingly taken a fall.

There was a huge line-up. Twenty-eight riders, with late flashes of sunlight touching the silks and throwing shadows along the track. The horses were snorting and blowing with excitement. The sheer number of them had some of them on their toes, skittering, impatient for the off. Then the starter let them go.

They flew into action. Duncan felt Ra-ho-tep pulling at the bit and had to fight to hold him back. The opening pace was too fast. Every single jockey fancied a last-race winner and the whole field was closely bunched.

Two fell at the second fence. It was already a mêlée. Duncan had to steer Ra-ho-tep around the early casualties. It wasn't until the open ditch that he began to creep forward.

Sometimes Duncan talked to the horses in order to coax himself. Stay calm, stay covered, stay focused. But it was hard for him to stay focused on this race. Many things ran through his head. There was his father's face as he tried to explain over and over to Charlie what he was doing and why he had to be in the detested colours of Osborne and on Cadogan's horse. There was Cadogan's eyes bulging beneath the rim of his fedora as he impressed on him the importance of losing. There was George Pleasance's complacent smile as he slipped into the warm pool in Marbella, and another image of the same man's face should Duncan win on Ra-ho-tep. Maybe Duncan would be a dead man. But then there was the unreadable lined face of Aaron, the Monk, jockey of integrity. They were all at his shoulder as he eased Ra-ho-tep further up the pack.

Duncan's broken rib had pained him all afternoon. Something in the gallop of Ra-ho-tep jarred him. He was finding it hard to get his full breath and he felt the horse pulling out of his control. He gritted his teeth and fought back.

He could tell that some of the early front-runners were already shot. As the pack thundered down the hill, it seemed there were lots still with a chance. Ra-ho-tep was still in the mix at three furlongs to go and a single jump. Then he saw Moonlight Serenade, second favourite, turn it on with some style, and it was right then that he knew he either let rip with Ra-ho-tep or took the easy way out, once and for all.

The two horses went together neck and neck up the hill and it seemed to go on for ever. The gradient and the heavy ground were taking their toll, trying to pull the horses back under the earth itself. Moonlight Serenade inched ahead. Duncan, trying to ignore the pain in his ribs, knew that he had to stay with him or it was all over. Part of him wanted it to be in the lap of the gods. He could ease the pain in his ribs. He could make George Pleasance happy. It would all be so easy. No one would ever know.

He was still a length behind Moonlight Serenade, Ra-ho-tep struggling in the heavy ground. He felt it all slipping away. But some instinct, some spark, or perhaps even a flash of pain in his ribs, made him raise his stick and lay it across the muscular flank of his horse. Ra-ho-tep quickened. He seemed to waken and pulled out of the mud, beat the hill and struck clear.

Had he left it too late? The two horses battled it out to the death. The finish line swept up at them. The noise of the crowd and the echoing tannoy was deafening.

Duncan Claymore on Ra-ho-tep won the finale of the Cheltenham Festival in high style.

21

'All I did was steer him home,' Duncan said to Mandy Gleeson as he trotted Ra-ho-tep into the winner's enclosure. 'He's a great credit to his trainer.'

'And we can have a chat with his trainer right now if we can go over to William Osborne.' Osborne was waiting in the winners' enclosure, but his face was white. Mandy hadn't noticed. 'William, well, you expected a result from the Champion Jockey on Ra-ho-tep, but you got the same result from Duncan Claymore, surely one of the up-and-coming jockeys of the Festival.'

Osborne struggled for words. 'He rode a fine race.' He turned and fiddled with Ra-ho-tep's cheekpiece.

'And he brought out the best of the horse at the last there. The sign of a great jockey?'

'We thought he'd do well for us,' Osborne said.

'And any news of the whereabouts of the Champion Jockey?' Gleeson asked, shoving the microphone almost in his mouth.

'Still no news.'

Mandy Gleeson decided she might get better chat from the trainer of the runner-up, so she whisked her team across to Moonlight Serenade.

By then Duncan had dismounted and they'd been joined by Cadogan, who was pretending to be all smiles. But if his eyes were bulging before, they were out on stalks now. 'Do you have any idea of what you've done?' he said in Duncan's ear.

237

'I've won you the pot,' Duncan said.

'You're a dead man,' Osborne hissed.

'Well in that case I'd better get weighed in.' He slipped the saddle off Ra-ho-tep. 'Nice horse.' Then, with the two men's eyes burning into his back, he carried the saddle over to the Weighing Room.

'Weighed in! Weighed in!' came the announcement over the public address. Duncan made his way to the presentation podium to take more plaudits. On his way back, one of the lads from Petie's stables said that Gypsy George wanted a word with him out by the horseboxes.

When he got there, three figures in black jumped out and bundled him into the back of a horsebox. They quickly pulled up the rear ramp. They all wore balaclavas and two of them were pointing guns at him.

One of them pushed him over roughly into the straw. Duncan winced as the pain from his broken rib shot through him. He thought he might vomit.

'So then, Claymore,' said one of the hooded figures, 'you just couldn't resist, could you? Couldn't resist winning.'

'Haven't you been warned about the dangers of winning?' This second figure had an Irish accent. It was a female voice. Although slightly built, she had a menacing manner.

Duncan held his throbbing ribs and looked coolly at his assailants. 'Well,' he said. 'It would make me shit my pants. Where did you get the firearms?'

The smallest of the three figures whisked off the balaclava. It was Roisin. 'Sports day starting pistols.'

The second to reveal himself was Gypsy George. The third, smiling, was Mike Ruddy.

'It all went off okay, then?' Duncan said.

'I don't want to do anything like that again,' said Roisin.

'You should have seen him, the shit,' said Ruddy.

Gypsy George looked at Ruddy in disgust. 'No one says *top o' the morning*,' he said.

'Yes they do,' said Ruddy.

'Your Irish accent was shite,' said Roisin.

'Ignore them. It was bang on. Where's Sanderson now?' Duncan wanted to know.

Ruddy looked at his watch. 'About now, he would be approaching home on shanks's pony. Working on what the fuck he's going to say. By the way,' he added. 'Great race.'

'I'm still worried about this George Pleasance business,' Roisin said.

'I think I can handle that,' Duncan said. 'You'd better get rid of these starter pistols and balaclavas.'

'There's a trap under the long box,' George said. 'I'll deal with it.'

'Okay,' Duncan said. 'Come on, boys and girls. I'll get showered and see you all in the owners' bar.'

'The first drink is on me,' Ruddy said. 'All this talking in Irish has given me a dry mouth.'

Mike was true to his word, and Petie was lavish with the champagne too. Petie had served notice on the racing world that he was an emerging force and that more, much more was to come.

Petie hadn't been in on the kidnapping, whereas Kerry knew all about it, though he couldn't be directly involved because he'd had to race. It was Gypsy George – who hated Cadogan and Osborne as much as Charlie did – who had engineered the plan along with Duncan when they'd spent some time talking in his caravan. Roisin had been pulled in by George, who knew she would be there for them. George was more doubtful about Ruddy, but they needed a third and Duncan had felt Ruddy's loyalty would be unquestionable. Ruddy had hated the way he'd been drawn into pulling up horses and saw it as a personal revenge.

It was audacious and it might not have worked, but they'd pulled it off.

Lorna was in the owners' bar with them, but her father was conspicuously absent, as was Osborne. The mystery of Sanderson's disappearance was almost flushed away by the flow of champagne.

At some point in the hurly-burly of the festivities Duncan spotted George Pleasance. He still wore that same wreathed smile but somehow this time his eyes gave him away. Duncan thought there was no time like the present, so he excused himself from the company and went to the gents' toilets, pretty certain Pleasance would follow.

He was right. Pleasance and his bald henchman and another stooge were there behind him within seconds. The bald man trapped the door.

'Nice race,' Pleasance said.

'I thought I'd lost it on the run-in.'

'You thought you'd lost it on the run-in? And you're going to tell me why you *didn't* lose it on the run-in?'

Duncan could feel Pleasance's sweet and rancid breath on his neck. He stood his ground. 'Last-minute instructions.'

'What last-minute instructions?'

'Cadogan told me in the paddock that things had changed.'

Pleasance laughed. 'You're lying.'

'No, for sure—'

'I still say you're lying.'

'—he'd been staking big bets on Tep. He told me that the bookies were refusing the lay bets. I know he made at least one big bet from his home because I was there with Lorna. I mean, a real monster bet. I just won him a huge payola. That's what he wanted. It was just after that Chinese guy left.'

'What Chinese guy?'

'How should I know, just some chap from Hong Kong. I assumed you were in on it all.'

Pleasance hovered over him, eyeball to eyeball. 'You do realise I can easily check this story out?'

'Of course you can. Why would I lie? You can find out yourself what he was betting down to the last cent.'

Pleasance patted his face. 'You bet I will, old son. And if your story doesn't check out, you know I'll be wanting to see you again.'

'All right,' said Duncan. 'All right.'

Pleasance left the toilets with his henchmen. Duncan turned to the mirror and threw a little cool water on his face. Then he returned to the party.

Epilogue

Six days later, the tabloids reported that Duke Cadogan had been killed in a gun incident during a clay-pigeon shoot on his estate. It was a tragic accident; according to the police, there was no suspicion of foul play. Some of the red-top papers tried to tie the incident to the disappearance of Champion Jockey Sandy Sanderson on Gold Cup day. But Sanderson maintained that the last thing he remembered was enjoying a drink in the company of some businessmen, only to wake up in a strange hotel with a terrible headache. Somehow the story became one about Chinese businessmen. Chinese or Hong Kong betting rings were suspected of skulduggery.

Lorna was bewildered at her father's demise. She knew that he'd never loved her, and she had little love for him. But he was still her father, after all. She also learned that she had inherited everything: house, grounds, capital, car collection and more than forty premium racehorses.

'But what will I do?' she cried to Duncan. 'What will I do?'

'I'll take care of you, Lorna.'

'Will you marry me?'

'Slow down. But if that's what you want, that's what we'll do.'

He went to Petie. 'You know any good builders?'

'Do I know any good builders? There's no such thing as a good builder.'

'You might need some new stables.'

'Why is that, then?'

'I know someone who pretty soon might be moving forty-plus head down to your stables.'

'Forty head? That's a lot of livestock.'

'Too much for you? Not ready for the big time?'

Petie didn't need to answer that.

Cadogan's funeral was a lavish affair with a sombre service at the local church filled to capacity and a reception in the mansion. It seemed to Duncan that almost everyone who had been at the Cheltenham Festival was there. William Osborne turned out in a new suit but his old fedora. Many of his senior training stable hands were in attendance; several of the major trainers came to pay their respects. Sandy Sanderson was there with his wife, Christie, looking immaculate in an impossibly tight black dress and large-brimmed hat. Sanderson read a verse from the Bible and the vicar gave a touching sermon in which he compared life to a horse race.

Even George Pleasance was there, smiling sadly, embracing the mourners and offering consolation to Lorna.

'If there is anything I can do to help, anything at all, you let me know.'

Lorna failed to return his sympathetic smile.

At some point in the proceedings Duncan was approached by Christie. She took him by the sleeve. 'Is it true you're getting married to Lorna?'

'News travels fast.'

'It does in the racing community,' she said. 'That would put you in a very useful position.'

'I can't think what you mean.'

'Maybe I underestimated you, Duncan.'

'Isn't that your husband calling you?'

She turned to see Sanderson glaring at them.

'He must be mad. You're a wonderful girl, Christie.'

He kissed her in full view of the Champion Jockey.

Gradually the mourners drifted away, until only Lorna, Duncan and the staff remained behind. Lorna gazed out of the window at the last of the departing cars. 'Most of those people who came didn't even like him.'

'I'm sure that's not true,' said Duncan.

'Oh, it is true,' she said. 'I'm not sure even I did. I'm going to take a long bath, do you mind?'

'Not at all. I thought I might go and see my dad. I'll be back in an hour or two.'

Duncan left his battered Capri parked in the yard and made his way to the garage. Once inside, he switched the lights on and again surveyed the lavish motor pool, just as he had the first time he saw it. The yellow Lamborghini seemed totally inappropriate for a funeral day, but then again ... He climbed inside, switched on the ignition and drove the purring Lamborghini out of the garage.

There was no way of knowing how much Charlie would remember. Duncan had told him everything. He'd had to do that, to explain to him why he would be riding Cadogan's horses and wearing Osborne's silks. There was always the danger that Charlie would forget what he'd been told and believe that Duncan had betrayed him. On the other hand, he anticipated a conversation where Charlie might say, in that knowing way of his, 'Odd, son, how things unfolded for Cadogan.'

And he would say, 'Yes, Dad. Very odd, that.'

They would leave it at that.

Of course, Duncan had had no idea of whether his plans would work out, or how things would turn out afterwards. He could never have anticipated Cadogan's 'accident' in the woods; not that he would ever shed a tear for the man who had ruined his father. And as far as he was concerned, he still had major unfinished business with Sandy Sanderson and William Osborne.

Because at the end of it all there was only the race. And just as the Monk had told him, in that race someone was always going to have to take the fall. It was just a question of making sure that *someone* wasn't you.

Sunlight flared in the open countryside. Duncan turned the radio up loud in the yellow Lamborghini. He booted the accelerator and the throaty engine gurgled with pleasure. The road stretched ahead like an unbroken beam of light.

About the Author

A.P. McCoy is a record-breaking Northern Irish horse-racing jockey with a series of impressive wins to his name, including the Cheltenham Gold Cup, Champion Hurdle, Queen Mother Champion Chase, King George VI Chase and the 2010 Grand National.

McCoy was named BBC Sports Personality of the Year in 2010, becoming the first jockey to win the award.